As Gil idly watched the ballroom scene, he was brought up short by the sight of his supposed fiancée—the girl who had refused to dance with strangers—the girl who had hesitated to waltz with *him*—waltzing breezily past in the arms of Lord Rival.

Gil was stunned by the violence of the emotions that gripped him at the sight. For a moment he forgot where he was. A loud and furious oath escaped his lips. Well, damn it all, why *shouldn't* he feel murderous? Chloe was his, confound it! He must have been mad to think he didn't want to marry her. Of course he wanted to marry her.

The revelation turned Gil to stone. He froze, staring at Chloe and Lord Rival. What a prime idiot he had been, thinking he wanted to weasel out of his engagement. Why, that was the last thing he wanted to do! Where was he going to find another girl he liked as well as Chloe? Where would he find a girl he liked *half* as well? Nowhere! There wasn't another girl to equal her. There never would be. Not for him.

But there she went, all aglow from the attentions of another man.

And there wasn't a blasted thing he could do about it. . . .

Coming next month

COUNTERFEIT KISSES
by Sandra Heath

Sir Gareth Carew was quite smitten by the attentions of London's lovely new arrival–until he recognized the charmer as Susannah Leighton, the woman who blamed him for the loss of her family's fortune. But can he win back her trust–and her love?

0-451-20022-5/$4.99

BURIED SECRETS
by Anne Barbour
"One of my favorite authors."–Mary Balogh

Love was for poets. Marriage was for fools. That was pretty much the philosophy of dashing rake Christopher Culver–until a scandalous spinster named Gillian Tate aroused his curiosity...and captured his heart.

0-451-20023-3/$4.99

THE NABOB'S DAUGHTER
by Dawn Lindsey

Anjelie Cantrell was the most sought-after heiress in Jamaica–and the most infuriating. Lord Chance is afraid the girl is more interested in mischief than marriage. That is, until their hearts were shipwrecked...

0-451-20045-4/$4.99

To order call: 1-800-788-6262

Falling for Chloe

Diane Farr

A SIGNET BOOK

SIGNET
Published by New American Library, a division of
Penguin Putnam Inc., 375 Hudson Street,
New York, New York 10014, U.S.A.
Penguin Books Ltd, 27 Wrights Lane,
London W8 5TZ, England
Penguin Books Australia Ltd,
Ringwood, Victoria, Australia
Penguin Books Canada Ltd, 10 Alcorn Avenue,
Toronto, Ontario, Canada M4V 3B2
Penguin Books (N.Z.) Ltd, 182–190 Wairau Road,
Auckland 10, New Zealand

Penguin Books Ltd, Registered Offices:
Harmondsworth, Middlesex, England

First published by Signet, an imprint of New American Library,
a division of Penguin Putnam Inc.

First Printing, April 2000
10 9 8 7 6 5 4 3 2 1

To Linda

my third sister
my second mother
my first friend

Chapter 1

Chloe shrieked when her posterior hit the mud. It was an extremely wet patch of mud, and the force of her landing sent her skidding backward. She ended up half lying, half sitting, where the puddle met the tangled roots of an ancient oak. She listened to the swift tattoo of Thunder's departing hooves with a calm born of despair.

Stranded. In the mud. She might have known her morning would end this way.

It was the first sunny morning in what seemed like ages, and Chloe had been so heartily sick of life indoors that she jumped at the chance to try out Father's new gelding. Wiggins told her the brute was too big for her. Wiggins had been right, as usual. Although she had held Thunder admirably for a good long while, even galloped him across the Two-Mile Run. She did wish someone had seen her then!

Well, no one had seen her then. But someone was about to see her now. That was unmistakably the sound of an approaching horse. Chloe struggled frantically to free herself from the squelching mud, managed to rise precariously to her feet, and discovered that her riding boots were stuck fast. She wished it were possible for a lady to swear. Chloe's vocabulary contained no words that did justice to this moment.

She stood in the icy mud, fuming. Who on God's green earth would be coming down this nameless track to nowhere? She supposed she ought to be grateful that anyone was, but somehow gratitude was not her dominant emotion. She was cold and wet and filthy, and she knew she looked ridiculous. She devoutly hoped that the approaching

stranger would prove to be female. She dared not try to free
her feet until she knew.

The horse rounded the bend and Chloe gasped, then bit
her lip. Thank God, it was Gil! Oh, dear—it was Gil! She
knew she would be handily rescued. But she feared she
would never hear the end of it.

Mr. Gilliland sat gracefully astride his mount, a beautifully groomed gray that, in other circumstances, would have
made Chloe green with envy. Gil was nearly as gorgeous as
the prime bit of blood he was riding. His London tailoring
looked out of place in the middle of Dobson's Thicket, but it
certainly was impressive. He looked every inch the gentleman, and, as he was a tall young man, there were a good
many inches to look it.

When he spied his childhood friend standing ankle-deep
in muck, wet, horseless, and muddy, laughter lit his azure
eyes. He promptly reined his horse to a halt and swept the
curly-brimmed beaver off his artistically arranged hair. The
muted sunlight in the wood struck the ordered waves of
guinea gold as he bowed, revealing the gleam of expensive
pomade.

"Chloe Littlefield!" he exclaimed. "Fancy meeting you
here. Lovely weather we're having, what?"

Chloe frowned crossly at him. "For heaven's sake, Gil,
get off that horse and make yourself useful! I am very glad
to see you, but *pray* do not tease me until you have finished
rescuing me."

"Oh, am I rescuing you?"

"Yes!"

He eyed her doubtfully. "What do you need me to do, exactly?"

She shivered. The mud had not penetrated the thick skirts
of her riding habit, but it had definitely seeped through her
jacket. And her feet had gone quite numb. "My boots are
stuck." Since it was only Gil, she lifted the wet hem of her
skirt and showed him.

"Step out of 'em."

"I can't."

Gil dismounted in a leisurely fashion and strolled up to

her. "Give me your hand," he ordered, and she did so. "Now try it. I've got you, Chloe."

Braced against Gil, clutching his hand and simultaneously holding her heavy skirts out of the way, she struggled to step out of the mud. Her right foot came out booted, although the boot was caked with filth. But when she stepped on her right foot and pulled her left free, her stockinged foot slipped out of the boot, leaving it behind. She clutched at Gil and squeaked as she nearly lost her balance. He held her with surprising strength—at arm's length. This did not offend her in the least; his anxiety to keep her at bay was perfectly understandable. She was extremely dirty.

"Thank you!" she gasped.

He steadied her, then let her go, pulling out a handkerchief to dust his gloves. "What a troublesome chit you are, Clo," he remarked. "I suppose you'll want me to retrieve that boot for you. It's ruined, you know."

Chloe gazed mournfully at her stranded boot, which looked absurdly small stuck by itself in the thick paste of mud. "Is it?" She wished again that her vocabulary were more extensive. "Blast!" she muttered. It seemed inadequate. "I suppose there's no point in retrieving it, then."

Gil chuckled. "It won't beggar you to buy a new pair of boots. I wish you'd let me pick 'em out for you."

Chloe sniffed and tossed her head, discovering in the process that portions of her hair were thoroughly caked. "In the village, no doubt, where the impropriety of you choosing boots for me would set everyone in a bustle!"

"No. In London, where no one would bat an eyelash."

That made her laugh. "I know you, Gil. You'd choose the most expensive boots you could find."

"Why not? You're swimming in lard. Do you good to spend a little of it. On *yourself,* Clo! Not on one of your godforsaken charities, and not on your father's horses, and not on Brookhollow! And, by the by, I hope you're properly grateful that I haven't laughed at you yet."

"Oh, I am," she assured him. "Do I look as silly as I feel?"

"Yes," he responded promptly.

Her lips twitched. "Beast."

Gil had a famously infectious grin. "Very well, what would you like to hear? You look quite fetching, for a girl who is covered in mud and blue with cold."

She did, actually. Chloe Littlefield was a little dab of a thing, and never spent an extra farthing on her appearance, but no matter how deplorably she was dressed she always looked just like a Dutch doll. The look was misleading, as Gil knew well. A keen intelligence was tucked beneath those flaxen ringlets, and that sweetly rounded chin had been known to assume a very stubborn tilt from time to time.

He watched as Chloe stepped gingerly to a slightly drier patch of ground and cast an anxious glance at the sky. "I feel half frozen, and it's going to rain again. We'd better start for home."

"Where's Thunder?"

The sudden scowl looked ludicrous on that doll-like face of hers. "After we parted company, Thunder took off for parts unknown. The stupid creature is probably miles away by now. He's very fast, I'll grant him that."

"Well, dash it, Clo—! Are you expecting me to put you up on my gray?"

She flushed. "I beg your pardon, but what else are we to do?"

Gil eyed her in dismay. She was filthy. As if reading his thoughts, Chloe began to chuckle.

"If you wish to wrap a blanket round me first, I've no objection."

"Yes, that's all very well, but I didn't bring a blanket!"

She patted his arm sympathetically. "Poor Gil! You weren't cut out for the role of knight-errant."

He shook his head glumly. "No. But you can't walk, I suppose, with only one boot."

She gave a little spurt of laughter. "I'm so sorry."

"I don't suppose my boots would fit you?"

"No, Gil. I should think it highly unlikely."

He sighed. "So would I. Very well! Up you go." He turned to seize Chloe round the waist, but then paused. "Most of the mud is on your backside. I say, would you mind riding facedown? I could put you across his rump, you know. On your belly."

She was so tiny, she had to tilt her head back to stare at him. "Would I mind *what*?" He saw the exact moment when she realized he had been teasing her. The china-blue eyes, round even when they weren't filled with astonishment, suddenly crinkled into laughter. "Gil, you unconscionable wretch! You don't mind sharing your horse with me at all."

He grinned. "Well, I wouldn't go that far! It will pain me to see you scattering dirt across this beauty's flanks. Not to mention the effect you will have on my new saddle. But here's for it! Up you go."

He tossed his wet friend into the saddle with some difficulty and took the reins from her. "I'll lead him, thank you."

She chuckled again. "Yes, no sense in marring that jacket of yours by sharing a saddle with me. It's very nice, by the way."

"Thank you," said Gil politely. "You'd stare if you knew what I paid for it."

"Oh, I've no doubt I would! And this horse is new, isn't he? What's his name?"

"Wager. He's new since you've seen me last, but I've been riding him 'round London for the past few weeks. He's a great one for attracting the ladies! I hope the two of us will soon be as famous as Lord Sheringham and his Gull-catcher."

She patted the animal's glossy neck. "He's certainly showy."

"Like his owner?"

Chloe's eyes sparkled mischievously. "I didn't mean to imply that he was *only* showy. I daresay he possesses other virtues."

"Ah. *Unlike* his owner." Gil shook his head reproachfully. "I'll tell you what, Chloe: it's a good thing you have no social ambitions. Never met a more rag-mannered wench!"

An ominous pattering sound began overhead. Rain was spattering the thick foliage that arched over the path. Gil greeted this development by muttering one of the words missing from Chloe's vocabulary. "And so much for my natty new jacket! Where are we, Clo?"

"Miles from anywhere, I'm afraid. Don't you know? What brought you into Dobson's Thicket?"

"You did, of course. Look out! I'm coming up." Gil gathered the reins in one hand and hauled himself into the saddle in front of Chloe. She clutched him round the waist. He was so tall, her face was completely muffled against the back of his coat.

"Gil, do you mean you were following me?"

"Tracked you like a Red Indian," he said, not without pride.

"Gracious! Whatever for? I didn't even know you were home."

"Wanted to see you," he explained. A flash of lightning caused Wager to dance nervously, and Gil steadied the animal, murmuring soothing blandishments. The crack of thunder followed almost immediately, and, with a roar, the heavens opened. Streams of water soon began to pour through the tree branches and strike them.

"I say, Clo!" shouted Gil above the racket. "Is there shelter anywhere about?"

"Barlow's cottage is less than a mile ahead," she shouted back. "There's nothing else, as far as I know."

"Good old Barlow," muttered Gil. His clearest memory of the cottager was unpleasant. Barlow had caught him stealing apples as a child. The consequences had been painful, and Gil had never forgotten it. But he urged his horse forward.

By the time they trotted into the clearing where Barlow's neat cottage stood, the day had turned nearly as dark as night and the downpour had become fierce. There was no light in the cottage. This was an ominous sign. Gil and Chloe slid off the horse, huddled on Barlow's small porch, and pounded on the door. There was no answer.

Chloe suddenly looked guilty and bit her lip.

"What is it?" demanded Gil, his heart sinking.

"I just recalled that Barlow's sister was taken ill last week. I believe he's gone to visit her."

With a despairing moan, Gil closed his eyes and leaned

dramatically against the door. To his surprise, it moved. He straightened hastily as it swung slowly open.

"Oh, thank goodness!" exclaimed Chloe, darting inside.

But Gil remained on the stoop. He peered apprehensively into the dim interior. "I say, Chloe, are you sure we ought to go in?"

"Whyever not? If Barlow were here, he'd take us in. We'd do the same for him. Anyone would! And of course we'll repay him for anything we use."

Gil's sense of foreboding did not diminish. "I don't know," he said uneasily. "Devilish queer fellow, Barlow. Rather keen on the idea of private property."

Chloe gave a little peal of laughter. "You're remembering those apples, aren't you? Silly Gilly! That was simply ages ago."

Gil winced. For the thousandth time, he wondered bitterly why his parents had burdened him with the name Sylvester Gilliland. The unfortunate juxtaposition of his Christian name and his surname had given rise to much merriment in his youth. Not, unfortunately, shared by him. But he had learned long ago that to show emotion upon being addressed as "Silly Gilly" only encouraged its use.

"Very well," he said darkly. "On your head be it!" And stepped into the cottage.

Two daunting facts struck him at once. The cottage consisted of one room only. And it was spotless. Chloe was bustling blithely about, heedless of her muddy skirt dripping on Barlow's meticulously kept floor. Gil shuddered. Chloe had thrown open Barlow's cupboards without a thought and was busily rummaging about. She was such a generous little soul, it was clearly inconceivable to her that anyone might object to her making herself at home.

He couldn't bear to watch. "I'm off to do something about Wager," he announced, and ducked back out into the storm. Gil found shelter for his dripping animal in Barlow's cow shed, removed the saddle, and rubbed him down as best he could. Since the only material to hand was hay, he was forced to rub Wager vigorously with handfuls of the stuff.

This took a good long while, but the exertion certainly kept Gil warm while it lasted.

The rain did not abate. By the time Gil returned to the cottage, Chloe had a fire crackling on Barlow's hearth and had put the kettle on. But what caused him to stop dead on the threshold was the sight of Chloe herself. She had somehow contrived to strip off her wet clothing and bathe while he was gone. A large tin basin containing a wet sponge and a cake of still-foaming soap gave mute testimony to her accomplishment of this feat. Her hair was piled anyhow on top of her head, the damp tendrils around her face curling riotously. Her pink and white skin glowed from scrubbing. And she was artistically wrapped in a kind of white toga.

The overall effect was deceptively angelic. Gil felt the hairs stand up on his neck.

"What are you wearing?" he demanded.

Chloe looked very pleased with herself. "It's a bedsheet."

"Good God!"

"What's the matter?"

"D'you mean to tell me you've torn up the man's *sheets*?"

"No such thing! It's merely tied." She raised her bare arms to show him how well it was tied. The toga did not slip, but the swell of Chloe's plump breasts above the tightly tied swatches was unnervingly evident. As he stood in the doorway and goggled at her in dismay, she broke into laughter. "Gil, do stop staring! Come in and close the door. You're letting the rain in."

"You're not dressed. It's indecent."

"Pooh! I've seen ball gowns that are far more revealing than this. The sheet is made of linen and it's ever so thick. There's another, too, if you'd care to get out of your wet things."

"What, prance about in a ruddy sari? No, thank you!" But he sneezed as he came in and closed the door behind him. "This adventure will be the death of me," he said gloomily. "Mark my words."

"Well, I do think you ought not to stay in those wet clothes. We don't know how long we may be stranded here."

Water was streaming off him and onto Barlow's floor. His

clothing was sticking to him, but pouring rivulets down his boots. The boots, at least, would have to go. Gil surrendered to the inevitable with a sigh. He plopped unceremoniously onto the floor and began tugging on his footwear, hoping grimly that this rough treatment would not ruin their shape forever. There seemed little point in searching Barlow's humble home for a proper bootjack.

"Why the deuce did you take Thunder out today, any-how?" he grumbled, wrestling with his boots. "And why did you take him so far? You might have known it would rain. It has done so every day for a se'nnight."

Chloe was carefully spreading her wet riding habit over the back of a wooden chair. "Yes, but the morning was so sunny! I couldn't bear to stay indoors another moment. I thought I should go mad." The golden head bent low over her task. "Don't scold me, Gil. You know how it is in that house," she said softly.

He did. Without another word, he finished yanking off his boots and placed them outside on Barlow's small, but rela-tively dry, front porch. As soon as he had closed the door again he padded over to his friend and patted her shoulder comfortingly, ignoring the fact that it was disconcertingly bare. "You always mean well, Chloe. I suppose today is not your lucky day."

She peeped up at him impishly. "This isn't my ill luck at work, it's yours. *I'm* here through pigheadedness. Wiggins told me the horse was too strong for me, but I *would* take him! So, you see, this situation serves me right. But I fail to see why you became entangled in my mishap."

"Following you," said Gil simply. His sodden clothing was wretchedly uncomfortable. He stood with his back to the fire and gingerly lifted his coattails, hoping the warmth would reach him eventually.

Chloe glanced curiously at him. "Did you follow me all the way from Brookhollow?"

"Yes, and I had the devil's own work to do so! You had left not ten minutes before I arrived in search of you, and Wiggins pointed me in the direction you had taken. I never guessed you would go so far, or I wouldn't have trailed you like a ninny! It was easy enough to see where you had gone, especially with the ground so muddy, but I was beginning to think I would never catch you."

"Well, I'm very grateful that you did! Only think what might have become of me if you had given up and turned back. I daresay I would be in that stupid wood yet, huddled under a tree and half drowned by now." Chloe carried a petticoat over to the basin and wrung it energetically. Bare toes peeped from beneath the hem of her bedsheet as she walked, but it was so voluminous on her diminutive frame that a train of bulky linen dragged behind her.

Gil grinned. "Is that modish ensemble comfortable?"

She tossed a saucy smile over her shoulder. "It's a deal more comfortable than wet wool, at any rate."

"Well, if informality is the order of the day, would you mind if I took off my jacket?"

"Heavens, no! Haven't I been telling you you should? No sense standing on ceremony with me, Gil. We're practically family."

He gingerly removed his jacket and spread it on Barlow's other chair. There were only two in the tiny cottage, both pulled up to the wooden table in the center of the floor. Gil lifted the clothing-draped chairs and set them closer to the fire. "I dare not remove my breeches," he remarked. "You might take advantage of me."

Chloe giggled. "Well, if *that's* what's worrying you, I should think you'd be in less danger if you did. A man looks far more attractive in wet breeches than wrapped in a bedsheet."

Gil turned to her with mock sternness. "And just how many men have you seen wrapped in bedsheets, miss?"

Her cheeks reddened, but she laughed at him. "None, of course! I was only trying to reassure you."

"Hm!"

"Gil, I really would feel terrible if you caught cold. And I can't think what has turned you so prudish all of a sudden." She removed her wrung-out petticoat from the washbasin and draped it over Barlow's dinner table, apparently completely unconcerned with the immodesty of displaying her undergarments to a bachelor.

He glared at her, exasperated. "Nothing sudden about it. We ain't children any longer!"

"Ain't?" she repeated, distracted by this linguistic lapse.

"It's the fashion," he explained. "But don't you follow it! Bad grammar is thieves' cant—all the crack in London, but not for females. Where was I?"

"Preaching decorum."

"So I was!" He resumed his stern demeanor. "If you have a fault, Chloe, it's that you are too trusting by half! Don't you know what people would think, if they knew we had paraded round Barlow's cottage dressed in his bedsheets? Don't you know what they would say?"

Chloe placed her small fists on her hips and sniffed at him. "I'm not completely birdwitted."

"Well, then?"

She sighed, rolling her eyes. "If *you* have a fault, Gil, it's that you simply aren't practical! You and I both know that you would never touch me. What does it matter what people might say? No one will know."

"I daresay old Barlow will be able to add two and two! He's always been fly to the time of day."

"Barlow is a dear. If he does figure it out, he won't say a word. He would no more harm me than you would."

Gil groaned, but his groan ended in another sneeze. Chloe marched to a cupboard and withdrew Barlow's sole remaining sheet. She tossed it to Gil. "Not another word! I shall turn my back on you until you tell me to turn round."

He caught the sheet. She turned her back. But Gil still hesitated. "You're absolutely certain old Barlow is away?"

"He left only yesterday, I believe, so if he's gone for a visit he can't possibly return for days yet."

"And we are going to buy him a new set of sheets?"

"Of course."

He sighed. The wet breeches were deucedly uncomfortable. And she was right—it was highly unlikely that any harm would come of it. Lord knew, they had done far worse things together and never been caught. He grinned reminiscently as he peeled off his nether garments. "You always were a fearless little thing. Remember the summer when I taught you and Tish to swim?"

Chloe's white shoulders shook. "Poor Tish! You had no mercy."

"Yes, but much you cared! You nearly drowned, trying to follow my lead. I was trying to teach you a lesson. A lesson you badly needed! You frightened me half out of my wits that day."

"You weren't trying to teach me a lesson. You were trying to put me in my place. I knew it, too! I couldn't let you win, Gil."

"*Let* me win? No such thing, you impertinent little snip! You may turn round now."

She did, and burst out laughing. The damp breeches and stockings were in a heap before the fire, and Gil stood before her clad only in his shirt and a kind of giant diaper that hung below his knees. "Charming!" she gasped. "Oh, Gil, I was right—you were far more fetching in your wet breeches!"

Gil grinned. "Beauty is as beauty does," he informed her piously. "And this beauty saved your groats today."

"Yes, indeed! I am in your debt. And Wager's, of course."

"Of course. Is that tea ready yet? You may pour me a dish, ma'am, and I'll tell you why I risked life and limb to seek you out."

Chloe poured the tea into two mugs of slightly cracked glazed pottery and, since Barlow's chairs were occupied by their clothes and the table by Chloe's petticoats, the two friends seated themselves cross-legged on the hearth rug. While Chloe was occupied in arranging her unwieldy bed-sheet skirts, Gil took a gulp of the tea. His face contorted into an extraordinary grimace. "What the deuce—!"

"What's the matter?"

"Clo, this can't be tea!"

"Of course it is tea! Oh, dear. Is it very bad?"

"Devilish!"

"Well, I daresay Barlow doesn't buy the *best* tea. Tea is

very dear these days." She took a cautious sip and immediately set the mug down. "Oh, my."

Their eyes met, and together they fell into whoops. "Well," gasped Chloe eventually, "now I know what to give Barlow on Boxing Day."

Gil's eyes traveled around the tiny cottage. He shook his head. "Phew! I tell you what, Clo, I wouldn't be poor for anything. It's too uncomfortable."

He seemed so earnest that she looked at him in surprise. Then she bit back another peal of laughter. "Gil, you are dreadful!"

He grinned. "Aye, we ought not to laugh at such things. We're a fortunate pair, Chloe."

"Yes, and Barlow isn't doing so badly. This is a very snug little home, I think." She waved a hand to indicate. "A bed, a table, two chairs, a serviceable wardrobe, cooking pots, dishes. What more does a single man need?"

"A valet, a card case, some letters of introduction, and a fat bank account," said Gil promptly. "Oh, and a cow."

"A cow! Why?"

"I don't know, but Barlow has one. He seems to have collected only the bare essentials, so a cow must be a necessity. Stands to reason."

Chloe choked. "Do you have a cow?"

"No, but I'm dashed well going to get one!"

Off they went into another fit of laughter. Chloe, wiping her streaming eyes with the edge of her bedsheet, finally managed to say, "Oh, Gil, it's wonderful to see you again! Why do you spend so much of your time in London? I miss you terribly."

He grinned affectionately at her. "I miss you, too, Clo. Why do you stay stuck down here in the back of beyond? No reason why you can't come to Town. All the world does so. In fact, I wanted to speak to you about—"

But Chloe was shaking her curls resolutely. "I cannot. The farmers cannot spare me."

"What, are you still ruling the roost at Brookhollow?"

"You know I am. Someone must."

Gil frowned. "I don't like to say aught against your father,

Chloe, but he ought to take a hand in managing Brookhollow's affairs. Daresay if you left him for a time, he'd be forced to do so. Good thing!"

Chloe shuddered eloquently. "It would *kill* me to come home and find everything at sixes and sevens, after all my hard work!"

Her friend's mouth set grimly. "I am strongly tempted to say something I know I will regret."

Affection lit her eyes. "Very well, I'll say it for you. You wish to tell me that Father ought to do the hard work, and I ought to lead the life of leisure! But talking pays no toll, Gil. Father has no interest in keeping up the property. Why should he, indeed? He is not really master at Brookhollow. The property was left to me, together with the fortune. I cannot blame him for his indifference. You must own, it would weigh heavily on any man to live as his daughter's pensioner."

"He's no one to blame but himself," said Gil with asperity. "Had he shown any disposition to lift a finger while your grandfather was alive, I daresay your mother's property would not have been left in that skimble-skamble way! At any rate, I don't like to see him punishing you for something you could not help. You are in no way at fault for the way things were left. In fact, you had nothing to do with it!"

A touch of cynicism curled Chloe's rosebud mouth. The worldly-wise expression sat oddly on her elfin face. "That was then. He blames me now."

"Why, for the love of heaven?"

"I am of age. Should I choose to do it, I could hand my property over to him. I could give him Grandfer's mill, or the glassworks, or one of the Harrowgate properties. I could make him a present of Brookhollow, for that matter. Well, I don't choose to do so."

Gil was appalled. "Good God, no! Why should you?"

She lifted one rosy shoulder in a slight shrug. "Why, indeed? And of course Father would never demean himself by asking me for anything. But I know exactly what he is thinking, and why he is so surly to me. I bought Thunder for him, you know, but he hasn't thanked me. And I don't believe he's even ridden the creature yet."

Gil clicked his tongue disapprovingly. "If your father was five instead of fifty, I'd call that behavior pouting."

Chloe smiled. "No one could accuse Father of pouting! His manner is far too elegant."

"His *manner* may be elegant, but his *manners* leave something to be desired!"

She threw up her hands in mock horror. "How can you utter such heresy? No son of Lady Maria Littlefield—née Westwood—*Westwood,* Gil!—can be apostrophized as 'ill-mannered'!"

Gil eyed her grimly. "Yes, he was reared to think too well of himself; that's the largest part of his problem. Westwood, my eye! I've no patience with it. I've witnessed the Turkish treatment he gave his wife and daughter—"

"Now, Gil, really—! Anyone would think he beat us regularly or locked us in our rooms! He was never brutal, you know."

"Aye, that's true. Just cold, and distant, and disapproving of everything you did. Or said."

"Or thought. Or was." Chloe's soft smile turned slightly bitter. "I have never understood how anyone could disapprove of my dear little mother. Mama had the most affectionate nature, and the sweetest ways! I daresay she wasn't very clever, and I know she wasn't wellborn, but still . . ." Her voice trailed off, and she stared into the fire.

"Her birth was perfectly respectable," said Gil firmly. "And if your father thought her connections were too deuced low for a man of his breeding, he ought not to have married her. A man should show his wife more courtesy than to criticize her day and night."

Chloe sighed. "Yes. My poor mother thought the sun rose and set in my father. And he felt nothing but contempt for her."

Gil eyed his friend shrewdly. "I'll say this for you, Clo— whatever he thought of your mother, he feels a healthy respect for her daughter! You've handled him very skillfully for a chit fresh out of the schoolroom. I was half afraid you'd let him browbeat you, but no such thing! I'm proud of you."

She blushed. "Thank you," she said with difficulty. "I couldn't let him overpower me. I couldn't bear to think of him squandering Mama's money on his latest mistress, or—or anything like that. I wanted to put some heart back into the land, and do good works, and keep the fortune safely out of the Westwoods' hands. I owed that to her memory. And to Grandfer's."

"Well, if your father ever tries to come the ugly over you, Clo, I hope you know you can always turn to me."

Her blue eyes widened in surprise at this unnecessary statement. "Of course."

Gil grinned. That was the best part of having a friend like Chloe. Each knew, without question, that the other could be counted on in any extremity. But that put him in mind of something. He slapped his forehead with an exclamation.

"Dash it all, I nearly forgot! I need a favor from you, Clo."

"It is just like you, Gil, to spend the better part of the day chasing me down and then forget to tell me what you needed!"

"Yes, well, it puts a man out, to have so many adventures piled on top of him. But I did have a good reason for seeking you out."

"Very well. What is it?"

Gil frowned and did not immediately answer her. "It's a rather delicate matter. Now that I must come to the point, I find it a bit difficult."

Chloe waited expectantly while Gil's eyes traveled round the room as if seeking inspiration. Finally he gave a little sigh and returned his troubled gaze to Chloe. "It's Tish," he said simply. "I'm worried about her."

"Tish! I thought she was perfectly happy."

"She was. She's not anymore."

Chloe's eyes widened in alarm. "Oh, do not say so! I haven't written to her in ages. We are both such wretched correspondents, you know, that neither of us thinks anything of it when we do not hear from one another. And she was so

aux anges at her wedding, I expected her to live in untram-
meled bliss forever after! I am sure she expected no less.
Poor Tish! Is Robert unkind to her?"

Gil snorted in disgust. "Lord, how would I know? If that's
not just like a female, to ascribe every misery to the state of
someone's marriage!"

"Well, for heaven's sake, Gil! What is it, then?"

"That's just it. I don't know. On the surface she's very
gay, dashes about town as if she hadn't a care in the world.
Well, she's shamming it. Don't ask me how I know. I just
do."

Chloe nodded. Gil always knew when one was shamming
it. "Have you asked her what's amiss?"

"I've tried. She won't confide in me, which makes me
deuced uneasy. What I mean to say is—Tish! Keeping secrets!" He shook his head.

Chloe, well acquainted with the former Leticia Gilliland,
was as alarmed by this departure from the norm as Gil had
evidently been. "Gracious! It sounds most unlike her. Tish,
of all people! She was never one to hide her feelings."

"No. Well, there you have it. Makes my hair stand on end,
thinking of all the things it *could* be and not knowing what it
is. But I'm only her brother. Perhaps she'd confide in you.
I'd give a great deal to be able to set things right." He leaned
forward and placed a beseeching hand on Chloe's linen-
swathed knee. "I thought if you paid Tish a visit, you could
learn firsthand what's what. I daresay between the two of us,
we'd be able to steer her away from point non-plus."

Chloe looked anxiously at her friend's worried countenance. "I know you would never ask me to come to London
if you did not believe it to be important. But I can't be
spared just now."

"What, from Brookhollow? A rubbishing *farm*? Chloe, I
need you!"

"It's a very *large* farm," she protested feebly.

"I daresay! But the crops will grow, or not grow, whether
you are here to coax them along or not."

"Oh, Gil! If you knew the first thing about land management—"

"Don't come for my sake, then. Come for Tish."

"I would do anything for either of you, or both of you! You know that."

"Well, then? Will you return to London with me?"

Chloe hesitated, biting her lip. It was very hard to turn Gil down. He had come to her rescue time and time again over the years, and he rarely asked her for anything.

He reached for her knee again, and gave it a friendly shake. "Clo. Don't let Brookhollow steal your girlhood. Are you never to have a life of your own?"

She straightened indignantly. "Not *that* again! Are we speaking of Tish? Or of me?"

Gil's grin was wholly unrepentant. "Both! You can't expect me to see both my girls in the suds and make no attempt to pull you out. You can take my word for it, Clo—London will do you a world of good. And Tish needs you, too."

Chloe's eyes narrowed in suspicion, but Gil looked completely guileless. "Very well," she said at last. "I will think on it."

"I leave tomorrow. With or without you."

"Tomorrow! Then it will have to be without me. I can't possibly be ready in one day!"

Gil's aspect became stern. "Are you thinking you need time to pack your things? You may rid yourself of the notion. Trust me, Clo! If you parade around London in those ghastly frocks Gertrude Tewksbury made for you, you'll be laughed out of Town!"

Chloe blushed. "The muslins aren't so very bad," she said defensively. "And poor Miss Tewksbury needed the work. She won't take charity—"

"Nor should you! I saw you in that monstrosity she called a dinner dress. Looked like something from the bottom of the missionary barrel! Yes, I see you are laughing, but *you* weren't obliged to sit at table across from the thing and look at it by the hour! Enough to put anyone off his dinner. It was all I could do to keep my tongue between my teeth."

"You did not do so, as I recall," said Chloe, twinkling mischievously. "You read me a lecture on the evils of frumpery the instant we were alone."

"Did I? I wish you had taken it to heart! It's more than flesh and blood can stand, seeing you in those frightful clothes of yours day after day. Besides, dash it all—people know you for a friend of mine! I daresay the knowing 'uns blame *me* for allowing you to go about looking such a figure of fun. Here I am, fancying myself a man of taste—I say! What's so deuced funny?"

"You are!"

"I? Why, I was never more serious in my life! Leave your things behind, Clo. Never saw anyone who needed a new touch more than you do. And it's not like you can't afford it! You're as rich as Croesus."

"That's all very well, but I still cannot be ready tomorrow! Nor can you, Gil. We are here, stuck in Barlow's cottage! What if we must stay the night?"

A brief silence fell, while the two friends listened to the rain drumming steadily on the roof. It was a sobering sound. Gil turned a little pale. "We can't stay the night. That *will* throw the cat amongst the pigeons."

"Well, what else are we to do? Our clothes won't be dry for hours."

"I shall have to sleep in the shed," said Gil gloomily.

"Oh, Gil, no!"

Exasperated, Gil raked a hand through his hair. "There's only one bed, Clo. I daresay you see nothing wrong with us sharing it!"

She dimpled. "Well, no. Not in any *real* sense. But I suppose you are right that we ought not."

Gil spluttered wordlessly. Chloe favored him with a kindly smile. "You worry far too much about the proprieties, Gil. After all, there is no one here to frown at us! I suggest we simply take it in turns to sleep. We must keep the fire going, since we are dressed in Barlow's only sheets and I haven't found an extra blanket anywhere. So one of us takes the bed, and the other tends the fire. Then, halfway through the night, we trade places."

Gil attempted to argue the point with Chloe, but her steadfast refusal to listen to reason, coupled with his own natural reluctance to bed down in a cow shed, resulted in his eventual capitulation.

He argued far more hotly over her insistence that she take the first watch. It seemed ungentlemanly to him to go to bed while she sat up, but Chloe finally convinced him that she actually preferred to sleep later, when she supposed she would be more tired. So Gil, grumbling, stretched out on the rickety wooden bed in the corner of the room and disposed himself on its straw mattress as comfortably as he could. He was certain he would not be able to sleep a wink, and said so.

And that was the last he remembered until morning.

Chapter 2

Bright daylight assaulted Gil's closed eyelids. He flung up a sleepy hand to shield them. It must be morning, he decided, his consciousness struggling slowly toward the surface like a diver fighting a strong current. Then a rough hand shook his shoulder and he opened his eyes, startled.

"Aye, you young varmint! You h'ain't outgrown yer rascally ways, have yer? Get up!"

Gil blinked, disoriented, at the stern face glowering down at him. "Barlow," he uttered at last, recognizing this individual. His bewildered gaze slid past his childhood's nemesis to the other persons crowding the tiny room. Wiggins, the Littlefields' groom, was there, and two or three others from Brookhollow. Also two women Gil did not recognize, and Betty Potter, the gossipy crone who was Barlow's nearest neighbor. Old Betty was the only person present who had anything approaching a smile on her face, but her creased grin struck him as oddly unpleasant. Malicious, even.

Memory rushed back, and Gil sat up, horrified. The modest, if ludicrous, diaper arrangement he had created with the bedsheet last night had come undone. He was in Barlow's bed with his shirt rucked up and his legs tangled anyhow in the sheet, which he was now wearing more like a long kilt than a baby's nappy. He hastily tugged his shirt down to cover his bare chest.

He glanced round, dazed. Clothing seemed to be strewn all over the cottage. They had made a rather spectacular mess of Barlow's spare and tidy home. Chloe's petticoats and Gil's breeches were displayed prominently across the dinner table, her riding habit was thrown across the back of one displaced chair and his jacket across the other, and four stockings—two male, two female—dangled from the mantelpiece like Christmas morning. It looked for all the world as if a pair of lovers had hurled their clothing about with reckless abandon and indulged in guilty pleasures on the hearth rug, which was conspicuous as the only bare spot in the room. Two nearly full tea mugs, side by side on the floor near the hearth rug, advertised the fact that this was where they had spent the majority of the evening. Miss Littlefield was nowhere to be seen.

"Wh-where's Chloe?" stammered Gil.

Wiggins' expression became wooden. He stared stoically at the wall. The others exchanged knowing glances.

Barlow's gimlet gaze seemed to pin the hapless Gil to the bed. "Where, indeed?" he growled. "What've you done with her?"

Betty Potter cackled. "I knew 'twas Miss Littlefield, the instant I seen he had a female wi' him! Didn't I say as much? Didn't I?"

"Save your breath to cool your porridge, you knaggy old Gorgon," ordered Barlow, addressing Betty Potter with the rudeness of long-standing acquaintance. To Gil's bemused surprise, she accepted the snub without a blink. But Barlow immediately returned his scorching glare to Gil. He wilted beneath it.

"Well?" demanded Barlow. "What d'you have to say for yourself? Aye, I know you're my better, and I ought to keep my place—but if you've wronged Miss Littlefield, I'll see you answer for it or my name's not Roger Barlow!"

Chloe's clear voice sounded from the doorway. "There is no need for these histrionics. Here I am, safe and sound, as you can all see."

The entire room turned as one to look at her. Gil stared, reluctant admiration causing his lips to twitch in unholy amusement. One had to hand it to her—Chloe Littlefield was full of spunk. She stood serenely in the doorway, regally ignoring the inescapable fact that she was clad in a bedsheet. And only a bedsheet. Her matchless poise also ignored the fact that everyone present must realize where she had been and what undignified errand she had been performing. By Jupiter, she was going to carry this off with a high hand. Good old Chloe! Pluck to the backbone!

"I am very much obliged to all of you for your concern," she said calmly. "Pray step outside now. I would like to dress."

The company seemed stunned to silence. Gil's shoulders shook as he watched all of them, even Barlow, file out without a word. But then Chloe turned to him and he saw the frantic signal she was sending with her eyes. "Yes, quite right!" he said hastily, scrambling up from the bed. "I'm going."

He scooped up his jacket on his way out the door, holding his linen skirts together with the other hand. It was difficult to walk with the sheet wrapped round his legs. As he shuffled out the door, Chloe closed it firmly on his train. One more step and his makeshift kilt would drop to the floor of Barlow's tiny porch. Gil halted and stood there foolishly, one hand clutching the linen sheet wound round his legs, the other stuck halfway through the sleeve of his riding jacket. He felt his face flush scarlet.

Wiggins glanced uneasily at him, hesitated, then stepped forward. "Allow me, sir," he said gruffly. He assisted Gil into his jacket, but then walked away without meeting Gil's eyes or acknowledging his thanks. Well, Gil knew this was serious. He would have to put things right. He cleared his throat self-consciously.

"I daresay you may be wondering what Miss Littlefield and I are doing here," he began.

Another cackle escaped Betty Potter. "No, that we're not!" She shook with senile mirth at this example of her own wit. Gil eyed her with disfavor.

"Well, whatever you may *think,* the situation is entirely innocent!" he said hotly. "The only person here to whom I owe an explanation is Barlow. We trespassed on your property, sir, and I knew dashed well it was wrong to do so. We'll put all to rights, of course—buy you a new set of sheets and all that."

Wiggins blanched. The two women whom Gil had never

seen before looked shocked. Barlow actually swore. Gil, suddenly made aware of the unfortunate implications of his offer, was struck speechless with indignation and horror.

"Oh, here, I *say!*" he gasped. "No, dash it! No! I mean—good God!"

The door opened behind him and Chloe stepped out, chin high, now modestly clad in yesterday's riding habit. It looked considerably the worse for wear. Gil took the opportunity to duck back into the cottage and scramble into his own clothing. He felt himself to be at a disadvantage, addressing a crowd of disapproving persons while wearing a sheet. On the other hand, leaving Chloe out there to deal with them alone was like throwing her to the lions. Gil was in the habit of spending a great deal of time and thought on his morning dress, but today he made an exception to the rule. He burst back out onto the porch in record time.

The party from Brookhollow was handing Chloe, stocking-footed, into a pony cart. Wager was tied to the back of it. Chloe's back was ramrod straight, her expression a nice mixture of reproof and hauteur. Her air of outraged martyr-dom made her look exactly like an aristocrat stepping into a tumbril for a journey to the guillotine.

Gil hastily snatched up his boots, which were still side by side on the porch. "Where are you taking her?" he demanded. "And, I say—that's my horse!"

"The both of ye are going to Brookhollow, young scamp," Barlow informed him. "Get you in, and not another word!"

Having thus reduced Sylvester Gilliland, that dashing man about town, to the status of a naughty schoolboy, Barlow reverted to surly silence. Gil, fuming, hopped into the cart and began pulling on his boots.

"Well, now we have a wolf by the ears!" he grumbled, for Chloe's ears alone. "Sorry I had to leave you to deal with the howling mob. Couldn't face 'em down in that dashed toga!"

"Pray do not apologize, Gil," said Chloe in a clear and carrying voice. "We have done nothing wrong, and we owe no explanation to these excessively vulgar persons."

He glanced at her apprehensively. The light of battle was flashing in her eyes, and he recognized the stubborn tilt of her chin and the two spots of angry color flaming on her porcelain cheeks. Storm signals.

"Now, Chloe, don't fly up into the boughs!" he begged her. "We can't blame these people for jumping to conclusions. Anyone would. But as soon as we're given half a chance to explain—"

"I see no need to *explain!* What business is it of theirs, I should like to know? What business is it of anyone's?"

"Keep your voice down, for God's sake! You need not answer to that lot that waylaid us at the cottage—"

"No, certainly not!"

"—but your father is another matter entirely! He's owed an explanation, Clo, and an apology. From me at least!" he added hastily, seeing the fury in Chloe's gaze.

"I do not desire you to apologize! Not to me, and certainly not to Father! Why, Gil, you *rescued* me! The only shocking thing about this situation is that you are being treated like a—like an abductor! Nothing could be further from the truth! You are my best friend, and anyone acquainted with us ought to know that."

"Aye. But some of those people who ambushed us *ain't* acquainted with us! At least, I never saw them before in my life. Who were those two platter-faced women hanging on Barlow's sleeve?"

"His sister, I believe, and a cousin of some kind."

"I thought you told me his sister was ill?"

"I was *mistaken!*"

"Well, don't comb my hair! I imagine we'll come about. As you say, it's not likely I'd do you a mischief. And even less likely that you'd let me! If you don't wish me to apologize, I won't. As soon as everyone comes down off their high ropes, I daresay they'll apologize to *us.*"

But this sanguine expectation was not destined to be fulfilled. Waiting for them at Brookhollow were Chloe's father and Gil's mother. Both of them had suffered some degree of anxiety when their children failed to return from yesterday's riding expeditions, and Mr. Littlefield had experienced an exacerbation of alarm when Thunder had returned to Brookhollow bearing an empty saddle. Discovering that his daughter was, in fact, safe and sound had naturally transformed his anxiety into rage.

Neither Mr. Littlefield nor Lady Gilliland was prone to vehement expressions of emotion. Nevertheless, there was no doubt in the minds of Chloe and Gil that their respective parents were profoundly angry. Mr. Littlefield delivered himself of a blistering scold, rendered somehow more terrible through understatement. Chloe visibly wilted under the bite of her father's sarcasm. This fired Gil's protective insincts and even roused him to anger, but his spirited defense of Chloe failed. Mr. Littlefield was deaf to all Gil's arguments, and Chloe was ignominiously banished to her room.

Then it was Gil's turn. He stood, mutely fuming, as his mother rose majestically to express her extreme displeasure with the conduct of her sole surviving son. She was far more compelling than Mr. Littlefield, especially since her affection for her children was consistent and strong, whereas Mr. Littlefield's affection for Chloe was erratic at best. Addressing Gil as "Sylvester," a name to which he had not voluntarily answered since the day he was old enough to throw a tantrum, Lady Gilliland favored him with several home truths, very pithily expressed. He was reduced to speechless chagrin, since he was perfectly aware of the aptness of her remarks. In fact, he agreed with them. He *had* let the informality of his relationship with Chloe lead him into inappropriate conduct. He *had* known better. He *ought* to have made allowances for Chloe's innocence and not permitted her to indulge in behavior that would paint a false picture to the world. And it mattered not a jot that he and Chloe had confidently expected their night together to remain secret.

By the time Gil bowed and left the room, he was scarlet-faced and greatly chastened. Lady Gilliland waited until her son had departed before sending an indulgent smile after him.

"He really is a very good boy," she remarked. "Although it is high time, of course, that he became a man."

She shot an amused glance at Mr. Littlefield. "And Chloe is an excellent young woman. I think they will suit admirably. Do not you?"

She saw the startled uplift of her neighbor's brows and laughed gently. "My dear Horace, I hope you do not mean to *accept* the children's explanation?"

Mr. Littlefield gazed hard at Lady Gilliland, an arrested expression on his aquiline face. "It seemed honest enough."

"Oh, yes! I daresay it is perfectly true. That is the danger, my friend, of rearing them together as playmates. Their relationship has always been completely innocent. I am sure it remains so. I daresay Gil would no more think of ravishing Chloe than he would Tish."

Mr. Littlefield looked shocked. Lady Gilliland smiled. "Come now, Horace! Sir Walter and I have always thought as one on this matter. And we need have no secrets from you, I am sure. May we speak frankly, you and I?"

"By all means." He bowed and indicated a chair.

Lady Gilliland seated herself gracefully. "Very well. First, let me assure you that Sir Walter and I have a great fondness for your little Chloe. It has always been the dearest wish of my heart that we might, someday, welcome her into our family."

"Aurelia, you surprise me."

"Do I? Not unpleasantly, I hope."

A short silence fell while Mr. Littlefield frowned, unseeing, at Lady Gilliland's serene smile. "No," he said at last.

"I thought not." She smoothed her gloves delicately, not meeting his eyes. "I am aware that you once had different designs for Chloe's future, but it seemed to me that you had abandoned those plans in recent years."

Her voice contained a question. She glanced at Mr. Littlefield and received a curt nod in answer to it.

"Yes," he said gruffly. There was bitterness in his expression. "I still believe Chloe could have married as high as she chose. But we won't speak of that. I was very displeased with her. Very."

Lady Gilliland adopted what she hoped was a sympathetic expression. She had strong opinions on the subject of Horace Littlefield's gross mismanagement of his marriage, his property, and his daughter, but expressing them now would hardly serve her ends.

"You are well aware of Gil's circumstances, Horace, so I see no need to enumerate them for you. His birth is not noble, of course, but the baronetcy will one day be his, and his fortune is far from contemptible. There can be no doubt that he holds Chloe in considerable affection. I feel sure he would make her an admirable husband."

Mr. Littlefield rose and took a turn about the room, his hands clasped tightly behind his back. "Pray do not take it amiss, Aurelia, if I seem a trifle—astonished. The notion of an alliance between our families had simply never occurred to me."

"Well, now that we have broached the idea, I hope you will give it your serious consideration. It's my belief there are advantages to the match on either side. But I must say, I never expected such an opportunity to—er—fall into our laps. I think we ought not to let it slip past us. Chloe and Gil have such a strongly established friendship, you know, that such a moment might never arise again."

She waited, covertly watching her neighbor's face. He was thinking furiously, and she could guess the direction of his thoughts. After a moment, she added softly, "Naturally, Sir Walter is prepared to discuss a handsome settlement."

Mr. Littlefield's eyes focused keenly on hers. He uttered a short, mirthless laugh. "Is he? Well, that's fair. That's only fair."

It seemed to her that Mr. Littlefield's breath quickened. He even licked his lips. She looked away in distaste. Horace Littlefield had always been a mercenary creature. One felt for him, of course, left dependent on Chloe by the terms of his late wife's will—really, a shocking arrangement!—but Aurelia was much inclined to think that a man who so blatantly married for money deserved his fate.

Still, Chloe was a very dear girl and it would be a pleasure to rescue her from the oppressive life she led at Brookhollow. And the Littlefield property would round out Gil's estate nicely. If Sir Walter had to pay through the nose to purchase an independence for Horace Littlefield, so be it. Chloe would bring ample funds into the family coffers to replace whatever they had to give Horace. Aurelia made a mental note that they must give Horace enough money to enable him to leave the neighborhood entirely. Otherwise, he would doubtless set up a local mistress and continue to make Chloe miserable. Chloe had borne enough.

"I shall ask Sir Walter to call on you," she announced, gathering up her reticule and tippet and preparing to depart.

Mr. Littlefield, still frowning slightly, clasped her hand briefly in farewell. It was difficult, Lady Gilliland supposed, for him to discard his dreams of a noble marriage for his only child. But unless Chloe's hand were forced, it was quite possible she would never marry at all. She had certainly been adamant on the issue, the only other time it had arisen.

At the door, Aurelia offered her host a gracious smile. "If the three of us—you, my husband, and myself—act in concert, I have every hope that we can turn this situation to good account."

She recognized the avaricious gleam in Mr. Littlefield's eyes and the rather obsequious bow he gave her. Horace's greed would always trump his lesser emotions, she thought cynically.

"Certainly, madam," he said, as if confirming her reading of his character. "I shall look forward to Sir Walter's visit."

Chapter 3

Gil sat at the breakfast table in his dressing gown, staring goggle-eyed at his copy of the *Morning Post*. A substantial repast sat before him, uneaten. The London traffic clattered by beneath his window, unheard. A stack of invitations and correspondence rested beneath his hand, unopened. Sylvester Gilliland appeared to have been turned to stone.

A sound of fierce pounding, as of urgent fists upon a not-very-distant door, eventually penetrated his consciousness. Voices sounded in the hall below, followed by the clatter of hurrying feet. Someone appeared to be racing someone else up the stairs. There were several other lodgers in the building, but Gil lifted his dazed eyes and, with a sense of bemused inevitability, fixed his gaze upon his own door. Within moments, it flew open, as he had been sure it would.

The two cronies in whose company he had just spent a convivial evening burst into the room as if shot by a cannon. One was a gangly fellow, as tall as Gil, his thin face dominated by a nose that gave him an undeservedly fierce and hawklike aspect. The other, younger and shorter, was a plump and genial soul with a perpetually startled expression. Each waved a newspaper.

"What the devil is this?" demanded Jack Crawley, in a roar that matched his bird-of-prey face. Gil winced. Barney Furbush, perceiving that Gil was still at breakfast and apparently not fully awake, set his newspaper on the table and turned to soothe his companion.

"Don't shout, old man. We'll soon get to the bottom of it. If anyone knows what this is all about, it's Gil. Bound to!"

He turned earnestly to Gil. "Suggest you make a clean breast of it, Gil. If you're under the hatches, dear old chap, you know you can always turn to me. No need to marry an heiress."

Jack dropped into the chair opposite Gil. "At any rate, you ought not to keep secrets from Barney and me," he said severely. "You never said a word last night. Shabby, I call it!"

Barney pulled another chair up to Gil's tiny table. "Now, Jack, don't fly into one of your miffs. Daresay he forgot. Anyone might."

"Forgot! Forgot he was getting *married?*"

Barney rubbed his nose thoughtfully. "Daresay he didn't care to remember it," he said wisely. "Happens all the time. Remember m'sister's coming-out party? I nearly went to Bath instead. If I hadn't happened to run into my mother in Bond Street that morning, I'd have missed it. Think of the dust they would have kicked up! A very near-run thing."

Gil's eyes, still wide with shock, swiveled to fix upon Barney's kindly face. He swallowed painfully but did not speak. Barney nudged Jack and pointed this out in an under-voice. "Why, it's my belief it's all a hum. Look at Gil! He's been landed a facer."

Jack's beetling brows climbed. "No. Really? I say, that's a rum go." He shook his head sympathetically and picked up Gil's coffeepot. "Some prankster must've planted the story in the *Post*, then. Daresay the chit doesn't even exist."

Barney, relieved, helped himself to a slice of toast and began buttering it. "Good thing, if that's all it is."

Jack frowned. "Yes, but who would want to do Gil such a mischief? I mean—notice in the *Post*! That's serious."

"Not if it's just a hum. Gil can't marry a chit who don't exist. Goes without saying."

Jack nodded, sipping coffee. Then his eyes narrowed in suspicion. "How can it be a hum? I mean—the *Post*, you know! That's a devilish starchy outfit. You can't slip a note under the door at dead of night and expect the *Post* to print it! Besides, if they start printing notices willy-nilly, what prevents your engagement being announced tomorrow? Or mine? A fellow might wake up any morning to find himself in the basket! Not likely the *Post* would lend itself to that."

Barney appeared much struck. "No, by Jove!" He turned his mild gaze upon Gil. "Crawley's right, Gil. You must have placed the notice yourself."

Gil made a sort of choking sound. The two friends waited expectantly.

"Chloe's father," he croaked. "Must have been Chloe's father."

"Ah," said Barney, satisfied. "That's all right and tight." He nudged Jack with his elbow. "Girl's father! *Not* a note slipped under the door."

Jack was frowning again. "Then the chit does exist."

"Lord, yes! I've known her all my life."

Barney swallowed a bit of toast. "Is she really an heiress?" he asked, interested. "Featherstone says she is."

Jack snorted. "Featherstone! When has he ever said anything worth repeating?"

Gil poured himself coffee with a hand that shook only slightly. "He's right this time, at least. Not that it matters. Chloe may have all the money in the world for aught I care. *I* don't want it!"

Barney nodded approvingly. "Quite right, old man. Oughtn't to have mentioned it. Beg pardon! Daresay we should congratulate you, though." A qualm seemed to shake him. He turned to Jack for guidance. "That's all right, isn't it? To congratulate dear old Gil? I've heard people congratulating fellows who were marrying perfect antidotes. Customary!"

"Of course it's customary, you nodcock!" said Jack scornfully. "But there's something havey-cavey about all this. Gil don't want to be married."

Barney looked shocked. "Yes, he does. Isn't that why we're here? Notice in the *Post*!"

Gil raked a hand through his hair. "But it's the most appalling thing!" he exclaimed. "I never offered for Chloe!"

His friends gaped at him. "How is that possible?" demanded Jack.

"You must have," said Barney simply.

"Dash it all, I ought to know whether I offered marriage to a girl or not!"

"You *ought* to," said Barney cautiously. "Perhaps you were a trifle disguised. A man might say anything when he's in his cups."

Jack rounded on Barney, annoyed. "Have you ever seen Gil foxed in the company of females?"

"Haven't seen him, foxed or otherwise, in the company of females. Come to think of it, I'm rarely in the company of females myself. Daresay a man needs a nip or two to bear it. Perfectly understandable."

Jack seemed inclined to argue the point, but Gil interrupted. "I don't need Dutch courage to spend time with Chloe! Haven't I just been telling you, I've known her all my life? But I don't want to *marry* her!"

Barney clucked his tongue sympathetically. "Rabbity-faced? All heiresses are, I believe."

Jack nodded. "It's practically a law of nature. Every girl with plenty of rhino is hideous."

Gil shrugged impatiently. "Not Chloe. She's a perfect little beauty."

His friends glanced at him in surprise.

"Is she, by Jove! Then where's the rub?" asked Jack. "Hot temper?"

Barney shuddered. "I say, Gil, if she's shrewish, don't marry her! Now, there's a horrible thing! My uncle's wife is an absolute harpy. Torments him day and night. Daresay he'll murder her one day and cause the very devil of a scandal. Frightful prospect for the family, but what can one do?"

"Chloe's not shrewish! She's the best-natured girl imaginable. Always full of fun and gig; never takes a pet about anything. Sound as a roast."

A brief silence fell. Gil's friends stared at him very hard.

"Well? Don't keep us in suspense," said Jack impatiently. "Does she smell of the shop?"

"The *shop*?" Gil gave a sudden crack of laughter. "I'd love to see her father's face if he heard you ask that! Very high in the instep, Horace Littlefield. His mother was a

Westwood, for God's sake. Chloe's great-uncle is the present earl."

"Then what's wrong with her?"

Gil's eyes widened in bewildered astonishment. "There's nothing *wrong* with her! Why the devil should there be anything wrong with her?"

Barney and Jack looked at each other, as if mutely seeking guidance.

Jack suddenly slapped the breakfast table with conviction. "Well, I'll tell you what, Gil—if you won't marry her, I will! She sounds like a deuced paragon."

Gil managed a rather shaky grin. "Oh, she is! If she ever came to Town, she'd have 'em all eating out of her hand. Chloe's a very taking little thing. But she won't come to Town. Chloe don't wish to be married any more than I do. In fact, far less! I do mean to marry someday, but Clo says she won't marry anyone, ever."

Barney looked at his friend uneasily. "I say, Gil, are you feeling quite the thing? I mean—*you're* going to marry her."

"Unless I do," said Jack hopefully. "If she don't appeal to you, Gil, would you mind introducing us? She sounds just the thing to me. Beautiful—rich—sweet-tempered—well-connected—"

"She won't have you, Crawley," interrupted Gil. "It ain't that ridiculous beak of yours, so don't poker up! Chloe won't have anyone. I'm telling you, the chit's determined never to marry."

Barney appeared doubtful. "She's female, ain't she?"

"Yes, I never met a female who didn't want a wedding. They all do."

"Not Chloe."

"Why not?" chorused Gil's friends.

Gil opened his mouth, then shut it again. "Don't ask me to betray a lady's confidence, for I won't do it!" He shoved his hands defiantly into the pockets of his dressing gown. "You may take my word for it, Chloe won't want to step into parson's mousetrap. With me or anyone else. Problem is—we are in the suds! No use hoping people won't see that dashed notice. They will."

Barney nodded sympathetically. "If they don't see that one, they'll see the one in the *Gazette*."

Gil paled. "It's in the *Gazette*, too? The devil! What am I to do?"

Jack frowned. "I suppose you'll have to send another notice, repudiating these."

"Repudiate an engagement to a respectable female?" Gil cried, aghast. "What kind of ugly customer do you take me for?"

Barney shook his head dolefully. "Scaly behavior. Very bad *ton*. But Jack's right, old fellow. There's nothing else to be done."

"Aye, and the sooner the better. Before everyone starts congratulating you, wishing you happy and all that."

Gil rose and took a hasty turn about the room. "But what about Chloe? What a shabby thing to do to her!"

"Humiliating," agreed Barney. "But I daresay she won't mind if you make a figure of her. No one else will have her, of course, once you turn short about. But you've already said she don't wish to be married."

Jack uttered a short bark of laughter. "People will always pursue an heiress, let alone a pretty heiress! You won't do her any lasting injury."

"I don't wish to do her an injury, lasting or otherwise! There must be another alternative." Gil pounded a fist into his palm. "I shall think of something."

His friends' silence, though sympathetic, was not encouraging. Gil wished to high heaven he could discuss the matter with Chloe. Common courtesy dictated that he consult her in something that concerned her so nearly. Besides, if he knew Chloe, she would have very strong opinions regarding what they ought to do.

If he returned and sought her at Brookhollow, however, he would run slap into Horace Littlefield. Gil felt fairly confident that if he met Horace Littlefield today, he would murder him the instant he saw him. He had no wish to spend the rest of his days hiding on the Continent, so a quick trip to Brookhollow was out of the question.

In the end, he decided to send Chloe an urgent private

message and await her reply. Although he did so immediately, this course necessarily engendered a delay before taking any action to dispel the rumors. Delay, he soon discovered, contained its own pitfalls. A saunter down Jermyn Street that morning brought home to him all the evils of his situation. Nearly everyone he encountered congratulated him and peppered him with what struck him as intrusive and impertinent questions.

He returned to his flat in a rare swivet, by this time feeling much the way he supposed a hare feels when set upon by hounds. He scarcely had time to draw a deep breath and savor his solitude, however, before he heard the sound of the knocker. He strode swiftly to his door and opened it, his gaze wildly seeking, and finding, his man Graves crossing the hall below.

"I am not at home!" he hissed.

"Very good, sir."

Gil retreated behind his closed door with a sigh of relief and poured himself a stiff brandy. A man needed a restorative after the sort of morning he had just had. He plopped into a wing chair and glumly regarded the fire. He was in the briars, and how to extract himself—aye, and Chloe!—was more than he could fathom.

The door opened. Graves stood there, evidently attempting to signal him, but Gil could not interpret the man's grimaces and winks. "What the devil is it?" snapped Gil.

"Females, sir!"

Gil straightened in his chair, horrified. "No! No!" he uttered feebly, but a small hand, fashionably covered in York tan, appeared from behind Graves, insistently pushing him aside.

"Pray do not block the door, Graves. I know perfectly well my brother is at home," announced a clear soprano voice in the hall, "and if you do not instantly permit me to have speech with him, I shall *scream!*"

And into Gil's sanctuary strode two invaders. Gil automatically rose from his chair at their approach, but his aspect was far from welcoming. One was his sister, Leticia, now Mrs. Dalrymple, a vivid brunette dressed very becomingly and in the height of the current mode. The other was Chloe Littlefield. Gil's jaw dropped.

"Clo, by all that's wonderful!"

Chloe glared speechlessly at him. Tish flew to her friend's side and placed a sustaining arm about her waist. "Now, don't rip up at poor Gil, Chloe," she said warningly. "I feel nearly certain he had nothing to do with it."

"If I thought he had," uttered Chloe passionately, "I would never speak to him again!"

"Take a damper," said Gil, exasperated. "You may go, Graves! And, mind you, if anyone else should call for me, for God's sake keep 'em out! I don't know what you were about, to bring these two up—"

"Do not blame Graves," interrupted Tish. "We saw you come in, so he couldn't fob us off."

"Yes, but it's the height of impropriety for you to be here at all! Females don't call on single gentlemen."

"That is what I told her," agreed Tish. "But she *would* come! So I had to accompany her, of course, to keep tongues from wagging."

"You mean this visit was *Chloe's* idea? Clo, in the name of heaven—!"

"Oh, hush!" cried Chloe, her face suffused with agitated color. "If you don't know an emergency when you see one, Gil, I do! I shall go mad if anyone preaches propriety to me, when we are in the worst scrape of our lives!"

Any lingering doubts Gil may have had as to Chloe's wishes vanished. Sobered, he begged pardon and waved his visitors into chairs, remarking as he did so that he wished it were permissible to offer them brandy. "For if I ever saw anyone in need of a bracer, Clo, it's you!" he said, observing her critically.

She sat tensely on the edge of her chair, her hands clenching and unclenching in her lap. She was dressed in one of the ill-fitting muslins that Gertrude Tewksbury had made for her, covered with a shapeless pelisse as practical as it was unflattering. Her soft, pale ringlets were crowned with a bonnet that was at least five years out of date. Sitting across from the dazzling Mrs. Dalrymple, she did not appear to advantage.

"I will drink brandy if you think it would help," she said.

Gil moved to bring her some, but Tish cried out against it, scandalized. "Really, Gil! You will only make bad worse! What possible use would spirits be in a situation like this?"

"You'd be surprised," he muttered, but dropped back into his chair.

Chloe turned wide, tragic eyes upon him. "You did not place that notice in the *Gazette*?"

He straightened indignantly. "No, nor the *Post*! You can't have thought *that*!"

"No," she said, her voice catching tragically. "But I had to *know*, Gil."

"I told you as much!" said Tish. She was perched gracefully on the edge of Gil's wing chair, her hands buried in an expensive-looking fur muff. Her dark eyes were bright with curiosity and excitement. What was high tragedy to her friend and her brother was clearly vastly entertaining to Tish.

Chloe's hands clenched again. "The devil fly away with Father!" she exclaimed miserably. "I am sure, now, it was he who placed the notices. But I would not have believed he could use me so!"

Gil snorted. "Why not? He's been trying to control you from the instant you were born! Although he never before had the effrontery to involve *me* in his attempts to bring you round his thumb. I suppose he simply did not think of it until now! For of all the high-handed, stiff-rumped gudgeons— but this bears the palm! Whatever possessed him?"

Her eyes blurred with angry tears. "Need you ask? It was that stupid incident at Barlow's cottage, of course. He's been saying ever since that you *compromised* me. Such stuff! But it wasn't only Father. You will not believe this, Gil—I can scarcely credit it myself—but your parents have been saying the same thing."

"What!"

"Yes! Only to me, of course, but still—"

"Good God! But they *can't* have thought—that is, why,

surely nobody believed—" Gil ran his hands wildly through his hair, heedless of the damage inflicted on his carefully arranged locks.

Chloe shook her own curls vehemently. "Of course not! That is what made the whole thing so absurd. I tried to laugh it off, you know—I was sure they would give it up once they came to their senses—but that only seemed to make matters worse. Father became absolutely unreasonable. He began insisting that I was 'damaged goods.' Did you ever hear anything more ugly?"

Tish cried out in horror. Gil only stared at her, dumbstruck. Chloe seemed to take comfort from her friends' indignant sympathy. Her spine straightened, and she sighed. "There was no bearing it, of course, so I came to visit Tish, as you asked me to. I only arrived last night. I was going to send you word this morning, but then Mr. Dalrymple saw the notice in the *Gazette*—"

Tish giggled. "Robert came in to breakfast and wished Chloe happy! You should have seen her face!"

"Tish, it is *not* funny!"

Gil moved impatiently. "No use trying to tell Tish something ain't funny; she'll laugh all the more. But, Clo, how could this have happened? Why would anyone—even your father!—announce our engagement without so much as a by-your-leave? I had nary a notion that this was in *anyone's* mind, let alone yours or mine! No one said a word to me."

"Nor to me! That is—well, Father went on about it until I was ready to scream, and Lady Gilliland did, too—but she only used the vaguest terms, I promise you! I never dreamed they were serious. And I never, *never* agreed to anything they said! On the contrary, I always insisted it was a completely harebrained idea and that I would have none of it."

Gil slapped a hand to his forehead. "If that isn't just like you, Chloe, to hear something told you over and over, and never listen to it simply because you don't care to!" he exclaimed. "Why the devil didn't you send for me? *I'd* have

scotched this precious engagement plan before it got
started!"

"Yes, but then Chloe would not have come to visit me,"
said Tish comfortably. "On the whole, I think this a very
good thing."

Chloe and Gil stared at her, revulsion writ large across
their faces.

Tish's irrepressible laughter bubbled forth at their horrified expressions. "Well, I *do!* I am in favor of anything that
produces such an excellent result. I believed nothing would
suffice to pry Chloe off that stupid farm and bring her to
Town, and here she is!" She tossed her head, setting her earrings dancing. "To my mind, you are both making a great
piece of work about nothing. You are both of age; no one can
force you to marry! Why not be engaged for a time? I daresay it would be quite amusing."

"Amusing!"

"You're mad!"

"No such thing. I enjoyed my own betrothal very much."
A shadow passed across Tish's sunny face. "It's far more fun
than marriage."

Gil, preoccupied with his own troubles, failed to observe
his sister's brief stumble. "Oh, excellent!" he said, with
withering sarcasm. "Hoax the *ton!* And then, I suppose, cry
off at the end of the Season! What a popular pair we would
be!"

"You need not cry off at any particular time. You need not
cry off at all. You could simply be engaged indefinitely."

"What, and never marry?" Gil looked as if he would like
to strangle Tish. "And good luck to us, trying to fix our interest with anyone else while engaged to each other! Of all
the corkbrained schemes—"

"Chloe doesn't wish to fix her interest with anyone. And I
daresay she would agree to jilt you, at whatever point you
met a lady who caught your eye."

Chloe sat up indignantly. "No! I will not *jilt* Gil. How can
you ask it of me? It would make him look such a fool!"

"Yes, by Jove, so it would!"

Tish gave a little crow of laughter. "What difference does

it make if you jilt him today, or a year from today? He will look nohow regardless."

Chloe turned anxiously to Gil. "That had not occurred to me. Must I jilt you? Why?"

He glanced uneasily into Chloe's troubled eyes. "I cannot jilt you, that's certain."

Tish nodded vehemently. "It isn't done. Now, don't argue, Chloe! A gentleman cannot cry off."

"But this is intolerable! Cannot you and I make some mutual announcement?"

Gil looked doubtful. "I suppose we could," he said at last. "We can put it about that we've decided we don't suit. Everyone will still assume it's my fault, but that don't signify."

Chloe's eyes were round with astonishment. "Why should anyone suppose it to be your fault? Good heavens! This is no one's fault but Father's! Why not simply tell the truth? I think we should publish a notice that my father announced our engagement without our knowledge or consent."

Gil's expression did not lighten. "That won't fadge, Clo."

Tish patted her friend's hand sympathetically. "Poor Chloe! She's lived so removed from the world, this all seems utterly gothic to her. Gil is right, dearest. You cannot tell part of the truth without the whole truth becoming known. If you announce that your father published your engagement against your will, everyone will wonder at it, and whisper, and before you have time to turn round it will be common knowledge that the two of you spent a night alone in a cottage."

"But that's nonsensical! How could anyone find out?"

Gil shook his head glumly. "It's a mystery how these things become known, but they always do. And if the tabbies don't find out the truth, they'll invent something even worse. No smoke without a fire, they'll say." His voice took on a high-pitched whisper as he imitated the gossips. "'There must be *some* reason why Horace Littlefield was anxious to marry his daughter to that ramshackle Mr. Gilliland! Some very *good* reason! Sss-sss-sss!'"

The bewildered expression on Chloe's face momentarily

turned indignant. "You are not *ramshackle!* But I do not care what anyone says, and I don't see why you should."

Gil threw up his hands in despair, and his sister turned patiently to their countrified friend. "You have never been the victim of such gossip, so you can't know how dreadful it can be. And, Chloe, pray bear in mind that it would injure my brother as well as you! He would figure in everyone's minds as the villain who compromised an innocent girl and then washed his hands of her."

"I own I would rather not make such a cake of myself," admitted Gil. "But if it's the only way out, I will do it. For Chloe's sake."

Chloe, with a bitter exclamation, rose and walked to the window. "We must do nothing that will blacken Gil's name," she said at last. "He has to live among these people, after all." She turned and bleakly regarded her friends. "But I cannot bear to let Father win, even temporarily. It was contemptible of him to place us in such a position. I thought if we denied the engagement, it would shame him."

"Yes," said Gil gently. Her distress was hard to watch. "But it will shame us as well."

Two large tears welled up in Chloe's eyes. "Gil, what are we to do?"

Tish flew to her side and hugged her. "Nothing, at present," she advised. "Oh, Chloe, don't cry! You'll come about."

Gil crossed the room and thumped Chloe vigorously on the back. "Buck up, Clo! We'll weather this," he promised her.

Chloe gave a rather watery chuckle. "Sorry!" she gulped. "I do hope, Gil, that the next lady who becomes engaged to you is less upset by the idea than I am."

He grinned. "Aye, it's a lowering experience to find myself betrothed to a watering pot."

Tish began pulling Chloe toward the door. "I do think, now that you're here, you ought to enjoy your visit," she said gaily. "I mean to show you the best shops in Bond Street."

She shot her brother a meaningful glance over Chloe's

head, and he nodded grimly. "The sooner the better!" he muttered, looking with distaste at Chloe's dowdy raiment.

Chloe brightened a little. "Now?"

"Now," promised Tish. Her eyes danced with mischief. "After all, every bride needs a trousseau."

Chapter 4

MMiss Littlefield, as the cherished guest of the dashing Mrs. Dalrymple, spent the next several days plunged into a whirlwind of pleasant activity. She was kept so busy, and so completely entertained, that it was almost impossible for her to remember the terrible trouble she was in.

Tish refused to allow Chloe to appear in public until she was suitably clothed and coiffed, and sent her beloved friend on such an intense round of shopping and sight-seeing that Chloe was exhausted at each day's end. This was deliberate. Tish was anxious to ensure that Chloe was in no mood for parties until such time as she could burst upon the scene with all the glory that Tish was secretly planning for her. But, as it turned out, Tish was fretting over nothing. It never occurred to innocent, reclusive Chloe that evenings spent quietly before a fire and going early to bed were an odd introduction to life in a fashionable London town house.

She saw very little of Robert Dalrymple. Tish informed her, with an elaborate show of unconcern, that fashionable couples were careful not to sit in each other's pockets. Chloe privately thought that this was one fashion Tish would have been glad not to follow. Tish had always been an open-hearted, affectionate girl, and Chloe saw no sign that her temperament had altered. She was very sure that Tish had loved Mr. Dalrymple when she married him, and it had certainly seemed that her affection was returned. Could matters have undergone so complete a change in less than three years? Chloe wondered. She knew little of such things. Having been alerted by Gil, she was covertly watching her friend. But she was given no opportunity to glimpse Tish and Robert's private life and none for intimate conversation with Tish. All she could do was promise herself that she would address the question later, after she had "settled in." For surely they could not keep up this hectic pace forever!

But Tish successfully thwarted her every attempt at reestablishing their former intimacy. Tish was sure she could hide nothing from Chloe if Chloe was allowed to look too closely, and she was desperately protecting several secrets. For one thing, she was guiltily aware that her friend would be horrified if she knew that Tish planned for her to join the ranks of the beau monde. Chloe had no social ambitions at all. The pleasure she took in her first spending sprees, and the delight in her eyes when she beheld herself clad in pretty clothes, were entirely guileless. Chloe was enjoying her transformation for its own sake, with no thought of how her appearance might affect others. But Tish knew something of the delights of popularity. She was determined that Chloe should experience all the pleasures in society that she herself enjoyed. To that end, she gently supervised the choice of Chloe's every gown and bonnet and glove, and even presided over the labors of the artist engaged to cut and arrange Chloe's hair. At last, Tish thought exultantly, Chloe's outward trappings would do justice to her beauty!

Tish herself was, as she laughingly confided to Chloe, an extremely sought-after personage. Blessed with vivacity and saucy good looks, married to a rich young man whom she adored, and with a healthy heir toddling about in her nursery, it was widely held that Leticia Dalrymple was the most fortunate of women. But Chloe thought she sometimes caught a hint of sadness lurking in Tish's eyes. At times there was a reckless, brittle quality to Tish's laughter that quite wrung Chloe's heart. She was both surprised and alarmed when it became more evident every day that Tish was disinclined to talk about whatever was bothering her. Chloe waited in vain for Tish to broach the subject and soon discovered that every hint she dropped would be carefully ignored.

She wished she could report all this to Gil. It confirmed the suspicions he had confided to her, and she would have been glad to receive his advice on the matter. But she never saw Gil. After that first disastrous morning in London, Tish kept Chloe on a very short leash. There was no time for anything but shopping, fittings, and more shopping. Enjoyable as all this was to a girl who had never experienced anything like it, Chloe began to chafe at being kept apart from her dearest friend. Just as she was about to insist that Tish at least invite her brother for dinner, Tish declared that Chloe was ready.

"Ready for what?" The two girls were closeted in Chloe's room, the Dalrymples' second-best bedchamber, crawling across the carpet on their hands and knees. This unladylike activity had been rendered necessary by the ingenious method the friends had recently devised for choosing dress patterns. It had proved impossible to compare and select patterns while sitting decorously at a table, since no table in the Dalrymples' house was large enough, so they now simply scattered them all across the floor. This answered very well. With the door shut against censorious eyes, the two girls spent many a contented hour crawling about, stacking and restacking the piles as if playing some elaborate game of Patience. Tish's young son often joined them, since crawling on the floor was one of the few skills at which he was an acknowledged master. His contributions to their pattern choices were generally overruled, but their rejection of his sartorial taste in no way dampened Bobby's enthusiasm for the project.

Bobby's participation had become, at this particular point, more of a hindrance than an amusement. Tish scooped him up and bounced him on her lap. Chloe, concentrating on the business at hand, lifted a sheet of paper from the floor. "I think this is rather pretty," she said.

"That's the one I had made up in orange sarcenet."

"Is it?" Chloe peered more closely at it. "I am picturing it in white gauze. Or perhaps pink."

"It would look entirely different. I don't mind a bit, if you should care to have it made up for yourself. Orange would not suit you, of course."

"No," agreed Chloe absently. "Sea green, perhaps, with satin piping—"

"Bah!" commented Bobby. Although his tone was forceful, this observation was not interpreted as an expression of criticism.

Tish chuckled. Her child was playing with her beads, and her friend was frowning at a dress pattern. They seemed equally unaware of the momentous import of her declaration. "Chloe, you are not attending!"

Chloe looked up in surprise. Her ringlets, now clustered becomingly round her face by the master who had cut her hair, emphasized her doll-like countenance and gave her wide-eyed expression an absurdly childlike appearance. Tish bit back a laugh. "I think it is high time you met a few of my friends. I am persuaded you will like them excessively. I have been invited to a drum this evening, and I really ought to attend. Would you care to accompany me?"

A troubled look crossed Chloe's face. "I never attend parties. Not parties with strangers."

"Only because you do not wish to be pursued," Tish countered swiftly. "But think, Chloe—no one will pursue you now. Even if people find out about your tedious fortune, everyone believes you to be engaged to Gil."

"That's true." Chloe sat back on her heels and regarded Tish thoughtfully. Tish immediately busied herself with smoothing Bobby's curls and straightening the collar of his dress. It would be fatal for Chloe to guess the size and nature of this party; she would surely refuse to go.

Chloe dimpled. "You are sure I won't disgrace you?"

"Well, not *sure*—but reasonably certain!" Tish kept her voice carefully casual, and was rewarded by the sight of interest lighting Chloe's eyes.

"I would enjoy it, I think. What should I wear?"

"I will come to you at half-past seven and help you choose, if you like."

Tish was so successful at downplaying the importance of the event that Chloe felt nothing but pleasurable anticipation. She donned a delicious silk gown that evening, its flattering hue the palest of pinks, and expressed unalloyed

delight in her own unaccustomed modishness. She laughed
at Tish's earnestness regarding the arrangement of her curls,
and clasped a string of chaste pearls round her neck with no
more thought than if she were simply going downstairs to
dinner. She was a little shocked by Tish's costume, a light-
weight and low-cut confection that left little to the imagina-
tion. But Tish only laughed when she saw the condemnation
in her friend's eyes, and assured Chloe that her gown was all
the crack.

"It would not do for you, of course," Tish added airily.
"But married women are allowed a great deal of license."

Chloe supposed that Tish was right—well, from what she
had already seen of London, she knew Tish was right—but
the faint blush that had crept up Tish's neck did not escape
her. She thought Tish shared her view that her gown was im-
modest, but for some undisclosed reason she had chosen to
wear it anyway. Chloe wondered at this oddity but was
silent.

They arrived downstairs and learned that Robert Dalrymple had gone, as he frequently did, to his club for dinner. The
news was delivered in colorless tones by the Dalrymples'
very correct butler. Chloe glanced at her friend, concerned
that Tish would feel hurt by this mark of her husband's neglect, but although an angry flush mounted Tish's cheek, she
shrugged it off. It even seemed that she felt oddly relieved.
Stranger and stranger, thought Chloe, puzzled.

They departed in the Dalrymples' carriage in grand style,
with two liveried and powdered footmen up behind. Chloe
was thus reminded that Mr. Dalrymple was the younger son
of an earl. She had never before seen his lineage trumpeted
in this way, and remarked, laughing, that she felt like Cinderella on her way to the ball. Tish offered only a nervous
smile in response to this sally. Chloe soon discovered why.
When the carriage halted behind a long line of similar
coaches, she lifted the curtain, peered out, and discovered
that her silly comparison to Cinderella's ball was, in fact,
distressingly near the mark.

"Merciful heavens!" she gasped.

They had joined a queue of elegant equipages approach-

ing the entrance of the grandest house Chloe had ever seen.
Light blazed forth from every window of its imposing edi-
fice, and flambeaux flickered on either side of its enormous
door. As each carriage reached the head of the line, footmen
sprang smartly forward to open the doors and hand out the
passengers. A parade of gorgeously arrayed persons was
processing slowly up the marble steps to the entrance.

Chloe turned accusing eyes upon her friend, and Tish
burst out laughing. "Now, Chloe, don't eat me!" she begged.

"You told me it was a party of your particular friends!"

"Well, so it is. Do not allow yourself to be overset! Beneath all the silk and linen they are only people, after all.
And pray remember that your own silk and linen is as elegant as anything you will see at Lady Paversham's drum!
There is no cause for anxiety."

But by the time the Dalrymple carriage had reached the
head of the line, Chloe's eyes had dilated into twin pools of
terror. Seeing this, Tish rapped her with her fan. "Remember
that you do not care a button for what any of them may
think! You have no desire to make a splash among the fash-
ionables. You have told me so any number of times."

Some color returned to Chloe's cheeks. She gave a shaky
laugh. "Thank you! I will bear it in mind."

It was true, Chloe reminded herself. And reminded herself. Still, she found it necessary to silently repeat, *These
people cannot harm me, these people cannot harm me,* like
a litany as she stepped from the carriage and entered the por-
tals of her first London appearance. The thought stiffened
her spine and enabled her to achieve a certain degree of
poise. Still, since she was unexpectedly facing the very sort
of gathering she had scrupulously avoided since her eigh-
teenth birthday, she could not help feeling a trifle tense.

To her surprise, everyone she met was extremely kind to
her. Lady Paversham took Chloe briefly under her wing and
introduced her to several persons, all of whom bowed and
smiled and said something pleasant. There was such a racket
of many voices all talking at once that Chloe caught none of
their names. It didn't seem to matter. Tish then guided her
firmly by the elbow as they made their way slowly through

the crowd, speaking first to this one, then to that, until all the smiling faces became a blur to Chloe.

The two friends finally arrived at a wall at the extreme end of the room, and stood their ground beside a set of French windows that opened onto a balcony. "It will be cooler here," explained Tish.

Chloe gratefully sank onto a tiny spindle-legged chair. Despite the unexpected amiability she had encountered thus far, it was not her notion of entertainment to join a horde of well-dressed strangers who all seemed to be well acquainted with each other, and listen to them converse, with gradually increasing volume, in an overcrowded room. It was obvious why this sort of gathering was called a "drum." Chloe's ears were already ringing with the noise.

It was also becoming quite warm. Lady Paversham's ballroom, or whatever this was, contained a vast quantity of candles and more people than Chloe had ever seen gathered in one place. Tish's careful steering toward the windows had been an excellent idea.

From the chair, Chloe hoped, her diminutive person would prove inconspicuous. For a time she sat quietly, watching the beautifully gowned women and impeccably tailored men swirl around her. She was not allowed to hide for long, however. Beside her, Tish was holding court. A steady stream of persons approached and hailed Mrs. Dalrymple, and Tish was soon thrown into the sort of infectious high spirits that Chloe irresistibly associated with impending disaster. During their childhood, whenever little Tish had burned with that reckless light she had inevitably run headlong into danger. Chloe's uneasiness was not alleviated when she noticed that the majority of persons with whom her friend seemed to be intimately acquainted were gentlemen. She was pulled to her feet and presented to a score of them. All of them were young, most of them had an indefinable air of rakishness about them, and some of them evinced the high color and loud laughter of men who had been drinking something stronger than lemonade.

Chloe had never thought of herself as a prude, but although some of Tish's acquaintances seemed agreeable, many of them made her hackles rise. She frequently found herself fighting an absurd urge to protect her friend, usually in the guise of wanting to pull Tish bodily away from the scapegrace who was frankly ogling her trim figure, or the drunken fool who was whispering something in her ear that made her blush.

Chloe was kept busy chatting with the group that surrounded them, but she saw Tish's eyes occasionally searching the room, as if looking for someone. When she did so, there was a kind of pitiful eagerness in her eyes that went to Chloe's heart. She found herself strongly tempted to give Robert Dalrymple a piece of her mind. Dinner at the club, indeed! She hoped, for Tish's sake, that Robert would make an appearance after all and gladden his young wife's heart. For all her popularity with this extremely fast crowd, Tish was unhappy, and Chloe thought she knew why.

Then, as she watched Tish adroitly extricate herself from the encircling arm of an admirer, Chloe saw her eyes, fixed on the crowd, light up. With an intense feeling of relief, Chloe turned to welcome Robert Dalrymple. She was still looking for him when she noticed a stranger languidly approaching their group.

All thought of Robert Dalrymple fled. Chloe's eyes, fastened on the unknown gentleman, caught and held like a fish on a hook. She stared. She could not help it. He was, quite simply, the most attractive man she had ever seen.

He was impeccably dressed but did not cultivate the formal, mannered stance of the other gentlemen in the room. He moved naturally, gracefully, like a panther. And like a panther, he gave an instant impression of lethal power, carefully controlled. He seemed older than the callow gentlemen surrounding Tish, but that may have been a trick of air and manner. He moved with a sort of nonchalant assurance, and had the air of a man accustomed to command. He pressed through the crowd effortlessly. It almost seemed to part for him.

Chloe's reaction to him was instantaneous, and shockingly physical. She was at a complete loss to explain it. He was not precisely handsome, at least not in the classical mode that she had been taught to admire. Dark hair, dark eyes, and strong features stamped with a faintly mocking expression were all she had time to note before he was upon them and Tish was performing introductions.

For once, Chloe made sure she caught the man's name.

"Chloe, pray allow me to present George Carstairs, Lord Rival. Lord Rival, this is Miss Littlefield."

The man turned to her. His eyes raked her, and something in her appearance caused his keen gaze to sharpen. One brow shot up. Then he bowed, murmuring something polite. At least Chloe assumed it was something polite—but then she noticed his mouth turning down at one corner, and her assumption was instantly cast into doubt. His expression, one brow flying high and his mouth simultaneously curving up and curving down, conveyed both salacious admiration and sardonic amusement. She had never seen anything like it.

There was something shockingly intimate in his gaze. Chloe felt as if she had just been stripped naked. Completely nonplussed, she offered Lord Rival a stiff little curtsey.

His eyes, so dark they were nearly black, bored into hers. "Miss Littlefield, is it? I've heard a great deal about you."

His tone was perfectly polite, yet somehow it conveyed an impression of mockery. And there was nothing one could reply to such a remark, of course. He had not given any indication of the sorts of things he had heard, nor where he had heard them.

It seemed he awaited a reply. "Really?" uttered Chloe, feeling like an idiot.

His eyes flicked over her again and his smile widened. His mouth was firm-lipped, muscled and sensuous. She caught herself staring at it, and blushed.

"Will you allow a stranger to wish you happy?"

So *that* was what he had heard! She turned to Tish, stammering and agonized, mutely begging for rescue. But no rescue was forthcoming. Tish appeared to have heard nothing. She was gazing at Lord Rival like a besotted schoolgirl.

With a shock, Chloe realized she had completely misinterpreted her friend's restless behavior all evening. She had *not* been hoping against hope that her husband would arrive. It was Lord Rival, not Robert Dalrymple, who had lit the glow of excited welcome in Tish's eyes a moment ago.

Chloe's stammerings halted. She sucked in her breath sharply and turned to look at Lord Rival with new eyes. He seemed to have forgotten all about Chloe Littlefield; he was now smiling softly at Tish and bowing caressingly over her hand.

The mystery of Tish's unhappiness was solved at one stroke. This man was the toad who was poisoning the well.

Chapter 5

Lord Rival murmured something inaudible, for Tish's ears alone. Tish uttered a breathless little laugh and touched his lordship's sleeve. The gesture was fleeting, over in an instant, but Chloe felt as if she had just witnessed something shocking. Sick at heart, she wondered bitterly what she would tell Gil. It might be more than a brother and a friend could do, to rescue Tish from such a dangerous diversion. And neither Chloe nor Gil had any expertise in this particular game.

She watched in mute frustration as Tish, her eyes now bright with excited happiness, flirted and preened for the amusement of this languid stranger. Lord Rival's enjoyment of Tish's infatuation was obvious, but Chloe could not rid herself of the impression that the caressing manners he adopted, and the sly intimacy that his every gesture implied, were false. Standing to one side, observing Tish and Lord Rival without being able to catch the actual words of their conversation, Chloe was vividly aware of the unspoken messages that seemed to escape Tish. There was mockery beneath Lord Rival's smooth and well-practiced attentions, she was sure of it. Mockery, contempt, and boredom, all barely beneath the surface. Why, the man scarcely bothered to conceal them. One moment his eyes sought Tish's, hot and filled with scandalous promises. The next, they flicked away to idly scan the crowd, as if seeking better entertainment elsewhere.

Chloe felt anger growing within her. Tish may fancy herself a woman of the world, she thought, but at heart she is still the innocent schoolgirl I used to play jackstraws with! And this terrible man is amusing himself at her expense.

As if hearing her thoughts, Lord Rival suddenly glanced in her direction. She had that odd sensation again, as if he could see right through her—or at least right through her clothes. Her eyes sparkling with anger, she lifted her chin at him, then pointedly turned her shoulder.

Any normal man would react to such patent dislike with chagrin. Even a coxcomb ought to have the good sense to recognize her hostility and keep his distance. She was horrified when Lord Rival's response was exactly the opposite of what it should have been. His faint air of boredom instantly vanished. He dropped everything, walked away from Tish without a backward glance, and approached Chloe.

From the corner of her eye, she saw him advance through the knot of fashionable people. Chloe felt herself filling with wrathful astonishment. How dare he! But Lord Rival, she thought nervously, had the appearance of a man who dared anything. She hastily looked away, fanning herself and feigning disinterest.

She knew the exact moment he arrived at her side. He did not touch her, but it seemed to her that the air around him crackled and sparked with palpable electricity. Neither of them spoke for what seemed a very long moment.

Rudeness was clearly called for. Chloe was unused to practicing deliberate rudeness, but Lord Rival made any other response impossible. She summoned it from somewhere, and began.

"Well?" she said coldly. And waited.

"Well, what?"

She dared not look at him. She addressed her remarks to the middle distance. "Why have you approached me, sir?"

"I am come to offer my assistance."

Now she looked at him, surprised. He was taller than she had thought; she had to tilt her head to meet his eyes. They danced with mischief. Really, the man was far too attractive! Small wonder Tish was making a fool of herself.

"Assistance?" she repeated blankly.

"Yes. You had the most extraordinary expression on your

face just now." He leaned one hand against the doorjamb behind them and leaned slightly toward her, lowering his voice. "I thought for a moment you had taken me in dislike. But of course that is impossible."

She stared into his dark, mocking eyes, feeling simultaneously transfixed and confused. Impossible? Impossible to dislike him? He was joking, of course. But Chloe was unable to smile. His words had hit too near the mark.

His voice became even softer. She had to strain to catch the words. "You couldn't have meant that scowl for me. So there must be something else amiss. I came to discover what it is."

He had insinuated his body so close to hers that she could actually feel the heat radiating from his person. His voice was mesmerizing, teasing and intimate. And she desired nothing more than to hear it again.

When she tried to speak, her voice came out in a whisper. "I don't know what you mean."

Dear heaven, that was the very look he had just given Tish. Now that she was on the receiving end of such a look, and felt her own reaction to it, her face heated with a sudden blush. She looked away again, fanning herself more vigorously in her agitation. It was impossible to think straight while looking at the man.

A pair of long, brown fingers reached out and stilled the beating of her fan. He is not wearing gloves, she noted in a detached sort of way. It was distracting, somehow, seeing the power inherent in those lean fingers and the way the muscles moved beneath the surface of his warm skin. The direction her thoughts had taken sent another flush of heat to her cheeks. She glanced fleetingly up at him, shamefaced.

"I am susceptible to drafts," he told her gently, indicating her fan.

Her blush intensified. She could think of nothing, absolutely nothing, to say. She did not believe for one moment that Lord Rival was susceptible to drafts. He had only said what he knew must embarrass her. The necessity of formulating some reply, and her complete inability to apologize for what she knew was a spurious injury, held her tongue-tied. Then annoyance came to her rescue, lifting her chin and loosening her tongue.

"What a rapper!" she blurted. "*You're* not susceptible to drafts—nor to anything else, I daresay!"

Too late, she remembered his rank. Chloe froze, horrified. She had not only used a most unladylike expression, she had addressed someone far above her with unbecoming familiarity.

Up went his eyebrow. Down went his mouth. "Oh, Miss Littlefield!" he purred. Laughter quivered in his voice. "You misjudge me."

"H-how so, my lord?"

His eyes flicked over her. His mocking smile widened. "I am very susceptible indeed."

He had somehow invested the word with a different meaning. Chloe stared at him, completely flummoxed. She knew she was out of her depth, and sinking fast.

Tish suddenly appeared beside them, lightly brushing Lord Rival's sleeve with her shoulder. The brief contact did not escape Chloe. She saw Tish's tiny, compulsive caress and instantly comprehended its significance. She knew exactly how Tish felt. She itched to touch him too!

Appalled, Chloe recognized that the moment of hot, sick anger that had flared in her heart at the sight was only partially the protective anger of a friend who was unwilling to see Tish victimized. Part of it was jealousy. She did not remember ever feeling the ignoble emotion before, but she recognized it at once. The shock sobered her. She watched with worried eyes as Tish recalled Lord Rival's attention, eagerly divulging what she had just learned—that Lady Paversham had set aside some rooms for cards, and wasn't that lovely?

It seemed to Chloe that his lordship turned his attention to Tish very reluctantly. His eyes lingered on her own a bit longer than they should have. But then she recognized the *thrill* that secret knowledge gave her, and her native shrewdness reasserted itself like a dash of cold water. Why, he probably gave that impression to every female! It was an easy enough trick to do.

The realization was strangely depressing.

Tish was inviting Lord Rival, whom she called George, to play piquet. He favored Tish with a smile that somehow managed to convey both tenderness and wickedness. "Very well, but bear in mind that I consider the game peculiarly my own," he told her. "Do not expect me to let you win. I shall have no mercy."

His sinful smile turned Tish's voice tremulous and heated the glow in her eyes. "I am not afraid of you, my lord!"

"Brave girl." Even the suppressed laughter in his voice was a caress.

Chloe watched, her wits returned now that Lord Rival's attention was claimed by another. She was amazed at the effect his smile had on Tish—and chagrined to acknowledge that it would have had the same effect on her, had she been its recipient. Oh, the man was a snake. Charming and evil and poisonously attractive.

Tish turned to Chloe, placing a beseeching hand on her arm. "Chloe, would you mind terribly if I disappeared for half an hour?"

The idea of Tish withdrawing to a private room with Lord Rival fairly made her hair stand on end. Chloe swiftly forced a helpless look, knowing well that her childlike features lent themselves to such an expression. "Well, I—I don't know, Tish. What shall I do while you are gone?"

"Oh, dear." Tish's eyes filled with concern.

Chloe spoke before Tish could think of something. "Might I come along and watch your game?" she pleaded.

"But, Chloe, that won't be amusing for you at all. You don't play piquet."

"I should like to learn. Oh, Tish, *pray* do not leave me out here with all these strangers! I promise I will not interrupt you. You won't even know I am in the room."

"Impossible," murmured Lord Rival. Chloe refused to look at him. She bent all her powers on Tish, who seemed to be wavering.

"Well, if—if Lord Rival does not mind. You don't, do you, George? Poor Chloe! I really cannot leave her to the mercies of this crowd. It was silly of me to even *think* of cards tonight. Perhaps we had better postpone—"

"Oh, by no means!" said Chloe quickly. "Not on my account, Tish. I couldn't bear it. I can stay out here without you. If I sit by the wall, I daresay no one will disturb me while you are away." She caught her lower lip between her teeth, assuming the look of a shy and shrinking violet who was trying to be heroic for her friend's sake.

A low laugh escaped Lord Rival. "Clever Miss Little-field!" he said, for Chloe's ears alone. Then he raised his voice to include Tish. "Let us include her, my dear. I've no objection to your friend's company." His eyes raked Chloe mockingly. "Quite the contrary, in fact. I look forward to bettering my acquaintance with her."

This outrageous man was flirting with both of them simultaneously! He was definitely playing Tish for a fool. And what's more, if she let him, he'd do the same to her. Chloe felt a flash of anger, but did her level best to hide it. She bestowed upon his lordship the sort of smile she supposed he expected from females—wide-eyed and adoring. "Oh, thank you, my lord!" she simpered.

An arrested expression crossed his features, but Tish seized his arm and began chattering happily, pulling him in the direction of the card rooms. He offered his other arm to Chloe and she took it silently, dropping her eyes in what she hoped was an expression of docile modesty. In fact, laying her hand on Lord Rival's sleeve caused her heart to pound with excitement. What *was* it about the man? The heat of his body seemed to warm her fingers, even through the layers of cloth that separated them.

Soon the threesome was ensconced in an intimate little room containing only one small table and a single branch of candles. It was awkward for Chloe, but she donned what she hoped was a sweet and simpleminded expression and pretended to be unaware that she was enacting the role of chaperone. She feared at first that Tish would see through her charade of innocence, but Tish's attention was clearly elsewhere. So Chloe drew her chair off to one side and watched the play, feigning absorbed interest.

The game of piquet proved incomprehensible, but no matter. It was the other game being played that truly interested Chloe. That game she was able to decipher fairly well, she thought. Tish was in a continual flutter of nervous exhilaration, betrayed by her high color and breathless laughter as she declared her points and played her cards. It seemed to Chloe that Tish played very carelessly. She had eyes only for her partner, and scarcely glanced at the hands she was dealt. It seemed that, to Tish, the chief purpose served by a rubber of piquet was that it made an excellent excuse to spend time with Lord Rival.

Lord Rival, on the other hand, was smooth, imperturbable, and largely unreadable. Chloe wondered if this reticence was for her benefit. It seemed to puzzle Tish, and even provoke her to more extravagant displays of flirting, as if she were desperately trying to engage his interest. Chloe blushed for her friend's pathetic eagerness. Every so often, Lord Rival would shoot Tish a secretive smile or make a suggestive comment, but Chloe formed the distinct impression that he was offering these sops to Tish's vanity in the hope that they would soothe her into more circumspect behavior. He seemed all too aware of Chloe's presence as an observer, and she was sure that her assumption of placid oblivion to their undergame did not fool him for an instant. He knew exactly why she was there, and which game she was watching.

Six hands were dealt and played, with the deal alternating between Lord Rival and Tish. Chloe could not follow the play at all, but it was clear that Tish had lost all but one hand. At the end of the sixth game, Lord Rival scooped up the cards with a fluid, practiced movement and offered Tish a tender smile.

"I make it 317. My sweet, your friend will think I have taken shameless advantage of you."

Tish giggled and tossed her head. "Nonsense, my lord! Chloe knows me too well. I do not regard a few losses at piquet, I assure you."

"Shall we play again? The cards were favoring you toward the end, I think. Perhaps your luck has changed."

Tish shot him a provocative glance from beneath her lashes. "Since I met you, George, I feel sure it has," she murmured daringly.

It was all Chloe could do to keep from shaking Tish. But Lord Rival's eyes were upon her, so she quelled her irritation with an effort.

"What say you, Miss Littlefield? Can you bear it if we play another round?"

She saw the amusement in his dark eyes, heard the mockery in his voice. A surge of dislike rose up to choke her, but she managed to smile brightly. "I am finding the game most interesting, my lord."

"You surprise me. I had thought it impossible to learn so complicated a game by simply watching others play it. The best way to learn is to practice it yourself—with an experienced partner, of course."

Chloe glanced at him again, her eyes narrowing in sudden suspicion. Which game did he mean? Sure enough, the amusement in his eyes was meant for her to see. You clever devil, she thought. Every sentence you utter has a double meaning.

She lifted a brow, then smiled blandly at him again. "But you play with such skill, my lord. It is an education merely to observe you."

An appreciative grin flashed across his features. He obviously understood that Chloe was not speaking of piquet any more than he was. "I own, I am held to be something of a master," he murmured, laughter lurking in his voice.

"My unfortunate friend is no match for you, sir," she said quietly. "You ought to spare her and seek a more worthy opponent."

Tish cried out at this. "I protest, my play is not contemptible! George, why do you not defend me?"

"You play very well, *cherie*. But Miss Littlefield correctly divines that you have not bested me yet." He ran the cards absently through his hands, shuffling them rhythmically, his eyes resting thoughtfully on Chloe. "What a pity that you have not yet learned the game, Miss Littlefield. I feel sure you have a natural aptitude."

Chloe could not suppress a flash of vexation. "You are wrong," she told him crisply. "I detest games. Of all sorts."

His shoulders shook with soundless laughter. "Then you haven't played the right game yet. When you find one that seizes your interest, and are finally matched with an opponent worthy of you, you will become as obsessed as any gambler."

Tish laughed. "Oh, not Chloe! She is far too level-headed."

Lord Rival's eyes never left Chloe's. Up went the eyebrow. Down went the mouth. "We all lose our heads sometime." He leaned slightly toward Chloe again, and she felt her cheeks grow hot. "The day it happens to you, Miss Littlefield, I hope I will be there to see it."

His voice was low, teasing, and intimate. It made her feel as helpless and angry as a beetle pinned to a card. Once again he had flustered her to the point where she could think of nothing to say. She was caught in a confusing swirl of fury and attraction. Impossible to like this horrible man! But equally impossible to resist his peculiar charm. It made a lady want to slap him, kiss him, do *something* that would break through that wall of cool mockery.

Whatever questionable enjoyment the evening had held was over for Chloe. She had to endure another hour of watching Tish's wretched card play and of witnessing Lord Rival making a May game of her. Chloe was stunned to learn, on the way home in the Dalrymples' carriage, that Tish had lost several hundred pounds to him that night.

"Tish, no! It is—it is *wanton!*" gasped Chloe.

Tish tossed her head and pouted. "Pshaw! I'm sure Robert loses far more than that at his wretched club."

"But—but—what is the point of it all? What does such a vast sum purchase? Merely an hour or two of entertainment?"

"Chloe, you don't understand. One must play. One simply must! It's the done thing. And often the cards run the other way, you know, so that it evens out in the end."

Chloe pressed her gloved hands together tightly to keep from saying something she feared she would regret. The idea that Tish would blithely hand over hundreds of pounds to Lord Rival, of all people, was more disturbing to her than she could possibly express. It seemed an enormous sum to Chloe, and she was absolutely certain that there was something wicked, something dishonorable, about a man winning that much money from a reckless, infatuated girl whose level of skill was far beneath his.

Chapter 6

The next morning Mr. Gilliland received a note. It appeared to have been written in the throes of agitation and with a very bad pen. The author had plainly written in haste, had employed frequent underlining and multiple exclamation points to disastrous effect, and had then completed the missive's annihilation by folding it repeatedly into a tiny square without giving it a chance to dry. What reached Gil was a muddy and blotted bit of creased foolscap that, to any other eyes would have conveyed no information whatsoever. Gil, however, had received similar billets in the past. Although the text was completely illegible, he knew an urgent summons from Chloe Littlefield when he saw one.

He immediately called for his curricle and arrived at the Dalrymples' door at what was, for him, a painfully early hour. The flicker of a curtain on the first floor caught his eye, telling him that he had been impatiently awaited. It was with a sense of foreboding that he strode, a few moments later, into his sister's morning room to meet Chloe.

He checked on the threshold. His jaw dropped. A vision of loveliness in which he, with difficulty, recognized his childhood playmate rose from a sofa near the fire and ran toward him.

"Gil, for heaven's sake! What took you so long?" the vision cried. "Tish may return at any moment!"

Miss Littlefield was garbed in a dainty morning dress of white muslin trimmed with fluttering sky-blue ribbons and flounces of lace. It was the first time in their adult lives that Gil had seen Chloe wearing a garment that actually fit her. He had always known that the clothes made for her by

Gertrude Tewksbury were unflattering, but until this moment he had not comprehended the enormity of what he now perceived was almost criminal incompetence. Miss Tewksbury, accommodating the fullness of Chloe's breasts, had somehow metastasized the feature into a general impression of plumpness. She had taken Chloe's petite and fairylike form and rendered it merely short.

One had always realized that Chloe was pretty, of course, despite her disfiguring wardrobe. One had simply assumed that her style did not appeal to one personally. It was a shock to see good old Chloe revealed as an exquisite and enchanting creature who definitely appealed to a man's baser nature. She looked adorable. Flaxen ringlets clustered becomingly round her seraphic countenance in a way that somehow, inexplicably, drew attention to the sweetness of her mouth. Gil had never looked twice at Chloe's mouth before. Now he found himself tempted to stare at it. Most unsettling.

She must have noticed his stunned expression, for she halted in midstride, her china-blue eyes wide. "What is it, Gil?"

He found it necessary to clear his throat before speaking. "Nothing," he stammered. "You look . . . you look different."

It was an idiotic thing to say, and probably rude as well, but Chloe correctly interpreted it as a compliment. She added to his stupefaction by beaming radiantly at him. "It's my new clothes," she confided. As if he didn't know. "But that's neither here nor there! I must tell you *immediately* what I learned last night, and I am in such a quake for fear Tish will return before I—*hist!* What's that?"

Chloe darted to the window, giving Gil a chance to admire the gracefulness of her movements, the pretty back of her modish gown, and the winsome way her curls tumbled down between her shoulders. He was moved to exclaim, "I say, Clo, that frock is slap up to the echo! Never knew you could look so well."

"Thank you," she said absently. She was peering intently down at the street. "Tish has gone to buy ribbons to match the silk we bought yesterday, but I told her I had the headache. I don't suppose she will be gone much longer. That is not her carriage, thank heaven!"

"Well, if you're so concerned about Tish overhearing us, why not pop on your bonnet and step out with me? I'll take you for a spin in my curricle."

"Oh, Gil, *would* you? I shall be back directly!"

He didn't suppose she would be, despite the rapidity with which she flew out of the room, but to his surprise she spent no more time in perfecting her appearance than was needed to fasten a tippet round her shoulders and tie her bonnet strings. Most females of his acquaintance would have fussed and preened a bit before allowing themselves out of the house. Of course, he acknowledged, it was hard to see how Chloe's appearance could be improved upon. The bonnet and tippet matched her frock, and were just as becoming. In less than five minutes they were seated side by side in his curricle and headed down Mount Street toward the park. Twice he had to admonish her not to turn round and peer behind them, but eventually she settled down beside him, heaving a tiny sigh of relief.

"I do not see Tish's carriage anywhere about, and I am sure we are not being followed after all."

"Followed! Why the deuce should we be followed?"

"Well, I don't know, but I'm sure Tish suspects that I disapprove of her goings-on, and she must know that I will do what I can to thrust a spoke in her wheel, so who knows but that she will set someone on to prevent me?"

"Good God! What's amiss? Never tell me that Tish is involved in something smoky, for I won't believe you!"

"No, not that, exactly, but—oh, Gil, she is in such a scrape!"

Chloe's voice caught, as if she were suddenly fighting tears. Gil felt his heart sink. "I knew it," he said grimly. "Give me the word with no bark on it, Clo. Is she scorched?"

She looked blankly at him. "Scorched?"

"In debt."

"Oh! No. Nothing so easy! We could pull her out of *that* sort of trouble in a trice."

"Well, then?"

"I will tell you, but you will be excessively shocked. And Tish must never discover that you heard it from me! Do you swear?"

"Of course I swear! Dash it, Chloe, have I ever betrayed any of your secrets?"

"No, but this is very, very important. Now, Gil, you must *attend,* if you please, and pray do not interrupt me or I shall make a mull of it!"

Gil, now thoroughly alarmed, assured her that he would hang upon her every word. Chloe folded her hands like a schoolgirl about to recite. She stared straight ahead, trouble in her face. "There is an odious man."

Gil exclaimed under his breath. She held up a warning finger. "Let me finish! There is an odious man who has—who has *insinuated* himself into Tish's good graces. You will think she ought not to have let him, but I met him last night, Gil, and I must say, it is difficult to blame her. Robert is so neglectful, and this dreadful man so attentive! He has wound Tish completely round his finger. And I feel sure it is deliberate. I don't believe he cares for her at all. I watched him very carefully, and it appears to me that he has entrapped poor Tish for—for *sport.*" Her voice had sunk to a shocked whisper.

She placed a hand on his sleeve, her expression tragic. "Is such wickedness possible, Gil?"

"Aye," he said shortly. Although he would have given a great deal to spare Chloe the knowledge.

She was shaking her head slowly, obviously perplexed. "Well. I would not have believed it, had I not seen it for myself last night. He set out to gull her, and she has fallen into his snare like a—like a—well, I don't know what. What falls into snares?"

"Never mind that! Does Robert know?"

"I don't know. His behavior toward her is certainly not what it was three years ago. But I don't see how he could know; he scarcely ever accompanies her anywhere! Why is that, Gil? Tish tells me it is the fashion, but how is that possible? To me it seems sad, and rather shocking for married persons to attend parties alone."

"Yes, it gives rise to all sorts of mischief. As you see! But I would have thought Tish the last woman on earth to—I say, who is the fellow?"

"His name is Carstairs. Lord Rival. Oh, Gil, mind your horses!"

At the sound of Rival's name, Gil had dropped his hands and the horses had shot forward. He controlled them again, clenching his jaw to keep from swearing aloud.

Chloe peeped anxiously up at him. "Do you know him, Gil?"

"I ain't acquainted with him, if that's what you mean! But the fellow is notorious. Worst rake in town! If he's come sniffing round my sister—" Gil ground his teeth in impotent rage.

Chloe's eyes widened in apprehension. "Now, Gil, pray do not do anything rash! If you're thinking of calling him out, or some such thing—"

"Well, I *am* thinking of it! Thinking of it with pleasure! But I'd only make a guy of myself. Besides, it's Robert's place to put a stop to this."

She bounced up beside him with a little shriek of alarm. "Gil, you *can't* tell Robert! Tish would instantly know you had done so! And that you had learned it from me!"

"Now, how would she know that?" argued Gil. "If Rival has been paying court to her, ten to one it's all over town! I suppose the only reason I haven't heard the tale is because I'm her brother." He paused, gloomily considering the matter. "It'll be a lesson to me. I'm forever receiving invitations from those beau monde biddies, and I never accept 'em. Dashed dull affairs! But if I had done my duty and showed my front at a rout or two, I daresay I'd have caught wind of this by now. How serious is it?"

"Heavens, I've no idea! But if you attend a party with us, you can decide for yourself. I own, it would be a great relief to me if you did. Now that I have gone to Lady Paversham's drum, it seems I am expected to attend other functions, and it would be dreadful to find myself thrust willy-nilly into the role of chaperone. Besides, Tish cannot blame me, whatever action you choose to take, if you have seen them together with your own eyes. But, Gil—there's more."

"Good God! What could be worse?"

Chloe toyed nervously with the fringe on her tippet. "I did not say it was worse. Indeed, I know so little of these things . . . perhaps this is silly."

"Out with it, Clo. I'll tell you if it's silly."

She sighed, and blurted it out in a rush. "They play cards together, and Lord Rival wins. I believe he always does so; he actually made some remark to that effect! Last night he won nearly five hundred pounds off her."

Gil whistled, long and low. "Pretty deep doings."

"Is it? Tish would have me believe it was nothing extra-ordinary, and that Robert loses more at White's, but I can't help thinking—"

"I daresay he may, but Robert doesn't always lose!"

"Well, perhaps I am making a mountain out of a molehill. And I know nothing of piquet, of course. When he said Tish had never bested him, he may have been speaking of—of something else. But it certainly seemed to me that Lord Rival is a superior player."

"Oh, he's the very devil at piquet! Known for it."

Chloe's blue eyes sparkled with indignation. "Why, then, it isn't *fair!* Surely he ought not to play Tish for such high stakes!"

Gil pursed his lips thoughtfully. "Hm. Very delicate question, that. I suppose she might feel insulted if he played her for chicken stakes."

"Oh, rubbish! She cares nothing for that, I am sure. Tish values piquet only as a chance to be alone with Lord Rival."

Gil shuddered. Chloe nodded in sympathy. "Yes, it was that obvious. To me, at least. I scotched it, though, by going off with them—so you needn't fear he made any progress with her last night."

"You're a right one, Clo!" said Gil approvingly, causing Chloe to blush with pleasure. "I'll come along on your next venture and meet the fellow myself. Unless—I say, you're not going to be presented, are you? For I won't go through that again, not for a monkey!"

"Well, I believe Tish may be planning that, but I don't know when. I think she said we are going to somebody-or-other's private ball tonight."

He nodded sagely. "Alverstoke House. The marquis is launching his cousin or some such thing. Very well, I'll join you after dinner and we'll go together. Bound to be a shocking crush, and I daresay I'll be wishing myself at the devil inside of an hour, but a fellow's got to sacrifice himself when his sister's in the basket."

Gil was as good as his word. He arrived promptly, and in very correct evening attire. Chloe had seen Gil in evening clothes any number of times, but apparently the items he donned in the country came from the second tier of his wardrobe. Tonight he was resplendent, and Chloe was agreeably surprised at how handsome he looked. It made her feel strangely shy, although she knew her own dress was faultless. A square-necked bodice of ivory satin, trimmed with seed pearls and cut daringly low—although not as low as Tish's claret-colored silk—flattered both her complexion and her figure. The long sweep of creamy fabric clung exactly where it should, and elsewhere fell in graceful folds to the floor, ending in a demitrain edged with seed pearls and satin piping. Her hair was dressed prettily, she carried an ivory fan, and, all in all, she fancied that she looked rather elegant. It was reassuring, however, to have this fancy confirmed by the admiration in Gil's eyes. She had seldom won approval from him on her toilette, so to have him stare at her through his quizzing glass and breathe, "By Jove!" when he saw her brought a flush of delight to her cheeks. She curtsied gracefully to him, snapping her fan open to display it, and fluttering her lashes with mock demureness.

"La, sir, you overwhelm me!" she declared.

He chuckled. "The shoe's on the other foot, I promise you!" He then bent his quizzing glass on Tish, and his features froze in condemnation. "I hope you mean to put something *on* before we leave the house," he said austerely.

Tish's eyes flashed. "This gown," she informed her brother icily, "is bang up to the nines!"

"It don't suit you. And neither does that expression! Females shouldn't use cant."

"How stuffy you are!" marveled Tish. "I hope you don't plan to inflict your gothic notions on *me,* because you'll catch cold at it!"

"Oh, I will, will I? We'll see about that, little sister! I don't intend to spend the evening watching you make a spectacle of yourself and putting us all to the blush! If you don't toe the line, I'll bundle you back in your carriage and send you home!"

Chloe flew to Tish's side and put an arm around her, throwing a warning look at Gil. "Oh, hush, Gil! You know you'll do no such thing, and Tish isn't putting us to the blush. You look lovely, Tish, really you do. And I'm sure you won't use cant expressions at Alverstoke House, will you?"

She sniffed. "Well, if Gil will stop being provoking, I will try to behave."

Gil scowled, indicating his sister's modish ball gown. "Gave me a fright, that's all," he said grudgingly. "Never saw you wear anything like that before. Not in public, at any rate."

Tish smoothed the wisps of silk hugging her slender form. "Does it really not suit me?" she asked anxiously.

Chloe patted Tish reassuringly. "It suits you beautifully. I would never dare to wear anything so—so fashionable, but you look quite fetching in it."

Gil shook his head gloomily. "*You* look fetching," he told Chloe. "Tish looks tempting. Playing with fire, Tish! Take care you don't get burned."

"Pooh! Would you have me dress like a dowager? You will see any number of women tonight who are dressed more scandalously than I."

"Oh, will Caro Lamb be present?" asked Gil, with withering sarcasm.

Chloe threw up her hands. "Stop it at once, you two! You are no longer in the nursery! Besides, I have never before visited the home of a marquis and I am shaking like a leaf. In fact, I have half a mind to run back upstairs this very in-

stant. You know perfectly well, both of you, that I never
wished to go to grand parties—"

As she had hoped, Gil and Tish instantly dropped their
quarrel and joined forces to soothe her. By the time they
reached Alverstoke House harmony had been restored and
Chloe felt at leisure to enjoy herself.

It was clear from the moment they arrived that Chloe was
going to enjoy her second *ton* party much more than the
first. Having Gil at her side added to her comfort on several
levels. It was delightful just to be with him, of course, since
she enjoyed his company for its own sake. And with him
present she no longer bore on her inadequate shoulders the
responsibility of monitoring Tish's behavior. It was a relief
to have Gil, whom all his friends described as a knowing
'un, available to nip his sister's wildness in the bud. She
could safely leave it to him to decide whether Tish's conduct
was beyond the pale, or if it was actually acceptable for a
dashing young matron. She devoutly hoped that Lord Rival
would be present. If he was, and Tish behaved more circum-
spectly tonight than she had at Lady Paversham's drum, that
would mean Tish knew her flirtation was wrong. If, on the
other hand, Tish did not adjust her behavior, Gil would either put a stop to it or reassure Chloe that there was no danger after all. Either way, the responsibility was no longer
hers.

She was also immensely grateful for Gil's hand lightly
supporting her elbow as she climbed a magnificent staircase
and was presented to the Marquis of Alverstoke and his ter-
rifying sister, Lady Buxted. The marquis was younger than
she had expected, and although he was perfectly civil, he
was such a superior personage that he quite intimidated her.
She was glad when his eyes slid indifferently past her to
Tish. She heard him inquire politely after Robert Dalrymple,
so it was clear that they owed their invitations to Tish's marriage. Chloe was embarrassed that Robert had chosen not to
accompany them, but fortunately the marquis seemed un-
moved by his absence. She could not help heaving a sigh of
relief when the introductions were over and the threesome
had escaped to the ballroom.

It was there, however, perceiving the size of the ballroom and the size of the crowd gathering in it, that Chloe suffered an attack of nerves. She halted in her tracks, clutching at her friends' sleeves.

Tish looked at her in surprise. "Chloe, what is it?"

"These people—all these people—will they have seen that wretched engagement notice?"

Gil patted her hand reassuringly. "Never mind, Clo. We'll introduce you simply as 'Miss Littlefield,' just as we did a moment ago."

Chloe tried to be content with that, but soon became miserably aware of the smiles and whispers that followed her as she clung like a burr to Gil's side. She felt like an imposter. It was terrible to mislead these kind strangers. The fewer acquaintances she made in London, she decided, the easier it would be when she left. Finally she announced that she had no desire to dance with strangers and that she would, in fact, refuse to do so.

Gil loudly deplored this as an unbecoming eccentricity in a chit still on the fringes of the *ton,* but when she proved adamant he delighted her by admitting that he disliked dancing with strangers himself. At any rate, he would remain at her side. "Lending you countenance," he told her severely. This caused her to squeeze his arm affectionately and call him "Silly Gilly," but fortunately no one overheard her.

Chloe soon discovered one completely unexpected way in which Gil's company added to her pleasure. He proved to be a capital escort. Gil had been on the Town for several years, but since Chloe had remained in the country she had not had occasion to observe the subtle changes wrought in him by the acquisition of what the beau monde called "Town bronze." For all his grumbling that attending a private ball was torture for him, and that he never did so, it was obvious that he had attended a sufficient number to know his way about and never put a foot wrong. It was just as obvious that Mr. Gilliland was well known and well liked. She was proud to be seen on the arm of this handsome and impeccably dressed young man who carried himself with graceful assurance, who was hailed good-naturedly from all sides, and who unobtrusively guided her through the unfamiliar social rituals. He seemed to know without being told exactly what a lady needed. If her shawl started to slip, he deftly caught it. When she tired of standing, he steered her unerringly to the only available chair. When she thirsted, he appeared like a genie at her elbow, with a glass of punch.

This she accepted with real gratitude, saying, "Thank you, Gil. How well you do this, to be sure!"

"Do what?"

"This." She waved her hand in a vague but comprehensive gesture. "I would be completely lost without you."

"Nothing to it," he assured her. "You'll be up to snuff in no time."

He was lounging gracefully beside her chair, surveying the crowded room through his quizzing glass. Tish had vanished into the throng long ago, spirited away by a couple of laughing young bucks. Gil and Chloe had caught a glimpse of her once, dancing the boulanger with a gentleman in a striped waistcoat, but she had swiftly disappeared again. Chloe and Gil had then walked the length of the ballroom, but to no avail, and finally they stationed themselves where they could watch the room's entrance and thus observe the comings and goings of the entire assembly.

Gil glanced rather doubtfully down at his petite companion. "I say, Clo, you ought to stand up. You'll never pick the fellow out in this mob."

But Chloe had concluded that Lord Rival was not coming. Latecomers had ceased to trickle in some time ago, and he had not been among them. For some reason, that made her feel cross.

She scowled at her punch glass. "I have no wish to spend my evening chasing wild geese. Besides, if he does show up, you will easily recognize him," she said tartly. "He leaves a trail of swooning females in his wake."

Gil grinned. "Married females, from what one hears."

Chloe looked up, startled. "Married! Why?"

"Lord, I don't know! He probably feels they are safer. Can't force him to the altar. Can't pretend they thought his intentions were honorable. Can't even kick up a dust when he transfers his affections elsewhere."

"So it is not just Tish? He—he hunts married women?" Chloe was appalled.

Gil looked uncomfortable. "Sorry, Clo. There are a number of other fellows who do the same, so don't go thinking it's unusual! If anything, I'm afraid it's rather commonplace."

"Commonplace wickedness." She shook her head, troubled. Then a thought occurred to her and she raised wondering eyes to her friend's face. "Gil, is 'Lord Rival' really the man's title? Or is it a soubriquet?"

Gil burst out laughing. "What an idea! No, it's his title, all right and tight. Originally 'rye vale,' I believe. Odd coincidence, though, isn't it?"

"Yes," she said, now thinking hard. "But, Gil, are you certain that he flirts only with married women?"

"That's what one hears. That's the way of the world, Clo. Married women are supposed to be able to handle themselves."

"But, Gil, he—I *think* he—well, it certainly seemed to me that he—" Chloe felt a blush heat her cheeks. "He flirted with *me* last night."

Gil rounded on her, staring. "The devil he did!"

"Well, I *think* he did," she said hastily. "He may have meant nothing by it. Or it could be second nature to him, you know—it may simply be the way he treats all females. He knows I am not married."

Gil flushed with anger. "He believes you are engaged, however—to *me!*"

"Yes, but—ooh!" Chloe bounced upright on the small chair, her eyes sparkling eagerly. "That gives me the most wonderful idea!"

"Aye, it gives me a wonderful idea too! I think I'll plant the fellow a facer."

"No, no, only listen! Gil, don't you see? If I am correct, and Lord Rival was flirting with me—and if you are correct, and he does so only with 'safe' women—oh, Gil, would you mind terribly pretending we are really engaged? Just for a time?"

"What, so the worst rake in London can cut me out?" spluttered Gil. "I can't say I think much of your *wonderful idea*."

"But, Gil, surely you care nothing for that. After all—"

"Not *care!*" exclaimed Gil, his voice cracking. "Not care if that ugly customer turns me into a figure of fun? Have you run mad? And I don't know what you mean by 'pretending' we are engaged. All the world thinks we *are* engaged."

"Yes, but I fancy if you pretended to be madly in love with me, it might pique his interest."

"Now, look here—!"

But Chloe was frowning intently, tapping her fan against her forgotten punch glass. "The more I think on it, the more it appears to me that Lord Rival might have another reason for preferring married women. They may be safe in some ways, but in other ways they present a challenge! I believe he enjoys that. In fact, he showed no interest in me whatsoever—or very little—until he saw that I *disliked* him."

"Oh, then you don't need me at all! The next time you meet the fellow, simply kick him in the shins. That ought to intrigue him."

"Now, Gil, *really!* Why are you biting my nose off? I think it is a famous scheme."

"What scheme? To throw me over for *Lord Rival?*"

"Why, yes! There's not a flaw to be found in it anywhere." Chloe began enthusiastically ticking the points off on her fingers. "It will snatch Tish right out of his clutches, because she will see that he cares nothing for her, and she will believe that her trifling with him wounds me. And whatever dangerous games she may play with her husband's affections—which, I own, I do not understand—Tish would never do anything to injure a friend. You and I can break our engagement, and no one will think for a moment that it was your fault, because it will be plain as a pikestaff that it was *my* fault. Everyone will say that you are well rid of me! And there is no danger that Lord Rival will lose his heart to me, because he never does so. And if he did, it would serve him right."

Gil's jaw set grimly. "What if you lose your heart to him?"

"Pooh! No chance of that. I dislike Lord Rival excessively." Chloe found that she suddenly could not meet Gil's eyes. The blush was stealing over her face again. She fanned herself, trying to assume an air of nonchalance.

Not unexpectedly, Gil's eyes narrowed in suspicion. Before he could speak, however, Chloe gripped his arm, her fingers tightening in warning. "Good gracious, here he comes! See? That is he, standing in the doorway. In the blue coat. And he has seen us!" Her fan flew faster and faster in agitation. "Yes, do continue to scowl at me, Gil—that is excellent! He will think we are having a lovers' quarrel."

Gil sputtered wordlessly, looking nauseated by the very idea. Chloe knew in her bones that Lord Rival would approach them. The appearance they presented of being surprised in the midst of a quarrel would be irresistible to a man of Lord Rival's predatory instincts.

Her intuition proved correct. Across the room, she saw the weariness in his gaze as it flicked idly round the room, and then she saw the weariness vanish as his gaze fell upon her and Gil. Amusement lit his expression, and he began to stroll toward them. Chloe discovered that she felt safer, somehow, if she continued to clutch Gil's sleeve. She rose nervously out of her chair as Lord Rival approached.

"Miss Littlefield, we meet again! Your very obedient," he said as he bowed. She thought the last thing on earth he appeared to be was an obedient servant, but of course one could not say so.

Instead, she curtseyed demurely. "Lord Rival," she murmured.

His dark eyes had shifted to her companion. "Your fiancé, one assumes?"

"Yes, my lord—Mr. Gilliland. Gil, this is Lord Rival."

The contrast between the two men could scarcely have been greater, thought Chloe, watching them exchange bows. They were very much of a height, but in coloring, air, and manner they were complete opposites. Gil's gleaming blond hair and youthful good looks appeared almost cherubic be-

side this dark, saturnine man. There was something sleek
and catlike about Lord Rival's handsomeness, and the almost cruel set to his mouth added to his habitual air of boredom and his frequent flashes of barely hidden mockery,
made everything he said and did seem double-edged. Gil's
frank, good-humored countenance and open manner con-
trasted oddly with his lordship's. The tableau the two men
formed looked like a portrait of Gabriel bowing to Lucifer.

"Your servant, m'lord," muttered Gil, barely able to mask
his antagonism.

Laughter shook Lord Rival, but so fleetingly that Chloe
almost wondered if she imagined it. "How do you do? You
are a lucky man, Mr. Gilliland," he said smoothly.

"Eh?" said Gil, startled. Then he flushed scarlet. "Oh, you
mean Chloe! Yes, of course! That is—certainly. Certainly I
am. Most fortunate."

The twinkle in Lord Rival's eye became pronounced, but
his grave expression did not change. "I would wish you
happy, of course, but the platitude becomes meaningless in
the face of such obvious good fortune."

"Oh—ah—exactly!"

"George!" cried a soprano voice at Gil's elbow. "When
did you arrive? I vow, I ceased watching the door an hour
ago! I decided you were not coming after all, and I have
been *desolate!* How could you frighten me so?"

Tish had materialized out of the crowd, leaning on the
arm of her latest dancing partner. The lad appeared to be a
shy and soft-spoken fellow, despite the flamboyance of his
chosen mode and the amazing height of his shirt points. Tish
stretched out her hand to Lord Rival and he took it, bowing
gracefully.

"The delicious Mrs. Dalrymple!" he uttered, raising
Tish's hand briefly to his lips. At the moment her gloved fingers came closest to touching his mouth, he shot Tish a look
from under his hooded lids that sent a vivid blush to her
cheeks. He retained her hand as he nodded to her partner,
who bowed, stammering something unintelligible.

"I hear a waltz beginning," said Lord Rival. "Tish, may I

hope for the pleasure? I daresay Wivenhoe will not object if I steal his charming partner."

Whatever objections the unassertive Wivenhoe might have had were disregarded, at any rate. Perfunctory leave was taken of the company, and Tish, with a high-pitched little laugh, was swept smoothly away to join the couples forming for the waltz.

Gil, rigid with disapproval, stared with almost comic fixedness at the spectacle of his sister bridling and giggling in the arms of a man who was not her husband. Then, as the couple disappeared into the milling crowd of persons on the dance floor, he abruptly came back to life. He seized Chloe's punch cup and thrust it at Wivenhoe.

"Here, Wivenhoe—do a chap a favor, won't you? There's a good lad!" said Gil, and before Chloe had realized what was toward, Gil was dragging her determinedly toward the center of the room.

"Gil, what on earth—"

"You waltz, don't you, Chloe? Of course you do. Come on!" And with these unromantic words, Gil swung Chloe into the most romantic of dances.

Chapter 7

Chloe hung back for a moment. "Gil, wait! Wait! I don't know if I ought."

"Ought to what?"

"Waltz."

Gil stared uncomprehendingly into her face. "Why the devil—Oh! Almack's! Never mind, Clo, this is a private ball. Besides," he said, seizing her grimly round the waist and propelling her doggedly into a circular motion, "the rules only apply to single females!"

"And what am I, in heaven's name?" demanded Chloe, struggling to keep up.

"Engaged!" said Gil bitterly. "Don't you remember?"

The top of her head did not quite reach his shoulder. She could see nothing but his starched shirt front before her. He suddenly spun her in a great swirl to the left, almost causing her to trip. She tilted her chin up and saw that Gil was not even looking at her; he was scanning the throng of dancers and glowering fiercely.

She pinched his sleeve. "Gil, pray look at your partner from time to time! We are liable to—gracious!" They had nearly collided with another couple. "Gil, you really must slow down! I cannot keep pace with those great, long legs of yours."

"Just give it a go, won't you? I think I see them over there." He pulled her tighter, the better to direct her steps, and began hauling her purposefully toward the opposite end of the room.

"Merciful heavens! Is that why we are galloping round

the floor like a pair of dervishes? Tish is a grown woman. You cannot—oh!"

This time, they had collided with another couple. "Sorry! Sorry! Beg pardon!" said Gil hastily, addressing everyone in the vicinity. Then he clutched Chloe again and would have danced off with the same reckless vigor had she not planted her tiny feet.

"What?" he said, harassed. He finally looked directly at his partner. She was glaring at him.

"When dancing with a lady," she announced, "it is important to give her the impression that you *wish* to dance with her!"

"I *do* wish to dance with you. Immediately! Come along!" ordered Gil and swept her back into his arms.

In deference to the indignant squeak she uttered, he moderated his pace, but only slightly. Chloe gave up, deciding that her most dignified course would be to pretend she shared Gil's apparent fondness for an energetic waltz. With that in mind, she pasted a pleasant look upon her face.

The effect was ruined, however, by Gil's persistent scowl. He soon began venting his spleen by muttering scathing remarks into Chloe's sympathetic ear. "Never saw anything to equal it. *George!* And *Tish!*" mimicked Gil savagely. "And right in front of me! I tell you what, Clo: it's bad *ton*. Not the thing at all!"

"I was afraid it was. I must say, that's exactly how it struck me. But I am not a judge."

"Well, I am!" declared Gil, not mincing matters. "Time I took a hand in the matter. Reflection on me! Everyone knows she's my sister."

"Yes, but what can you do?"

"Going to have a talk with her."

Chloe's face puckered with worry. "Oh, Gil, do you think that's wise? She's bound to take snuff—"

"D'you think I care for that?" he interrupted. "Let her! At least I will have done my duty. And if I know Tish—which I do!—after she's done ripping up at me, she'll think it over and realize I'm right."

They had reached the opposite side of the room and, just

as Gil had said, found Tish and Lord Rival. They were very near the wall, taking small steps and dancing at half tempo. Tish was gazing dreamily into his lordship's eyes. Lord Rival was holding Tish much too close for propriety, and it was clear that the waltz—once he had danced her away from her party—had become a public display of the intimacy of their friendship. Gil bristled at the sight.

Chloe was afraid Gil would accost Lord Rival on the spot, but Gil's social skills were too deeply ingrained for any such breach of conduct. He confined himself to a careless greeting as they approached the pair, which forced them to look up and acknowledge Gil and Chloe's presence. Tish looked disgruntled, but Lord Rival seemed merely amused by the interruption. Neither appeared ashamed in the least, nor even self-conscious. The two dancing couples fell apart, but Lord Rival kept Tish's hand, tucking it into his elbow.

Gil managed to keep his expression civil. "I say, Rival, would you mind if I had a word with my sister? Something important I forgot to tell her. Family business, you know."

Lord Rival raised an eyebrow in what appeared to be polite inquiry, but Chloe saw the spark of laughter in his eyes. "Indeed? Nothing too serious, I hope. No death in the family?"

"Oh, no! Nothing like that," said Gil carelessly.

Tish looked cross. "Tell me later, Gil."

"It's urgent."

"Urgent, but not serious? That's absurd!"

But Gil was bowing perfunctorily to her escort. "You'll excuse us, won't you, m'lord? Quite right! I know you will." And he firmly removed his hotly protesting sister, pulling her into the set that was forming on the floor.

Chloe found herself abruptly left alone with Lord Rival. She had not foreseen this result of Gil's impetuosity. She tried to appear perfectly at ease, but could feel the telltale color stealing across her face. His observant lordship clearly noticed it, too. A chuckle escaped him.

"Dare I hope that this maneuver was of your contrivance, Miss Littlefield?" he murmured.

Her eyes widened in startled confusion. "Mine?"

"Ah. I thought not. How lowering, to be sure."

Her blush intensified as she realized what he meant. "Did you think I asked Gil to take Tish away so I could be alone with you?" she exclaimed. "How dare you!"

"Oh, I do not dare. Nor did I think it. I merely hoped." His eyes scanned her and his smile widened. "You don't like me, do you?"

Chloe, quivering with indignation, opened her mouth to tell him exactly what she thought of him—and then remembered the scheme that had seemed so appealing not fifteen minutes ago. She closed her mouth with a snap and struggled with herself.

"I— I scarcely know you, my lord," she managed to utter.

"We must take steps to rectify that. May I have the next waltz?"

A thrill compounded of excitement and terror choked Chloe. Reminding herself that Lord Rival's interest might depend upon her own unavailabilty, she cast her eyes modestly down.

"Oh, my lord, I only waltz with Gil," she said demurely.

She lifted her gaze in time to see the grin splitting his features. It was an oddly attractive grin, lopsided and mischievous. "If that is so, I imagine you would welcome a chance to waltz with anyone else. Even me."

She found she had to bite her lip to keep from laughing. "I'm sure I don't know what you mean, my lord."

"I'm sure you do! And you may stop calling me 'my lord.' My friends call me George."

"You and I are not friends."

"We will be."

What a strange man he was! Such arrogance would be intolerable, if one did not suspect that he was joking more often than not. She regarded him doubtfully, wondering if she ought, in fact, to call him by his Christian name. It seemed vastly improper—but, of course, if she intended to flirt with him she could hardly cavil at a little impropriety.

He was grinning at her again. "You look just like a little bird, with your head on one side."

"Considering a worm," she said tartly, once again forgetting her role.

But his lordship was in no way discomposed. "I hope you decide to pounce, little bird." He startled her by leaning in, whispering so his hot breath tickled her ear. "They tell me I'm a very tasty fellow."

And with a last, low laugh, he strolled away. Chloe stared at his departing back, shocked to the core of her being. She had no clear idea what he meant, but she could still feel his breath in her hair and hear the soft seduction of his voice. It was as if the brief whisper was too momentous for her to have taken in all at once, so it was repeating itself like an echo, shivering through all her senses. *Pounce, little bird . . . pounce, little bird . . . they tell me I'm a very tasty fellow.*

Oh, the man was dangerous. No doubt about it.

She heard a tiny sound and turned her dazed eyes to the wall sconce nearby. A moth was fluttering and dancing in helpless confusion round the candles. Chloe knew just how the poor, doomed creature felt. Irresistibly drawn to the light but frightened by the heat. Eventually it would be too dazzled to resist, and would blunder into a fatal encounter with that bewitching brilliance.

Chloe certainly hoped she had more sense than a moth. But she was contemplating just such a delicate dance, and she knew she could afford no stumbles. She stepped forward with her fan, reached up, and gently herded the foolish creature out of danger. "With my thanks for the warning," she told it softly.

As if on cue, she heard the orchestra striking up a waltz. She squared her shoulders and turned. Sure enough, Lord Rival was approaching through the crowd, smiling at her. Gil and Tish were nowhere to be seen.

Chloe took a deep breath and returned his lordship's smile. She could do this. She was sure she could. But then he was upon her, lifting her hand audaciously to his lips, and her smile slipped as she went suddenly hot and breathless.

"My waltz, Miss Littlefield," he said, his voice as soft as velvet. His smile caressed her. "My style differs somewhat from Mr. Gilliland's. I hope you do not find it too tame."

Tame! The absurdity surprised a shaky little laugh out of her. "I hope not, indeed."

She felt his touch on her waist. His left hand took her right. Even through their gloves, she was aware of his skin beneath the cloth in a way that had never occurred to her with any other dancing partner. Trembling, she placed her left hand lightly on the blue broadcloth sheathing his upper arm. His body was almost too well muscled. It felt strong and hard and warm beneath her fingertips. Then she looked into his smiling eyes—and was lost.

As he swept her into the dance, Chloe felt the breath sigh out of her, and she melted against the strong arm at her back. What a handsome man. What a perfect dream of a man. For a time she would throw caution to the wind, and just enjoy the dance. No harm in that, was there? This was going to be wonderful.

Step, two-three, turn, two-three—a flash of light and puff of smoke caught the corner of her eye, and she glanced behind her.

The moth had blundered into the candle after all.

Chapter 8

Like many of his gender, Gil was rendered instantly helpless by feminine tears. He thumped his sister's shoulder clumsily. "Buck up, old thing. I daresay you haven't made a *complete* fool of yourself."

Tish snatched the handkerchief out of her brother's pocket and, with an unintelligible exclamation, buried her face in it. He watched, very ill at ease, as she restlessly paced the tiny balcony. A row of these ran along the length of the ballroom at Alverstoke House, and, at the first sign that Tish's emotions threatened to make them both conspicuous, he had thrust his sister hastily through the velvet draperies masking the entrance to this one. Although the windows had been thrown wide to permit the marquis's guests to avail themselves of these retreats, the balconies were clearly intended by their designer to be more decorative than useful. A short stroll, or even a thorough escape from the ballroom, was unobtainable here. Light and music, both muffled, still reached them through the thick folds of drapery behind them.

"Men!" uttered Tish at last, in accents of loathing.

This struck Gil as an incomprehensible change of subject. He seized on it, therefore, with relief. "We're not such a bad lot, really," he said cheerfully. "Many of us are thoroughly decent chaps."

Her face emerged from the depths of white linen long enough to cast her brother a glance of pity and scorn. "You are complete *rotters!*"

Gil was startled. "Who? Me?"

Tish swept her hand in a tragic, comprehensive gesture.

"All of you! You are all alike! I daresay if you were not my brother, you would treat me as shabbily as all the rest!"

Gil thought it best to quell his natural impulse to argue with her. She was clearly beyond the reach of reason. He held his tongue, therefore, and waited in sympathetic silence for Tish to tell him what, in God's name, was wrong. For the next minute or so, however, all she did was sniffle and brood.

Gil could stand it no more. "What, in God's name, is wrong?" he demanded.

She shook her head woefully. "You wouldn't understand."

"I understand that you are behaving like a widgeon! Which I know you are not," he added hastily, as Tish rounded on him. "Now, *come* on, Tish—there's a good girl! Tell us what's the matter, won't you? It can't be anything I said. I only recommended that you stop tying your garter in public."

"Why should you care?" cried Tish passionately. "It doesn't matter what I do. Nothing matters anymore. I might as well be *dead!*"

"Oh, here, I *say*—!" Gil was genuinely shocked.

"I told you you wouldn't understand." She slumped in defeat. A shiver, whether of cold or despair, wracked her slender person.

Gil placed a brotherly arm around her shoulders and silently hugged her. He searched his mind for something comforting to say, but felt himself to be at a disadvantage; he hadn't a clue what was causing his sister's disproportionate misery. So he swiftly examined his recollection of the events leading up to this scene, trying to discover what, exactly, had set her off.

He had wrested her from her paramour's arms, but that had only annoyed her. He had then read her a stern and brotherly lecture. That had naturally infuriated her, but not to the point where she had lost control. If anything, she appeared to have expected it. But then he had threatened to tell her husband of her misconduct. Aha! That was the moment when her face had started to crumple and he had thrust her out onto the balcony.

He glanced speculatively down at the woebegone creature huddled in the circle of his arm. "Never mind, Tish," he said kindly. "I won't tell Robert. But you'll have to keep Rival at arm's length from now on. I wouldn't say a word to you if it wasn't important, you know; I've never been one to meddle in what don't concern me. But this game will ruin you, sure as check, if you don't put a stop to it."

To his consternation, her tears immediately welled up again. "You may as well tell Robert. It won't make a particle of difference."

"Now, that's where you're wrong," he said firmly. "Robert's not the sort of care-for-nobody who will let his wife run wild, making her name a byword and him a laughingstock! You may count yourself fortunate that your husband is still in the dark. I know you fancy yourself to be up to all the rigs, but you're not. There's a deal you don't know about men, Tish, and this in particular is a subject that was omitted from your education! If he gets wind of this escapade, little sister, you'll find yourself at point non-plus."

"Oh, it's not *fair!*" exclaimed Tish.

"Fair or unfair, that's the way of it. I wouldn't be surprised if Robert bundled you off to the country or sent you on a long visit to that harpy with the poodle—you know the one I mean. In Bath."

Tish shuddered again. "Aunt Honoria."

"That's the one. She's the very reason men have aunts in Bath, Tish. Gives us someone to send our erring wives to."

She greeted this sally with a faint smile, but it faded immediately. "If he sends me away, it won't matter where he sends me. That will be the end," she whispered bleakly. "The end of everything."

The depth of her unhappiness was unsettling. Lord Rival had obviously stolen too much of Tish's heart, if the thought of being sent away from him, no matter where, plunged her into such despair. "Damnation!" muttered Gil. "Does he matter that much to you, Tish?"

She nodded miserably.

"Think of your own little Bobby," he urged her. "Think of your family, and your friends, and all the people who care for you and hold you in esteem. Think of Chloe. Think of me! Why, there are any number of people who have your best interests at heart. Lord Rival ain't among them."

"I suppose that's true," she said listlessly. "But George makes me feel—oh, I can't explain it to you, Gil. I know there is really nothing in it. But he makes me feel like a—like a woman."

Gil was so relieved to hear her say there was nothing in it, he scarcely cared what she meant by her last remark. "That's the dandy!" he said approvingly. "Now you're seeing more clearly, what? A woman. Aye, and likely to remain so."

Tish gave a rather watery chuckle. "You have no idea what I mean, do you?"

"No, and I don't care to," admitted Gil, grinning. "If some chap made me feel like a woman, I'd be more likely to darken his daylights than weep over him."

Tish giggled a little, but then shivered violently. Gil frowned. "You're going to catch your death, out here in the night air wearing next to nothing. Mop your cheeks; we're going back in."

After mendaciously assuring her that no one would guess for a moment that she had been crying, and reluctantly accepting the return of his damp handkerchief, Gil succeeded in shepherding Tish back into the ballroom. She was hailed with delight by a group of young men standing nearby, which seemed to lift her spirits somewhat. When they started teasing her about going out on the balcony with her own brother, arguing about which of them should have the privilege of escorting her back onto the balcony, and begging her for dances, she visibly brightened. Gil, satisfied that Tish would survive the evening without a return to the slough of despond, wandered off to see what had become of Chloe. He felt a pang of guilt at leaving her alone, even in such a good cause. The poor girl must have found herself among the wallflowers.

The ballroom seemed even more crowded than it had

when he and Tish had left a few minutes ago. Between the throng of persons on the floor and the massive bouquets of flowers packed into every nook and cranny, Gil wondered how it was possible to find space to dance. It would be useless to search for the diminutive Chloe until the music had ended.

As he leaned against a column, idly watching the scene and calculating how much longer it might be before supper was served, he was brought up short by the sight of his supposed fiancée—the girl who had refused to dance with strangers—the girl who had hesitated to dance the waltz with *him*—waltzing breezily past, in the arms of Lord Rival.

Gil was stunned by the violence of the emotions that gripped him at the sight. He glimpsed them for only an instant: Chloe, eyes sparkling and cheeks flushed, looking prettier than he had ever seen her, and Lord Rival, smiling lazily down at his partner as he swept her round in a circle. Then they vanished from sight among the multitude. But it seemed to Gil that the image had been burned into his brain.

For a moment he forgot where he was. A loud and furious oath escaped his lips, startling a nearby dowager into spilling her punch. She turned to favor him with her opinion of his language, but he was off, striding heedlessly through the groups of chattering people as if he would mow them down in his haste.

He soon realized the futility of attempting to chase the dancing couple, especially since he had no notion where they had gone. He halted, therefore, breathing hard through clenched teeth. It seemed that a red miasma clouded his vision. He was struggling to recover some semblance of control when he became aware of a jocular voice hailing him.

"Gil! I say! Gil! What the devil are you doing here? Never thought I'd stumble across you at one of these dos!"

Gil bent his ferocious gaze to his left and saw Jack Crawley at his elbow. Crawley's jovial expression changed ludicrously to dismay, and he fell back a pace. "I say, are you all right?"

"Fine!" barked Gil.

"Good, good! Glad to hear it," said Jack hastily. He eyed

his friend, doubt and concern in his face, and finally blurted, "You don't look it."

Gil audibly ground his teeth. Jack stared at him. Then light dawned. "I see what it is, old chap. You're in a temper."

"Well, what if I am?"

"Don't bite my head off, dear boy! I'm sure it's no concern of mine."

Gil growled something that sounded like rude agreement. His eyes were furiously scanning the crowd.

"Unless I might be of service," suggested Jack cautiously. "Happy to do anything in my power, of course."

Gil's head swiveled back to face his friend. His frown altered slightly, to one of fierce concentration. "Is Barney with you?"

"Lord, no! Can't get Furbush out to one of these ghastly affairs; he don't need to marry an heiress. I'm here with m'mother and sisters. Been paying court to Miss Sowerberry." Jack shuddered eloquently. "Fellow needs something stronger than negus after dancing attendance on that antidote for the better part of an hour. I say, Gil, have you danced with the beauty?"

"What beauty?"

"Chit Alverstoke's bringing out. The cousin, or whatever she is. Daresay she hasn't a penny to bless herself with, but—"

"I've danced only with Chloe." Gil returned his irascible scrutiny to the crowd of dancers.

Jack brightened. "Oh, is she here? Gel you don't wish to marry? I've a fancy to meet her, if you wouldn't mind doing the honors." He waited, but Gil seemed not to have heard him. He cleared his throat delicately. "Where is she, old man?"

"Who?"

"Miss Littlefield. You said she was here."

"She's dancing with Lord Rival." The words were uttered in a voice of suppressed fury.

Jack looked shocked. "Rival! What's his interest in her?"

"He has no *interest* in her! What the devil are you implying?"

"Nothing, nothing, dear boy! Don't fly into a pelter. I only thought—that is, I daresay you might not know—"

"Know what? Out with it, man!"

"Well, I'll tell you. But don't shoot the messenger, Gil!" Jack took a deep breath. "That fellow, Rival. You don't know him. No reason why you should; he's one of the Corinthian set. But, Gil"—Jack leaned forward impressively and tapped his friend earnestly on the chest to emphasize his words—"he's *devilish attractive* to females."

"Oh, for God's sake!" yelped Gil, swatting Jack's hand away in a frenzy of impatience. "Tell me something I don't know! Chloe's off making sheep's eyes at the fellow as we speak, and I don't know where they've gone."

Jack clucked his tongue sympathetically. "That's a bad business."

Gil gave a short, mirthless laugh. "So it is! But one can't call a man out for waltzing with a girl."

"No. Pity." A thought occurred to Jack, and he turned to stare at Gil. "Is that why you asked me if Barney was here?"

Gil grinned sheepishly. "Looking for a pair of seconds. Lost my head for a moment."

"Good Lord! Never knew you to go off half-cocked. You feeling quite the thing, Gil?"

"Oh, I'm all right now," Gil assured him. "After all, I don't suppose Chloe can get into too much mischief at a place like Alverstoke House. Trouble is, she's such a babe in the woods—not up to snuff at all! Never know what a girl like that will do."

"No. But if she's an innocent soul, I daresay there's nothing to worry about," said Jack soothingly. "Rival don't pursue fledglings. He prefers women who know their way about."

Gil's mouth set grimly. "If Chloe throws herself at him, however, I expect he'll be glad to catch her."

Jack wheezed with laughter. "Pshaw! Innocent girls don't throw themselves at men. That's why they're innocent, what? Ha! Ha!"

"Aye, but Chloe is *setting out* to do so. My hope is, she won't have the foggiest notion how to go about it."

Jack frowned at Gil, his brows nearly meeting over his beaklike nose. "I can't have heard you right," he said at last. "Could have sworn you said Miss Littlefield was going to throw herself at Lord Rival."

"That's what I said."

Jack digested this information in silence. "Why?" he finally asked.

"Oh, she fancies she's doing me a favor!" Gil gave a crack of bitter laughter. "And just try telling her otherwise!"

"Doing you a—? Oh, I see." Jack cocked an eyebrow knowingly. "You must've told her you don't wish to marry her."

"Yes, but if you're thinking she's gone off in a fit of pique because I injured her feelings, let me assure you that I didn't! She was in a worse pucker than I was about that dashed notice."

"Then why—?"

"It's to put a stop to the business, that's why! She plans to throw dust in everyone's eyes by pretending to be head over heels for Lord Rival. Believing I will then be able to jilt her with a clear conscience! Did you ever hear anything to beat it?"

Animation returned to Jack's features. "Well, congratulations, Gil!" he said warmly. "You know, I wondered how you would get 'round this engagement thing. Miss Littlefield going to get you off the hook, eh? Very sporting of her."

Gil glared. "If you think I should be *grateful* to her, you're fair and far off, my friend! If she succeeds in this crazy scheme of hers, how do you think it will make me look? Like a complete gudgeon, that's how!"

"Yes, I suppose it might do that," Jack agreed. After a moment, he added, "Make *her* look nohow, at any rate."

"I know it will! Of all the crazy, shatterbrained ideas—but that's Clo all over! She gets a notion in her head and runs away with it. Never a thought for the consequences!"

Jack looked thoughtful. "On the other hand, of course, it should do the trick."

"Do what trick?"

"Why, scotch your engagement! You can't expect to get out of it without some sort of dust being kicked up. May as well try this plan as any other. Rival willing to play along?"

"If you mean does he respond when she bats her eyes at him, yes, he does! Chloe's a devilish pretty girl. Didn't I say he's waltzing with her even now? I'm sure he'll be only too glad to ruin her reputation—and mine! Come with me, Jack. I've got to find them."

Jack shook his head, puzzled. "Seems to me that if Miss Littlefield is willing to sacrifice herself, the least you could do is stay out of her way while she does it."

Gil's expression became mulish. "If you won't come with me, I'm going without you. But I mean to put a stop to this if I can."

"Daresay you can't," said Jack calmly. "Good thing, if you ask me. You're being too chivalrous by half."

"I'm not being chivalrous!"

"Yes, you are. You say you don't wish to look foolish. Well, you won't. It's Miss Littlefield who will suffer for her conduct, and you know it! You're going to save her from social ruin."

Gil's chin began to jut alarmingly. "And what if I am?"

"Why, it's chivalrous, that's all. Acting against your own interests! You don't want her. She don't want you. What the devil are you meddling for?"

Gil fumed, searching for an answer to this home question. He found none. Jack was right. He should, in fact, be doing what he could to promote this plan of Chloe's, not thwart it. It was a good plan, as far as it went. His reaction was nonsensical.

It didn't matter. Every time he thought of Chloe throwing herself at Lord Rival, steam started coming out of his ears. "Are you coming, or aren't you?" he snapped. "You said you wanted to meet her. Well, let's find her! I'll be only too happy to introduce you. And, for God's sake, Jack—ask her to dance!"

Jack, brightening, linked arms with his crony. "I've no objection to dancing with her. In fact, I'll be happy to pay court to her, if you think it would help."

Gil tore his eyes from the crowd of dancers to stare at Jack. "How the deuce would that help?"

Jack coughed vaguely. "Oh, I don't know—divert her attention from Rival, if you really think she's in any danger. And you know, Gil, if I must marry an heiress, I'd as lief marry a pretty one. Besides—friend of yours! Daresay I shall like her."

"Haven't I been telling you forever that Chloe don't wish to be married?" Gil's voice nearly cracked in exasperation.

"Yes, you've said that. Thing is, I don't believe it," explained Jack. "Now, don't fly out at me! Never saw you so testy in m'life. You been in the sun, dear boy?"

But the music had ended, and Gil, distracted, was scanning the crowd again as groups of dancers, laughing and chattering, left the floor. He suddenly spotted Chloe not far from where he and Crawley were standing, fanning herself beside a marble pillar. The pillar supported an enormous stand of flowers, and she made a lovely picture in her ivory ball gown against the background of riotous color. Lord Rival was still beside her, and seemed to be saying something terribly amusing. Chloe was laughing up at him in a way that made Gil feel suddenly, irrationally, murderous.

Well, damn it all, why *shouldn't* he feel murderous? Chloe was *his*, confound it! That was the long and the short of it: Chloe was his. He must have been mad to think he didn't want to marry her. Of course he wanted to marry her.

The revelation turned Gil to stone. He froze, staring at Chloe and Lord Rival, heedless of Jack Crawley tugging at his arm. He felt hot and cold and sick with rage. What a prime idiot he had been, thinking he wanted to weasel out of his engagement. Why, that was the last thing on earth he wanted to do! Where was he going to find another girl he liked as well as Chloe? Where would he find a girl he liked *half* as well? Nowhere! There wasn't another girl to equal her. There never would be. Not for him.

But there she stood, his own precious Chloe, all aglow from the attentions of another man.

And there wasn't a blasted thing he could do about it.

Chapter 9

Lord Rival wearily let himself into his flat. It was very late, and he was dog-tired. Unfortunately, sleep did not lie in his immediate future. A lamp was burning in his sitting room, and the sprawling figure of a lanky young man occupied his favorite chair. As the chair's owner entered the room, this individual straightened somewhat and gave a prodigious yawn.

"Heigh-ho, George, is that you at last? Thought you was never coming home. Done with another night's raking, eh? Good God, the sun's rising! Time for breakfast. And a good thing, too. I'm famished."

"I wonder why I gave you a key to this flat?" mused Lord Rival, closing the door behind him and advancing to the fire. He stretched his chilled hands toward the blaze. "It is not time for breakfast, brat. It is time for bed. And you are invited to neither."

The young man grinned, unaffected by this chilly reception. "I daresay you'll relent, at least as far as breakfast. I'm devilish hard to snub."

"So I have noticed. What brings you here, Sid? Outrunning the constable again?"

"In a manner of speaking. Landlady shut the door in m'face, if you can believe that."

"Easily! I find myself in sympathy with the woman."

"Yes, but you wouldn't change the locks on a fellow, would you? Shabby treatment! The wonder is that she dared. Why, all my things are in that room!"

"You failed to pay the rent, I suppose."

A shadow flitted across Sid's habitually smiling face, and

he hunched a shoulder. "Luck's bound to turn sometime," he muttered defensively. "I'll pay her rubbishing rent eventually, and so I told her. Why can't she give a chap a chance to come about?"

"Why not, indeed?" said George with mock compassion. "Landlords are such a distrustful lot."

He seated himself in the chair opposite his uninvited guest and regarded him cynically. Sidney Cheyne was a well-born, charming ne'er-do-well, too handsome for his own good. He was, in fact, exactly what George Carstairs had been ten years ago. They resembled each other neither in appearance nor in manner; Sidney's slightly-too-calculated boyishness differed from his own suave urbanity as day from night. Yet, somehow, looking at Sid was almost like looking in a mirror. George felt for Sid as much contempt as he felt for himself, and nearly as much affection.

"I hope you don't mean to touch me for a loan. Surely you know me too well for that."

Sid gave a short laugh. "Yes, I do! Besides, you never have a feather to fly with."

A slight smile briefly lit George's saturnine features. "Oh, I have a *feather*, these days. I am even occasionally airborne. Still, finding myself aloft is such a pleasant and novel experience, I am loath to relinquish any portion of my small store to a wastrel like you."

Sid opened his eyes in startled chagrin. "I say, coz, that's rather a case of the pot calling the kettle black, don't you think?"

"Yes," agreed George blandly. "Which is why I have no hesitation in saying it. The pot and the kettle share a certain affinity, after all. But you really must give up this notion that we are cousins. We most decidedly are not."

"Oh, as to that—! I consider you quite one of the family." Sid grinned and stretched out his long legs. "Wouldn't presume like this on a stranger, George! Wouldn't dare! But since our great-grandmothers were cousins—"

"By marriage only!"

"—I know I may call on you in any crisis."

George held out his hand peremptorily. "Give me back that key at once! I was mad to give it you."

Sid winked. "Not on your life! A man never knows when he may need a safe haven."

"You won't find it here, brat. If the water's too hot for you in London, why the devil don't you go home?"

"Because I don't wish to hand my head to my father for washing, that's why!"

"Nonsense. You're the prodigal son. He'll kill the fatted calf the instant you appear on the horizon."

Sid snorted. "I'm not the prodigal son. I'm the black sheep! They'll skin me alive if I show my face at Cheyne. You don't know how lucky you are to have no family."

"No family? I thought you had decided we were cousins," mocked George.

Another grin split Sid's features. "You're my cousin when I want something from you," he explained. "Otherwise, our connection is really too remote. I generally don't think of you as family at all."

"I would take offense, of course, if I didn't realize you meant that for a compliment," remarked George. He reached a languid hand for the brandy decanter resting on a nearby table and held it up to the light. "Oh, did you leave me a dram? You are the soul of courtesy."

"I even left you a clean glass."

"A model guest," murmured George, pouring himself the drop that remained in his decanter. He regarded Sid over the brim of the glass as he rolled the amber liquid meditatively back and forth. "If you won't go home, will you take some advice? I am older, and presumably wiser, than yourself."

Sid looked wary. "You may give your advice, if you must. Whether I take it or not is another matter. What is it?"

"I can tell you how to change your luck at the gaming tables. At least, I can tell you how I changed mine."

Sid's jaw dropped. He leaned forward eagerly. "Now, that's something like!" he exclaimed. "I thought you seemed a trifle plumper in the pocket than you were a year ago. I wondered how you had managed it, but I didn't care to ask."

Sardonic amusement lit George's eyes. "You thought I was fuzzing the cards or some such thing."

"No—no, of course not!"

"Good," said George, his voice as soft as silk.

Sid flushed. "I—I only thought you might have stumbled upon something, you know. Some trick you didn't want to share."

"I have. And I will tell you my secret. But you won't like it." George tilted the brandy down his throat, swallowed, and wiped his mouth with the back of his hand. An enigmatic smile lit his features as he regarded Sid's avid expression. "I stopped drinking."

Sid's eyes slid, in doubt and surprise, to the brandy decanter. George's smile widened. "At the table. I never touch a drop at dinner, nor when gaming. In fact, I never drink at all until the evening's end. And that, my friend, is why my luck changed. I told you you wouldn't like it."

Sid's face had indeed fallen; he looked almost ludicrously disappointed. He laughed uneasily. "You're right. I don't. Hang it all, a man must drink when his companions do so! I always keep a clear head."

George shrugged, bored. "By all means, delude yourself. It's not my concern. Unsolicited advice is never welcome; I don't know why I offered it in the first place. I ought to know better. But it's late, and I'm tired."

As he set down his glass, preparing to rise from the chair, Sid leaned forward and laid an urgent hand upon his sleeve. "George—you know I hate to ask, but—really, I am utterly rolled up! Might I pay you a visit?"

George frowned. "Here? Good God, man, I've only two rooms."

"No, I know that. I meant your place in Sussex. If I could stay there until next quarter-day—"

"No."

The terse monosyllable caused an angry flush to mount Sid's cheek. "It's—it's not like I'd *steal* anything!" he exclaimed, mortified.

George uttered a short bark of laughter. "There's nothing there to steal. I only wish there were! Over the years, everything of value has been either stripped away or mortgaged. Don't look so cast down, lad! I'd send you there, but the place is all in holland covers and there's only a caretaker on the premises. No staff at all. I can't afford one." His mouth twisted in bitter humor. "Being a baron isn't what it used to be."

Sid flung himself back in the chair, scowling. The veneer of charm that he wore like a cloak slipped for a moment, revealing the sulky, spoiled boy beneath it. "At least you have an estate," he said resentfully. "And a title! I haven't anything of my own."

George's lips compressed into a thin line. His young friend was incapable of appreciating the gifts he possessed that George did not. George had had a father, and a grandfather before him, whose idea of estate management was to wring every last groat out of the land, mortgaging everything that was entailed and gambling away whatever was not. The result was that George Carstairs was the proud owner of an ancient title, a crumbling house, and a mountain of debt. He was the last of his line, and utterly alone in the world. His only sibling, a much-loved sister, had died in childbirth four years ago. Sidney Cheyne was a younger son and would never have a title, since he seemed unlikely to earn one on his own. But he had a prudent and prosperous father, a large family who cared enough about him to fret and scold and threaten him whenever they saw him, and personal gifts that might someday dupe a nice girl into marrying him. He would certainly never be destitute.

Or lonely.

George rose abruptly. "I'm for bed. You may stretch out on that sofa if it's long enough for you, or sit by the fire and brood over your wrongs, or leave. It's all one to me. Breakfast won't be served until noon, but you're welcome to share it."

"I'm obliged to you," muttered Sid. He did not look grateful. He had obviously counted on that invitation to his friend's Sussex estate.

George gave a short laugh and withdrew to his bedchamber. No valet awaited him; he had had to dispense with such luxuries long ago. He loathed the menial work of polishing boots and pressing linen, but he had become quite adept at it. The expensive wardrobe was not a luxury, it was a necessity. So he spent whatever money he had on his clothing and accoutrements, and he cared for his gear himself. No one must guess the depth of Lord Rival's poverty.

He stood wearily before the pier glass and tugged at his cravat. What the devil had possessed him, preaching temperance to the likes of Sidney Cheyne? He must be going soft. And if a man goes to the trouble of dispensing advice, he ought not to give away only half the secret. Gambling with a clear head was important, but the company in which one gambled was even more so.

Well, he was less proud of that particular key to his recent success. He tossed his cravat aside, a rather ugly expression twisting his features. No, he wasn't proud of that at all, but needs must when the devil drives. A man must have funds. And women were such easy pigeons to pluck. No one taught them, as young men were taught, to beware of sharpsters like himself. Most of them did not even play especially well. And if a man was handsome enough, all he had to do was bow and smile and whisper a few words of flattery, and the silly creatures fell into his hands like ripe peaches.

Leticia Dalrymple, for instance. He owed the pair of gleaming Hessians in the corner of the room, two coats by Weston, and four bottles of excellent brandy to Tish's folly. Not to mention six months' rent. If her husband ever deduced how much money she had lost to her friend George, friend George might find himself meeting Robert Dalrymple at dawn some fine morning with a pistol in his hand. But George really didn't think it would come to that. He trod very carefully where young wives were concerned. Young husbands were notoriously hotheaded.

He would have to tread even more carefully now, at least for a while. Mrs. Dalrymple had acquired a watchdog. Temporarily, he hoped. The Honorable Robert Dalrymple was a fool who never accompanied his wife anywhere. But that

Miss Littlefield was no fool, and she apparently meant to accompany Tish everywhere.

Unless he was much mistaken, it was Miss Littlefield who had dragged Tish's brother into the game. That, too, might prove tricky. Ordinarily, he would have dismissed young Mr. Gilliland as no threat at all. A callow youth was no match for a man of the world. But brothers—ah, brothers of any stripe were often more of a hindrance than husbands.

He frowned as he hung up his jacket. What game was Miss Littlefield playing? He generally found young and inexperienced girls completely uninteresting, but she evinced flashes of intelligence and oddly contradictory behavior that intrigued him. Perhaps she was a bit older than she appeared. She looked a veritable child, transparent as glass. She was frequently as tongue-tied and stammering as the tiresome little schoolgirl she looked to be. But she would occasionally blurt out some caustic, and apparently heartfelt, remark that surprised a laugh out of him.

Her treatment of him was hardly appropriate for a duenna, and even less appropriate for a respectable young man's fiancée. Last night she had veered wildly and obviously back and forth between angry dislike and unwilling attraction, with spurts of gushing admiration thrown in for good measure. What struck him as peculiar was that both the dislike and the attraction seemed genuine, and the gushing admiration utterly false. It was almost as if she were attempting to ignore both her dislike of him and her attraction to him, and—with dreadful ineptitude—set up a flirt. But why?

He gave a mental shrug and climbed into bed. Tish Dalrymple was his prey, not Chloe Littlefield. Miss Littlefield represented only a hurdle he must leap in his pursuit of the charming and gullible Tish. Flirting with Miss Littlefield might lull her, or it might not. If it did, her gaucherie would add a welcome element of the unexpected into the game. If it did not, he could always protest that he only meant to be friendly. Either way, the next week or two were shaping up to be more amusing than he had anticipated.

When he arose six hours later, he was not surprised to find Sid Cheyne still present and snoring on his couch. The smell of food was the only thing that finally served to wake him, at which point he joined his host for a mutually bleary-eyed and silent breakfast.

Sid finally pushed his tankard away with a sigh of contentment.

"Feeling more the thing?" inquired George solicitously.

He grinned. "Aye. Amazing what a difference a few slices of ham can make to a fellow's temper. Strange, isn't it? Pigs are the meanest beasts in creation, but ham is jolly stuff."

"I daresay that's why they speak of ham as being 'cured.' "

"Yes, it's cured me, at any rate! Thank you, George. Very good of you to let me stay and all that. Sorry if I seemed a bit peppery earlier—"

George held up a graceful hand. "No, no, do not apologize! Finding oneself at point-non-plus is naturally disconcerting. You are speaking to a man who has been there himself on more than one occasion. Matters always seem less bleak in the morning—although one is hard pressed to say why, since one's situation has changed not a whit."

"No. But I daresay something will turn up. I'll have another go at persuading the landlady to let me in. Dash it all, I can't be expected to pay her if she won't let me change my clothes! I can't touch anyone for a loan looking like this!" He ruefully indicated his rumpled garments.

"Fatal," agreed George. "You have the look of a man who would instantly abscond with any monies entrusted to him."

Sid laughed unwillingly. "The trouble is, I haven't enough friends. And the friends I do have are as badly dipped as I am! I don't count female friends, of course. One can't ask women for money—more's the pity! I know any number of rich women who'd be only too glad to help if I dared let 'em know I needed it."

"You will have to offer for Miss Sowerberry."

"Good God, I hope not! I'm such a charming fellow, you know, that she might actually accept me."

"Well, if it does come to that, don't put a period to your

existence. There are worse fates than marriage to a respectable female. Or so I'm told." He took a thoughtful sip
of coffee. "I can't think of one, of course."

"No! I don't notice *you* offering marriage to any of the
beauties who have thrown themselves at your feet! If you
have managed to escape the net all these years, I imagine I
shall find a way."

A faint, ironic smile flitted across George's shadowed features. "Heiresses don't come along as often as one could
wish. And the ones that do come along are inevitably surrounded by a pack of guard dogs."

Sid chuckled. "Aye! It was dashed difficult to get near the
Sowerberry. Had to turn her aunt up sweet, and her mother
as well. And after I finally muscled my way into the inner
circle, I found half a dozen other gentlemen there before me.
Thought at first she must be a matrimonial prize of the first
water! But it was all a hum, of course."

George lifted an eyebrow. "No such thing. She is an only
child, and I have it on the best authority that her father is
worth—"

"Oh, I don't mean the fortune! She's full of juice, all right
and tight. But she's dull as dishwater. No conversation at all,
and nothing to look at. It does sicken a man, to watch everyone scrape and fawn and make cakes of themselves over her
as if she were a beauty. Which she ain't! And then to find
oneself doing the same—well, it's a humbling experience, I
can tell you! I'll say this for you, George—you're an honest
fellow. You never pay court to ugly women."

"Certainly not. Where's the sport in that?"

Sid opened his eyes at his friend. "One doesn't do it for
sport. It's the money, man, the money!"

George made a grimace of distaste. "It hasn't come to that
yet, thank God. I pity the poor sods who sell themselves into
marriage for the sake of a soft life. It sounds a disgusting op-
tion, to me. As long as I am able to scrape two shillings together, I prefer my rather precarious existence on the fringes
of society."

"Fringes!" Sid snorted. "You're found in the best ball-
rooms in town. But I must agree with you, old man, that

there is much to be said for bachelorhood, even with creditors beating down the door. Go where you please, do what you please, embroil yourself in all sorts of dangerous mischief—"

"Yes, the constant sense of impending doom is part of the appeal! Nevertheless, I suppose the day will come when I shall have to marry. I'm the last of my line, you know."

Sid grinned and leaned across the table to punch his friend playfully in the arm. "Better start looking now, George! The only thing you can offer a female is your *beaux yeux!*"

George was startled. "I am not yet in my dotage."

"No, but if you wait until you are, you'll find the pickings slim." Sid pushed himself back from the table and stretched his limbs, not noticing the arrested expression on his host's face. "Well, I'm off," he said, with cheerful abruptness. "Thanks for the breakfast. I'll see you at Manton's later, I daresay."

George nodded absently and bid his young friend farewell. He then walked to the window and frowned, unseeing, at the street.

He would turn thirty-four this year. He had inherited the title at the age of twenty-two. Which meant—good God, he had been living here in London for twelve years. Where had the time gone?

No wonder he felt bored and restless lately. Twelve years was a long time to spend adrift. And that's exactly what he was: adrift. Anchorless. Passively allowing the wind to blow him wherever it would.

This unfettered life had been exciting at first. It had grown gradually less exciting, but that was probably inevitable. One grew accustomed to a life of idleness and intrigue, and adept at dodging the dangers of angry husbands and angrier creditors. So life naturally held fewer and fewer challenges.

The main source of his income had proved, until lately, wildly unreliable—but interesting. Now that he had hit on a system that paid off more often than not, gaming was a bore. Dalliance with married women, together with its attendant mix of dangers and satisfactions, he still found entertaining. But he had become so awfully good at attracting women, that was slowly turning into a bore as well. When he tried to recollect the various flirts he had enjoyed, all the faces seemed to blur together. None stood out. They were just a succession of pretty smiles and cold hearts.

But it was his heart that had grown cold.

He tried to think of someone or something he really cared for, and came up blank. His sister's face floated briefly in his memory, but he thrust the image away, shaken. Poor Susan. Married at eighteen, dead at twenty. The world was a harsh and hostile place.

For the first time, he wondered how long he could continue his way of life. Another five years, perhaps. Ten, at the outside. Perhaps there would always be women who found him attractive, and he could continue fleecing them indefinitely. But surely, as Sid's bad joke had pointed out, the list of possibilities would shorten as time went on. How long would he retain the ability to be choosy about his victims?

That was a disquieting thought, to say the least. Sid had complimented his "honesty" in eschewing ugly women, and he had stupidly prided himself on making conquests of the prettiest women in the *ton*—well, good God, how long would that last? What an unthinking imbecile he was! What a hypocrite, to jeer at the men who were pursuing Miss Sowerberry! He would find himself among such supplicants one day. It would be that, or starve.

Besides—and this was the truly surprising thing—the notion of succeeding at the game indefinitely was unappealing. Even distasteful. He did not *want* to continue this way of life forever. Or for another ten years. Even five years more struck him as a profoundly dreary prospect.

Well? What, then?

George began pacing the room restlessly. What, indeed. He had no profession, no calling to give his life meaning. He was unsuited to be anything other than what he was. A pity one could not work and remain a gentleman! Why was that? A line he had read somewhere echoed faintly in his mind:

"Idleness is the appendix to nobility." The only occupations open to him were philanthropy, which required funds, or managing his estate, which required funds. He hadn't any. If he had, he would return to Sussex and try to put some heart back into the land. Now, *there* was a prospect to warm the coldest heart.

For a moment he halted, picturing it vividly. He generally avoided thinking about his estate, but the memories were as fresh as yesterday. Bitter memories and futile dreams. Dreams of his childhood home, restored to what it must have been three generations ago. Fertile fields. Healthy sheep. A bustling village, its prosperity reborn. A land of peace and plenty. And himself, home at last. Children at his knee. A wife at his side.

Suddenly his crooked grin wryly twisted his features. Go ahead, old boy, he told himself. Focus on the woman's face. Who is it? She'll have to have the chinks, if you expect to make this hopeless dream a reality.

He was not surprised when her face refused to come into focus. He had never yet met a woman who inspired him with any desire to form a permanent connection. Did he really want to search for such a person now?

Perhaps he did.

This was a novel idea. He rubbed his chin thoughtfully, mentally perusing the list of young women making their come-out this Season. A dismal lot! Miss Sowerberry and the other Homely Joans were out of the question for a connoisseur like himself. But all the pretty girls were too young. Too chattering. Too giggly.

Good God, if they struck him so at thirty-four, what would they seem to him at forty? He had better, in fact, start looking about! George sank into the nearest chair, unnerved.

But this was absurd. If he could think of no one he wished to marry, what of it? He had no desire to marry. None.

Back came the memories, tormenting him with their sweetness, and their utter unattainability. He could almost smell the wind off the sea. *Home.*

Damnation. If he could think of a rich girl who was halfway interesting, he might well pounce. It would be worth it. And he would be so grateful to her, and so sick of enduring empty flirtation after empty flirtation, that he might well learn to care for her.

Pounce. The image rang a bell, faintly, in the back of his mind. He had invited some female to pounce on him, not so long ago. Who was it?

Why, of course. Of course! Chloe Littlefield.

Chapter 10

The day was fresh and fair. It was difficult for Chloe to restrain herself until the "fashionable hour," but it arrived at last and Tish decreed that *now* they might hack sedately round Hyde Park. Chloe rolled her eyes at the silliness of letting the beau monde dictate the proper time for air and exercise, but she soon discovered that air and exercise were completely beside the point. In fact, they were unobtainable. She was forced to abandon her hope of cantering briskly down Rotten Row, but could not regret it; Hyde Park during the fashionable hour was a sight well worth seeing.

The paths and lanes were choked with elegant carriages, strolling dandies, and gentlemen mounted on expensive horseflesh. It was not unlike watching a very beautiful parade, except that one became, oneself, part of the show. Chloe was agreeably surprised by how many faces she recognized. It was pleasant to greet acquaintances as they traversed the pretty pathways, bowing and smiling; it made Chloe feel that she was becoming almost at home in London.

There were fewer ladies than men on horseback, so Tish and Chloe were instantly conspicuous. Tish enjoyed this for its own sake and was thrown into giddy high spirits—but as soon as Chloe realized the degree of attention they were attracting, she felt a trifle shy. She was thankful that she was an experienced rider and that she had just purchased an extremely becoming, and shockingly expensive, riding habit. At least she knew she had nothing to blush for, so when a pair of dandies raised their quizzing glasses as the two girls rode past, she was able to keep her composure.

"Why must they do that?" she asked Tish crossly. "It puts me out of countenance to be stared at so rudely."

"It's meant to, goose! Just ignore them."

"I have half a mind to turn round and stare back at them."

"Oh, no, you mustn't do that! Heaven only knows what would happen. Men are such unaccountable creatures. But Chloe, just look at the women in that barouche over there! Who can that harridan be? Did you ever see such eyebrows? The beauty beside her is Lady Whitlatch. What a ravishing bonnet, to be sure! I have only met her once or twice, but of course one instantly recognizes her. They say her mother was one of Louis XVI's mistresses, but I, for one, do not believe it. People are so spiteful, you know; let a woman be *that* beautiful and they will find dreadful things to say about her on the slimmest of pretexts! One can scarcely credit it, but she must be on the shady side of thirty by now. Oh! Why, here comes Barney Furbush!" Tish interrupted her own chatter to wave her riding crop merrily. "Have you met him yet? No, of course you have not, for he never goes to parties. Not the parties *we* are invited to, at any rate! Mr. Furbush, how do you do?"

A young man stopped politely at the side of the path as Tish reined in her hack, and lifted his hat to them. Chloe blinked a little at the gentleman's attire, which was exquisite to the point of absurdity. Mr. Furbush's addiction to the extremes of fashion was unfortunate, since his silhouette did not conform to the wasp-waisted model necessary to display his apparel to advantage. In contrast to his costume, his person was soft and unassuming. He had a pleasant, undistinguished face and a completely vapid expression.

"Ah de do?" said Mr. Furbush, bowing.

Tish performed the necessary introductions. "Mr. Furbush is a great friend of my brother's," she added.

Chloe looked at the young man with renewed interest. "Why, so am I!" she told him cordially.

Light appeared to dawn in Mr. Furbush's brain. "Littlefield, did you say? You the gel he's going to marry? Very happy to make your acquaintance!"

Color flamed in Chloe's cheeks. "Well, as to that, Mr. Furbush—"

"Not much in the petticoat line, myself, but I daresay Gil will manage to pull it off. Wedding, you know!" he explained, as the girls looked mystified. "A great lot of people gawking at one and hurling rice in one's face and so forth. Unnerving, I should think. On an empty stomach, too! But Gil's always been full of pluck."

Tish giggled. "You are so droll, Mr. Furbush!" she exclaimed, a compliment that seemed to surprise its recipient. "But where have you been hiding yourself? I haven't seen you for an age."

He waved a hand vaguely. "Oh, I've been here and there. Round about. Walking with Jack Crawley just now, you know. He wanted to come; met a chit last night he wished to see again. Heiress! Means to dangle after her, I suppose, though he didn't care to call on her. I didn't quite follow that part—wasn't particularly attending. Delicate business! Not my cup of tea. At any rate, he fancied she'd be in the park, and here we are."

In proof of his assertion, Jack Crawley came walking round the bend. He brightened visibly when he saw his friend conversing with Tish and Chloe, and advanced eagerly upon the group, sweeping off his hat as he approached.

"Mrs. Dalrymple, how do you do? Miss Littlefield! Your servant," he said, executing a very creditable bow. "Beautiful day, what?"

The girls politely agreed. Jack beamed. Chloe had to hide a smile at the picture the two friends presented, side by side. Jack Crawley was as tall as Barney Furbush was short and as angular as Barney was round. He was one of those young men who seem to outgrow their frames in adolescence and spend the next decade or so catching up. His legs were spindly, his shoulderblades stuck out like wings, and his Adam's apple was visible even through the folds of his tightly wrapped cravat. His thin face was dominated by a nose that, had he been a woman, would have

caused everyone to think him a witch. Chloe privately
thought that if Mr. Crawley meant to catch an heiress, he
would have to choose a nearsighted one. And court her
from a distance.

The group conversed for a few minutes on inconsequen-
tial matters, and then, just as Tish and Chloe were preparing
to ride on, Mr. Crawley looked earnestly at Chloe, swept off
his hat again, and blurted, "Miss Littlefield, will you be present at Lady Bartlett's ball?"

"Why, I hardly know," said Chloe, startled. "Tish?"

"I believe we will be there," said Tish cautiously.

Mr. Crawley had turned a little red. "I wonder if I might
have the first waltz?" he stammered. "If no one else has
claimed it, of course."

Chloe stared at Mr. Crawley in astonishment and dismay.
"Gracious!" she said faintly. Then inspiration struck. "I
think I may have promised it to Gil," she murmured apologetically, blushing for her lie.

"Then may I have the second?"

"Well, I—I—"

"She has promised the second waltz to me," said a
smooth baritone from just behind her. Chloe jumped, and
had to prevent her hack from dancing nervously. She
looked over to see Lord Rival pulling up beside them on a
showy chestnut. He touched his hat to both her and Tish,
smiling lazily. Chloe caught her breath, dazzled. She had
not seen him in daylight before. Heavens, he was handsome.

How long had he been there, eavesdropping? She had no
more promised a waltz to him than she had promised one
to Gil! What an audacious creature he was! She hardly
knew whether to scold him or thank him. After all, she
would far rather waltz with Lord Rival than poor Jack
Crawley.

But beneath them, on the path, Mr. Crawley looked both
crestfallen and chagrined. "Oh, well. Another time, perhaps," was all he said, placing his hat back on his head.

Chloe's conscience pricked her. "If there is a third waltz,
Mr. Crawley, you may have it," she promised. He bright-

ened a little, bowed, and went off down the path, arm in arm with Barney.

Chloe stole a glance at Lord Rival, her mouth prim. He quirked an eyebrow at her. "No point in rescuing you, fair maiden, if you willfully tie yourself to the stake."

"You had much better mind your own business, then," she replied tartly. "Nobody asked you to rescue me."

"Come, come! Knights-errant cannot wait to be asked. They must rush in, you know, where angels fear to tread."

A little spurt of laughter escaped Chloe. "That's what fools do."

His dark eyes gleamed. "What fools do, Miss Littlefield, is beg for waltzes a week in advance of a ball."

"What fools do, Lord Rival, is claim waltzes that were never promised."

"And did you really promise the first waltz to Mr. Gilliland?"

Chloe bit her lip. "No. But you cannot have it!"

"I don't want it."

Chloe choked in surprise, but Lord Rival was grinning down at Tish, who looked saucily up at him.

"Well, George?" she said demurely.

"Must I ask?"

"Yes, you must."

"Very well, sweet tormentor!" He placed one hand over his heart. "May I have the honor of dancing the first waltz with you at Lady Bartlett's ball?"

Tish nibbled the tip of one gloved finger, pretending to consider the matter. "I don't know," she mused. "I never willingly dance with fools."

"Fools?"

Tish opened her eyes innocently. "You said only fools request dances a week in advance of a ball, did you not?"

Chloe and Tish both laughed at Lord Rival's expression of comic chagrin.

"I did say that. The more fool I! Never mind. Only promise that you will not give it to another, and I shall be content to wait and ask you at the ball."

Watching him banter with Tish, Chloe was struck by a

subtle change in him. On horseback, easily controlling the
animal beneath him, his air of weary mockery seemed less
pronounced, his teasing remarks more mischievous and
less dangerous. She found this side of him, the daylight
creature, more likeable than the jaded man she had met at
Lady Paversham's drum. Still, she could not like the predatory way he looked at Tish, and even less did she like the
way Tish looked at him. Tish had always been one who
wore her heart on her sleeve. It was pinned there now, for
all to see.

Lord Rival rode between them for a few minutes as they
continued down the path, to Tish's obvious delight. Chloe
found herself nervously watching the other persons crowding the park. Were they taking note of Tish's infatuation? Or
were they all completely preoccupied with seeing and being
seen? That certainly seemed to be everyone's purpose in
coming here. If only Gil would chance to appear! Once
again, Chloe had been thrust into the role of chaperone. She
disliked it very much indeed.

Her best hope for protecting Tish was to distract Lord
Rival and turn his attention to herself. That was, after all,
what she had told Gil she meant to do. But she could think
of no way to accomplish it. She rode silently along, lost in
thought, casting about in her mind for something she
could say or do to lure his lordship away from Tish. Her
lack of experience in the art of dalliance was definitely a
handicap.

But Lord Rival himself was turning to her, drawing her
into the conversation with his lazy smile. "You are silent,
Miss Littlefield," he observed.

"Yes." Chloe felt the monosyllable fall into the conversation like a stone and realized that something more was expected of her. "I have nothing to say," she explained,
blushing faintly.

"Really? Now, that's an unusual virtue."

"What is?" asked Tish, leaning forward in her saddle to
peer past Lord Rival at Chloe.

"Miss Littlefield, sweeting, keeps silent when she has
nothing to say."

Tish laughed. "If I followed her example, I would scarcely utter a word from dawn to dusk, I daresay. I chatter like a magpie."

"Oh, never that." Lord Rival shot Tish a tender look that made Chloe's hackles rise. "Like a brook, perhaps. Bubbling over stones."

"Very good," said Chloe bracingly. "A much pleasanter image. Although a magpie pauses from time to time, and a brook babbles incessantly. For my own part, I should prefer a magpie outside my window to a brook."

"What, and wake each morning to the sound of screeching?" Lord Rival's eyes still rested on Tish, and now the look he gave her brought the color into her cheeks. "I would rather sleep and wake to the sound of my babbling brook."

As Tish subsided into giggling confusion, Lord Rival bent his wicked gaze on Chloe. "Or silence," he added. "Perfect silence." His eyes flicked briefly to her flaxen curls. "They do say silence is golden. Were they referring to you, Miss Littlefield?"

Despite her resolve to be blithe and breezy, Chloe was knocked off balance. "I hardly think so, my lord," she stammered, dismayed by his sudden reversion to double-edged remarks. She could easily understand Tish's fascination for the man; it was oddly exciting to engage in this racy banter. And he was so terribly attractive! One felt an almost overwhelming urge to draw those dark eyes to oneself, to feel the powerful thrill of capturing such a man's undivided attention.

But his attention *was* divided, and her lame reply had turned him back to Tish. Chloe inwardly berated herself. Well, what might she have said? Yes? She tried in vain to think of a clever answer to his silly question, frowning abstractedly at the path ahead. Try as she might, she could think of nothing. Perhaps it was simply not in her nature to encourage a near stranger, egging him on to say outrageous things. She was more the douse-him-in-cold-water type.

To her surprise, Lord Rival continued to turn his attention to her from time to time, despite her awkwardness at the game of raillery. At first, she supposed it was simply good manners on his part, and her heart warmed to him. But then she noticed a calculating, considering look in his eyes as he smiled at her. He seemed to be watching her, weighing her for some secret purpose. It was disconcerting, and added to her tongue-tied ineptitude. But the more convinced she became that she was actually boring him, the more he persisted in including her. Watching, always watching. She could almost see the wheels turn in the brain behind his eyes, but could receive no clue as to what he was thinking, or why.

When she saw Gil coming toward them in the distance, she felt a surge of such tremendous relief that she was half afraid he was a mirage. He had not seen them yet, and it took a great effort of will to keep herself from waving and calling out to him, as she would have if they were back in the country lanes at home. He was mounted on Wager and rode easily along, touching his hat and smiling at chance-met acquaintances. Gil has always had a graceful seat, she thought, admiring the way he sat his horse and the way the sun glinted on his hair, burnishing it to the gold of a new-minted coin every time he lifted his hat. He looked so handsome that her heart swelled with affectionate pride.

Eventually he did see them. His start of pleased surprise was unmistakable. So was the slight stiffening that followed, as he perceived the identity of the girls' escort. He rode up at once, however, and managed to greet the party civilly enough.

Lord Rival seemed completely unperturbed by Gil's barely cloaked animosity. He nodded, indicating Wager, and complimented Gil on the animal's quality. Gil thanked him and glanced at the chestnut Lord Rival was riding, seeking to return the compliment.

Lord Rival smiled humorlessly at the doubtful expression crossing Gil's face. "A hired hack," he informed Gil. "Showy, but short of bone."

"Oh," said Gil.

At first he seemed undecided as to whether to join the

group, but when Chloe invited him to do so, with desperation in her eyes, he responded immediately. He turned Wager to fall in beside Chloe's mount, and the party progressed at a decorous pace. Tish drew her hack into step beside Lord Rival's, leaving Gil and Chloe to bring up the rear. They did so rather glumly, both watching, with a jealous eye, the interplay of the couple ahead. Tish was very gay, but her trills of delighted laughter at Lord Rival's remarks grated on the ears of Chloe and Gil.

"What a humorous chap he must be," said Gil caustically.

"He is," agreed Chloe listlessly. "A very quick wit." There was no pleasure in her voice.

Silence descended again.

"Gil," asked Chloe, frowning, "how does one learn how to flirt? Tish was never a flirt when we were growing up."

"Lord, no! Couldn't flirt with the boys at home; they all knew her too well. Her technique only works with strangers."

Chloe looked thoughtful. "I wonder why that is?"

Gil snorted. "Because it's all a lot of rubbish! Good luck batting your eyes and giggling at a man who's well acquainted with you; he'll tell you point-blank you're behaving like a blithering fool."

"But men seem to like it."

"Oh, yes! Very flattering, you know, to make a woman behave like a blithering fool. One fancies it's all due to one's devastating wit, or dazzling appearance, or some such thing."

Chloe digested this information in silence, watching Lord Rival display his devastating wit and dazzling appearance, and Tish evidence her resulting devastation and dazzlement.

"So the trick must be," she said slowly, "to focus one's attention on the man and behave as if one were besotted. And not to think about how silly you look doing it."

Gil looked alarmed. "Here, now—why are you asking? I hope you don't mean to start behaving like Tish! One's enough for any family!"

"Well, not like Tish, precisely—" Chloe stopped short,

and turned to stare at Gil. "I'm not a member of your family!"

To her surprise, Gil had turned beet red. "Misspoke!" he said hastily. "What I meant was—well, don't pattern your behavior on Tish's! I don't like to say it of my own sister, but you know as well as I do that she's wild to a fault. Not the thing at all! I don't need *two* of you raising eyebrows all over town. I've enough on my hands, trying to decide what to do about Tish."

"But that's why I need to learn how to flirt," said Chloe reasonably. "Surely you remember! I'm to draw Lord Rival's attention away from her. Only I don't seem to know how to go about it."

"I don't *want* you to learn how to go about it! Dash it, Clo—"

"Do you suppose I need to dress more revealingly?"

"No!"

"Well, I'm glad to hear you say so, for I do think I would feel *most* uncomfortable in the sort of frocks Tish wears. Those ball gowns! I would never be able to look anyone in the eye without blushing."

"So I should hope! Now, Chloe—"

"But it's the verbal sparring I should like to learn. That seems to be at the heart of it."

"The heart of what?"

"Flirtation, of course. At times I can do it, but as soon as Lord Rival says anything too risqué, I back away from him. I can't help it; it embarrasses me."

"Well, thank God for that, at least! Chloe, the man's a *rake!* You mustn't encourage the fellow! You don't know what you're dealing with."

"I can learn, can't I? If Tish can do it, so can I."

Gil made a sort of gurgling sound. But there was no time for further discussion; Lord Rival and Tish had pulled to a halt, and Chloe, looking about her, realized they had reached the edge of the park nearest the Dalrymples' town house and were bidding the gentlemen adieu.

Gil seemed to have more he wished to say, but Chloe pressed his hand reassuringly at parting. "Don't worry so much!" she whispered, under cover of Tish's cooing farewell to her cicisbeo. "Not about me, at least." And she rode off with Tish, her resolve strengthened to do what she could to help her dear friends through this frightful hobble.

Chapter 11

Tish found some way to encounter Lord Rival on almost a daily basis, so Chloe had plenty of opportunity to experiment with her new theory of flirtation. Whenever she was around the man, she gushed and cooed and flattered—and tried very hard not to think about how idiotic she must appear. She even managed to unblushingly call him "George" from time to time, although such familiarity went very much against the grain.

It did seem to work, in a way. She was almost always able to distract him from paying court to Tish. While she struggled to appear infatuated with him, Lord Rival would always give her his full attention. But it was a little disconcerting that his face, as he watched her gyrations, expressed only fascinated disbelief.

It was hard work, this flirtation business. She tried to appear consistently besotted, but Lord Rival seemed to take a perverse delight in provoking her temper. This frequently caused her to slip and say something cutting. The odd thing was, whenever she dropped her mask and scolded him, or made some tart remark, he seemed to enjoy it more than her flattery! She could not understand this at all.

And she had not realized that concentrating so hard on trying to *appear* attracted to him would make her forget that she actually *was* attracted to him. It was only in those moments when he would goad her into forgetting her role that she became aware of it. She would snap at him, and he would laugh at her, and suddenly the charade would fall away and genuine heat would spark between them. This was utterly confusing.

Her thoughts were so filled with Lord Rival that she forgot to tell Gil that she had promised him the first waltz at Lady Bartlett's ball. In fact, it was only after her arrival at the ball, when her eyes fell on Jack Crawley, that she remembered. Since she and Tish had been escorted by one Mr. Choate, an inoffensive gentleman who was some sort of Dalrymple connection, she had no real expectation that Gil would even be present. She knew he loathed balls, and he did not seem to have enjoyed the Alverstoke affair nearly as much as she had.

"Oh, dear," she murmured, clutching the printed program the hostess had given her guests, listing the dances. Well, this would teach her not to tell deliberate falsehoods! She was going to look extraordinarily foolish, maintaining that she had promised a waltz to a man who was conspicuously absent.

Mr. Crawley approached, all enthusiasm, and greeted the party punctiliously. "The third waltz, Miss Littlefield!" he reminded her, beaming.

She glanced at her card and discovered that there would be, in fact, a third waltz near the end of the evening. She dutifully assured him it was his, and jotted his name next to it with the little pencil that was cunningly tied to the card with a bit of ribbon. It would not harm her to dance one waltz with an unattractive man, she reminded herself stoically. But the first waltz was slated to follow the opening quadrille. Since she was obliged by her ill-advised evasive maneuver in Hyde Park to keep that waltz open for Gil, she found herself without a partner as the orchestra struck up for the first waltz.

She feared she looked as ridiculous as she felt. Her color somewhat heightened, she pressed herself as inconspicuously as possible against the wall and tried to hide behind a potted fern. It was not as if she lacked for partners; the result of the hostess's clever program-and-pencil idea was that all the men had rushed about at the start of the evening, cajoling the young women to write their names next to the dances, and she had been pleasantly surprised by the number of gentlemen who had good-naturedly surrounded her. Her

objection to dancing with strangers had been rendered moot
by the fact that she was now acquainted with them all. In
fact, all the rest of her dances were spoken for. But that was
small comfort at the moment.

With a pang, she saw Lord Rival leading Tish to the floor.
He was the handsomest man in the room. Watching them together, she could not hoax herself into thinking she had succeeded in drawing his attention away from her friend. His
demeanor toward Tish was as attentive, as charming, and as
seductive as ever.

And she ought to have known she could not escape Jack
Crawley so easily. Sure enough, he spied her behind the fern
and advanced delightedly toward her. Chloe flushed scarlet
with shame. Why had she snubbed this inoffensive and well-
meaning young man, merely because he had the misfortune
to be ugly? One of Gil's friends, too! She deserved this mortification.

While he greeted her with every appearance of goodwill,
she grasped her fan, took a deep breath, and addressed the
third button on his waistcoat. "Mr. Crawley, I'm afraid I owe
you an apology," she began.

"What's that? What's that? Oh, nonsense!" he assured
her, laughing amiably. "What you owe me, Miss Littlefield,
is a waltz."

Feeling absurdly relieved, she obediently followed him
onto the floor. "It's very good of you not to take offense,"
she told him shyly.

His eyes twinkled kindly down at her. "Not at all. Can't
blame you for preferring Gil to me, you know. But if Gil's
fool enough to stay at home, you may as well dance with
me—eh?"

He proved so droll and friendly that she found herself
warming to him, and felt perfectly at ease by the time their
dance ended and he had led her in a gentle promenade to a
row of chairs. She was looking about for Tish, fanning herself, when she spotted Gil near the entrance of the room. Her
heart gave a joyous leap. "Gil is here!" she cried.

Jack's eyes followed hers. "Well, that's lucky," he remarked. "Fancy him arriving after the first waltz! I'm in-

clined to believe it's an omen, Miss Littlefield. What do you think?"

But Chloe was not attending. "Pray take me to him, Mr. Crawl—oh! He has seen us."

Gil strolled up to them. "Hallo, Clo. Hallo, Jack. What a row those violins make! Every dog for miles around must be howling."

"Gil, why have you come so late?" demanded Chloe.

He gazed at her in mild surprise. "Am I so very late? Never tell me Lady Bartlett started the ball on time!"

"Well, she did, and you are quite out. I saved the first waltz for you, too."

Gil appeared genuinely moved by this news. "Did you, Chloe? I say, that's splendid!"

"Yes, but it's already been danced."

Jack guffawed at the expression on Gil's face. "I took it!" he said gleefully. "Couldn't let Miss Littlefield stand out."

"Jack, you're a dog," said Gil, resigned. "Put me down for the second, Clo."

Faint color tinged Chloe's cheeks. She looked away. "It is promised to someone else," she said primly.

Jack snorted with laughter again. "And the third, too! Aye, you may well stare! But you told everyone at the outset she was a taking little thing. Well, she is! What the deuce d'you mean by leaving her alone at a ball? It'll be a lesson to you, Gil, old chap!" He dug a playful elbow into his friend's ribs.

Gil snatched at the program hanging from Chloe's wrist and held it up to the light, turning a little pale. "You haven't left me a single dance!"

"Well, good gracious, you never even told me you were coming!"

"The devil! What am I to do with myself all night?"

"Here comes Lady Bartlett," remarked Jack. "I daresay she'll find partners enough for you. Plenty of wallflowers lining the room."

Gil turned round, his eyes nearly starting from his head in horror. True to Jack's prediction, Lady Bartlett soon bore him inexorably off to be introduced to the awkward and un-

attractive females who still lacked partners. Chloe could not
help giggling as she watched Gil bowing to a bony and
freckle-faced girl in puce. They joined the same set as Chloe
and her partner, the shy but sartorially magnificent Mr.
Wivenhoe. Good manners forbade anything more than a
speaking glance as she and Gil briefly joined in the figures
of the dance, but it was all Chloe could do to keep a straight
face as she watched Gil's silent suffering.

For her own part, Chloe was having a marvelous time.
She enjoyed dancing, the orchestra was excellent, and there
were distinct advantages attached to everyone believing she
was engaged to Gil. None of the gentlemen who danced
with her was anything other than friendly, and Mr. Crawley
was the only man who attempted to dance with her more
than once. Since she ascribed this gallantry to his friendship
with Gil, she felt quite comfortable.

Once, between sets, Gil found her and brought her a cup
of negus. He looked very hot, and Chloe burst out laughing
when she saw his hunted expression.

He eyed her glumly. "I'm glad you find it amusing. *One*
of us ought to salvage some enjoyment from this ghastly
evening."

Chloe's eyes danced as she took the cup from him. "Poor
Gil! But you knew you would have to dance at a ball. Why
did you come?"

"I came to dance with *you!*"

Believing that this statement represented a heroic sacrifice on Gil's part, Chloe was touched. "Thank you, Gil," she
said warmly. "You are the best friend anyone ever had."

He did not seem overly gratified by the compliment.
"Your last partner was not so very bad," she offered.

"It's not that I mind standing up with every ape-leader in
the room. After all, someone has to do it! But I don't enjoy
making conversation with a great crowd of females I don't
know and don't care to know. I was never so thankful in my
life to be *ineligible!* I'll tell you something, Chloe—if it
weren't for this betrothal of ours, I believe that tallow-faced
chit would have set her cap for me." Gil shivered.

"It is very comfortable to be engaged," agreed Chloe, sipping her negus contentedly. "Tish was right about that, if nothing else."

"By the by, where *is* Tish?"

"I don't know." Chloe glanced around the room, troubled. When was the last time she had seen her? Then she remembered: Tish had been waltzing with Lord Rival. Suddenly some of the pleasure went out of Chloe's evening. She frowned. "I hope she is not off somewhere with Geor— with Lord Rival."

Gil looked very hard at Chloe. "Did you say *George*?"

"No! I said Lord Rival." She felt a blush stealing up her neck and inwardly railed at her wretchedly fair skin.

"You started to say 'George.'"

Her blush was betraying her. "Oh, very well! What of it?" she said, as airily as she could. When he did not immediately reply, she stole a glance at his face. What she saw there made her instinctively place her hand on his arm. "Oh, Gil, it is nothing! Pray—do not look so! Remember, I am trying to draw him away from Tish. He said I ought to call him George, and—"

But Gil shook her hand off roughly. "I must dance with Miss Endicott. I will speak to you later," he said, in a queer, flat voice Chloe had never heard him use. She stared after him as he moved away, stunned and frightened by his strange reaction. She had to quell an impulse to run after him. It was a dreadful, lonely feeling to stand here in this press of people and watch the person she loved best in the world walk away from her in anger.

Her partner for the next country dance approached, and Chloe had, perforce, to summon a smile and move through the figures. As she and her partner promenaded up the set between the other couples, a movement at the edge of the room caught her eye. A flash of cherry-colored silk. Tish. She turned to look and saw Lord Rival escorting her friend back into the room.

Where had they been? Had they been gone a few minutes only, or half an hour, or an hour? She saw them for the briefest of moments before she had to return her attention to the dance, but in that moment she saw Tish's gloved hand reach up and lightly smooth the edge of Lord Rival's lapel. The tiny gesture was somehow intimate, possessive. Chloe felt a surge of wrath at the sight. She'd been behaving like a perfect idiot for days, making a complete fool of herself— acting very much like Tish, in fact!—and for what?

She no longer knew what portion of her anger could be ascribed to her protective love for Tish, what portion to her sense of humiliation over throwing herself at a man whose interest was plainly elsewhere, and what portion to jealousy. She knew only that she was furious.

And the next dance was the waltz! The waltz she had promised to that snake, that toad, that *scoundrel.* She bade farewell to her current partner and stood tensely, eyes glittering, as Lord Rival approached her unhurriedly through the crowd. There was a moment when he accurately interpreted her expression. Up went the eyebrow, down went the mouth, in his incomparably mocking smile. She lifted her chin and tried to stare him down.

In vain, of course. No mere female could penetrate that wall of arrogance. He arrived before her and bowed smoothly, one hand on his heart. "My dear Miss Littlefield." His eyes gleamed. "What have I done to incur your displeasure?"

With an effort, Chloe choked back her anger and somehow managed a rather ghastly smile. "La, sir, nothing in the world!" she simpered, curtseying.

The eyebrow flew upward again, but he said nothing. Instead, he swept her into his arms and compelled her resistless body into the graceful sweep of the waltz. Chloe felt her instinctive response to his touch and hated herself for it. If only he weren't so wickedly handsome!

"How well you waltz, Lord Rival," she cooed, fluttering her eyelashes bashfully. "I vow, you are the best dancer in the room."

"You overwhelm me, my dear," he said dryly.

"Oh, *George!*" she breathed daringly. "If only I could!"

He muttered some exclamation under his breath. "This is too much," he said aloud, and, to her astonishment, pulled her out of the dance.

"Wh-where are we going?" she stammered, as he pro-pelled her firmly toward a door.

"Somewhere where we can talk," he informed her. His eyes were still lit with amusement, but there was a grim set to his mouth.

Chloe accompanied him, willy-nilly, out the door and onto the coolness of Lady Bartlett's back terrace. Blinking in the sudden darkness, she clung to his overly muscled arm and stumbled along beside him as he led her into the garden, away from the light and away from the other couples strolling and conversing on the pavement. He did not halt until he had drawn her down a side path where dense foliage hid them from the house.

"Now," he said firmly, grasping her by the shoulders and turning her to face him, "suppose you tell me what the devil your game is?"

"M-my game?" she faltered.

Her eyes were adjusting to the dimness. He loomed over her, formidably tall and powerful, his shirtfront gleaming white in the moonlight. She could not quite read his face.

"You are playing some game with me, and I am tired of fencing in the dark. You're a gently-born, respectable fe-male. Why are you behaving like an opera dancer?"

"Oh!" gasped Chloe, scarlet-faced in the darkness. "How dare you? I have no idea how a—how an opera dancer be-haves!"

"Well, I do. And your behavior toward me would put the most shameless lightskirt to the blush! You were angry with me a moment ago, but you still tried to empty the butter boat over me. What the deuce do you mean by it?"

Chloe was trembling with angry mortification. "I don't mean anything by it! You're wicked, and vulgar, and hateful, and I wish—"

"Go on," he prompted her. "You wish?"

Suddenly the words tumbled out of Chloe in a rush. "I wish you would leave my friend alone!"

"Ah." His head tilted consideringly. Even in the uncertain moonlight, she could feel his eyes boring into hers. "Your friend. The delectable Mrs. Dalrymple. You would like me to remove myself from her—er—circle of admirers."

"Yes, I would!"

"Why?" he asked simply.

Confused, Chloe took a step backward. His hands left her shoulders and slid behind her, and she unconsciously leaned back against the circle of his arms, blinking puzzledly up at him. *"Why?"*

"Yes. There must be a score of men who buzz round Tish like so many bees. Why single me out?"

Chloe waved a hand impatiently. "The rest are just a lot of silly boys. You are different."

His shoulders shook with silent laughter. "I am glad to learn that you think so."

She clasped her gloved hands pleadingly. "Sir, will you not heed me? Be a little less particular in your attentions, I beseech you. You do more damage than you know—and I do not think you care for her. To you, it is all sport."

"Certainly it is sport. And what do you think it is to Tish? I am as much her toy as she is mine."

Chloe shook her head vehemently. "You do not know her as I do. Tish was ever one who followed her heart, not her head. And she does not realize—she does not think how it must appear to others, this—this fascination with you."

"So I am harming her reputation."

"Yes, my lord. As you are well aware!"

"And you would save her from me by turning my attention to your own sweet self?" Amusement quivered in his voice. "What a noble creature you are, Miss Littlefield."

Mortified, Chloe covered her face with her hands. Honesty was *not* the best policy when dealing with a heartless rake! Had she no common sense at all?

"I don't know why I am even speaking to you in this way!" she exclaimed despairingly. "I must be mad."

She moved to free herself from his hold, but he tightened it a little, the laughter still shaking in his voice. "Do not go! I assure you, if you wish to divert my amorous attentions away from poor Tish, you are making better progress here in the garden than when you were smirking and winking at me in the ballroom."

Chloe blushed again in the darkness. "Was I smirking and winking?"

"I'm afraid so."

"I—I'm not very good at prevarication. Of any sort," she confessed.

"No, I see that."

"It was difficult for me, trying to flirt with you when I had actually taken you in dislike." The instant the words left her lips, she realized how extremely uncivil they were, and was thrown even deeper into confusion. "Oh, I'm so sorry! I hope—I hope I have not hurt your feelings?" She peered anxiously into the dark face looming above hers.

Chloe did not know whether to feel reassured or offended when he suddenly burst out laughing. "No," he finally managed to say, "no, you have not hurt my feelings. I know just what you mean."

Chloe sighed with relief. "I am glad."

His teeth gleamed white as he grinned down at her. "It has been written all over your face, my dear. Half the time, you wish that Tish had never seen me."

"Yes," she admitted.

He lifted one hand and gently tilted her chin up, forcing her to meet his eyes. "But the other half of the time," he told her softly, "you merely wish that you had seen me first."

Instantly, there was a subtle change in the tension running between them. Chloe stared into his face, stunned by the recognition of this truth. Part of her did, in fact, wish that she had seen him first!

Heat seemed to flash between them. It shot through her, swamping her senses. Closing her eyes against a confusing rush of unfamiliar feelings, she waited for—she knew not what.

And then he was kissing her. His kiss was forceful, as commanding and unyielding as he himself was. Her own response seemed completely irrelevant, although she felt the primitive shock of it clear down to her toes. There was nothing for her to *do*, she had only to cling to him, dizzy and startled, and experience it. Like a match to gunpowder, his kiss ignited the fierce attraction she had sternly repressed; it burst immediately into all-consuming flame. She pressed against him, trembling with longings she did not understand.

He lifted his mouth from hers eventually and held her at arm's length. She swayed limply in his grasp, panting and shaken. And utterly bewildered.

"Oh, Chloe," he whispered hoarsely. A wicked grin split his features. "I think you *do* like me a little."

Dazed, she lifted one hand to her mouth. Dear God in heaven. She had let him *kiss* her. Reality suddenly struck her like a fist. With a gasp, she broke free of him and ran, stumbling, back toward the house. Her ears rang with the mocking laughter that followed her.

George laughed aloud from pure enjoyment as he watched her go, her pale gown a flash of light against the rustling darkness of the foliage. It was rare that anything or anyone made him laugh out loud. But what an odd amalgam of contradictions this girl was: frankly duplicitous, mysteriously transparent! Foolish and clever. Sweet and tart.

He wondered again if this odd and intriguing child might make a tolerable wife. He was inclined to believe she would. He generally found blondes unappealing, but apart from that minor detail Chloe was a pretty little thing. And his discreet inquiries had confirmed that she was, in fact, a considerable heiress. Mistress of her own fortune, too, which was unusual.

And now he had another valuable piece of information. Whatever her relationship to Sylvester Gilliland might be, it wasn't romantic. Until a few moments ago, Chloe Littlefield had never been thoroughly kissed. He was sure of it.

Chapter 12

Chloe was afraid she would feel awkward and embarrassed when next she saw Lord Rival, but, to her relief,
he took pains to put her at her ease when she and Tish encountered him in Hyde Park the next day. He certainly did
not seem to think any worse of her for her dreadful display
of wantonness. If anything, he treated her with more deference than before. But then, just as she was beginning to
breathe easier, a moment came when Tish's attention was
drawn away to greet an acquaintance—and he took advantage of the opportunity to *wink* at her! She blushed furiously,
but had to own that his audacious gesture gave her a secret
thrill. It would have been rather lowering, she supposed, had
he pretended that their encounter never happened.

She tried in vain to think of a way to open a conversation
with Tish about Lord Rival, and then was taken completely
by surprise when Tish introduced the topic herself. They
were sitting at breakfast together and Chloe had just swallowed a mouthful of tea, when Tish suddenly said, "And
what do you make of our George?"

Chloe choked. When she recovered her breath she gazed
at her friend, eyes watering, and saw that Tish was laughing
at her.

"He's a handsome fellow, don't you think?" Tish said
teasingly.

"Yes," said Chloe faintly, still coughing a little.

Tish sighed dreamily over her teacup. "I just adore him,"
she gushed. "Those eyes!" She rolled her own eyes for em-
phasis. "And the wicked things he says! Makes one feel—
oh, I don't know—pretty, I suppose."

Chloe stared at her friend. Tish seemed completely un-
selfconscious. There was no hint of shame in her confession.

Tish looked expectantly at Chloe. "Well? Don't you think
so?"

"I? Well, I—yes, I do." She hesitated, unsure of her
ground, then plunged ahead. She dared not mention the kiss.
Not yet. But it would be a relief to inform Tish of at least one
important fact. "You know, Tish, you are not the only
woman to whom he says wicked things. He says them to me,
too."

But instead of looking vexed, Tish smiled the smile of a
conspirator. "Oh, I'm sure he does! George is never at a
loss."

Chloe must have had a very queer expression on her face,
for Tish burst out laughing. "My poor Chloe! I forget how
inexperienced you are. Does he shock you?"

"Sometimes," said Chloe cautiously.

"Well, do not let him see it! He will only become more
outrageous." She sipped her tea contentedly.

Chloe was baffled. "But, Tish, doesn't it—doesn't it
bother you, that Lord Rival says outrageous things to me?"

Tish looked surprised. "No. Why should it?"

"Well, I—I thought he was a particular friend of yours."

"Oh, yes! Certainly he is. But George will flirt with any
presentable female, you know. He doesn't mean anything
by it."

Now what was she to make of that? Chloe, feeling unaccountably nettled, struggled to keep her temper. For a
woman who professed to *adore* Lord Rival, Tish seemed utterly unperturbed by his attentions to other women! Was she
so sure of his regard? If so, Chloe had very good reasons for
believing she was mistaken! But what would it take to shake
Tish out of her complacency? Chloe was severely tempted
to blurt out the story of the kiss George had given her. *That*
ought to wake Tish up!

But what if it didn't?

Before she could think of a way to delicately probe further, the door to the breakfast room opened to admit Robert
Dalrymple. Chloe saw him hesitate for a fraction of a second

before entering, almost as if unsure of his welcome. Robert was a broad-shouldered, sandy-haired young man with a distinct air of breeding, and he had completely captured Tish's heart a few years ago. It pained Chloe to see the reserve with which Tish bade her husband good morning and Robert's distant nod as he seated himself at the head of the table and shook out his napkin.

He inquired politely as to the girls' plans for the day, but did not display any real interest in their comings and goings. His life seemed completely separate from his wife's. No wonder George had been able to make such inroads in Tish's affections! Her husband had obviously withdrawn from her. And Tish must always have someone to love.

Chloe frowned absent-mindedly at the tablecloth, tracing the pattern in the linen with the edge of her teaspoon. She wished she were better acquainted with Robert Dalrymple. It was impossible to speak frankly to him, but she would dearly love to know what had distanced him from his once-adoring wife. For all she knew, it was Lord Rival's attentions that had angered Robert.

If that were so, it was doubly important that she lure the rascal away from Tish. She could not help glowing a little at the thought. The more she thought about George's kiss—and the memory did seem to intrude fairly frequently, at the oddest moments—the more she wondered if she might have been a bit hasty in dismissing outright the idea of marriage. Perhaps it contained compensations of which she had been unaware.

Chloe was roused from her musings when she gradually realized a quarrel was brewing over her head. She looked up to see Tish smiling overly brightly at her husband.

"Well! What's sauce for the gander is sauce for the goose. I shall follow your example, Robert, and amuse myself as I see fit. I believe I shall attend Mrs. Budleigh's party tonight."

A muscle jumped in Robert's jaw. "Mrs. Budleigh? Can it be possible? Are you actually acquainted with that woman? Who, may I ask, had the effrontery to introduce *my wife* to Mrs. Budleigh?"

Tish shrugged, assuming an air of indifference. "I don't recall precisely. One meets a score of persons every week during the Season; I cannot remember every introduction! But I must have met her somewhere. She has sent me an invitation to her card party, and since it appears I will not have the pleasure of your company, I mean to go. I daresay it will be very diverting."

Robert set down his fork, tight-lipped. "If that is your idea of an evening's entertainment, I can tell you it is not mine."

"No? But I'm sure I need not hesitate to attend the party without you. Nothing new in *that!*" Tish's assumption of nonchalance was rapidly crumbling.

"And what of Miss Littlefield? Will you leave your guest alone all evening? I knew you had become a hoyden, but I did not think you had sunk so far!"

Two spots of angry color were flaming on Robert's cheeks, and Tish's eyes were flashing daggers. Chloe was uncomfortably aware that the combatants had completely forgotten her presence.

Tish snapped her fingers at her husband. "Pooh! An almond for a parrot! Chloe will not grudge me one evening. Besides, she may come along if she wishes."

"Good God! Have you lost all sense of decency? If a tenth of what one hears is true, Mrs. Budleigh's parties are nothing to inflict upon a green girl."

"Why, how stern you are!" marveled Tish. "And while I am at Mrs. Budleigh's, what sort of party will you be attending?"

"You need not concern yourself with that! It will be a gentlemen's party."

"Yes! Cards and tobacco and drinking, and everything carried to excess! But apart from the cigars, it will be not so very different from Mrs. Budleigh's party, will it?"

Chloe cleared her throat self-consciously. Tish and Robert turned startled eyes upon her. "If—if I might excuse myself," she said in a small voice, "I think I should write a letter to Mr. Fanshaw this morning. I left him in charge at Brookhollow, you know, in my absence."

"Oh, certainly," murmured Tish, sounding rather dazed.

Robert merely turned a dull red and gazed at his breakfast plate. Chloe fled.

Although she thus avoided hearing the end of the quarrel, the upshot was painfully apparent. Tish soon marched into the morning room, where Chloe was writing her letter, and, with angry tears glittering on her lashes, announced her resolve to attend Mrs. Budleigh's card party that evening. Chloe had never heard her mention the invitation prior to this morning's row with Robert, so she feared that Tish's whole object in going was to defy her husband. It seemed there was something disreputable about this party. And after hearing the things Robert had said about Mrs. Budleigh, Chloe was absolutely certain she had no desire to attend it herself.

She looked up from her letter, consternation in her face. "Oh, Tish, must we go?"

"Yes!" Tish flung herself onto a sofa, scowling. "At least, I must. You need not, if you don't wish to."

"Does—does Robert accompany you?"

"No, he does not, and I don't care!"

The addition of that unnecessary information fairly shouted that the opposite was true. Chloe set her pen carefully down, not looking at Tish's face. She feared Tish would see the pity in her eyes. "Well, I had rather not go, if you don't mind. I'm frightfully sorry, Tish, but you know I have no head for cards."

"Very well," said Tish indifferently.

Chloe stole a glance at her friend, hoping that her own refusal had helped Tish change her mind. After all, it *would* be unmannerly to leave a guest to her own devices all evening. Not that that would matter between such old friends as Chloe and Tish. But at the very least, if Chloe stayed at home and Robert went to his own party, Tish would be left with no one to accompany her. And a lady could not jaunt about the town alone.

Tish was staring into the fire, her shoulders tense and her hands playing nervously with the fringe of one of the sofa pillows. Chloe watched her face for a moment, worried by

what she saw there. "Tish, you cannot go alone," she said
tentatively.

Tish offered her a brittle smile. "Mr. Choate will take me
up in his carriage. I have already sent round a note. So, you
see, you need not apologize for declining the invitation. Suit
yourself! It is a matter of complete indifference to me
whether you come along or not."

And with this, Tish flounced out of the room. Chloe
stared after her in dismay. Worse and worse! Really, it was
enough to make one wish one had stayed safely at
Brookhollow, to be thrust into such a sticky situation! The
last thing Chloe wanted was to find herself plunged into the
midst of a marital dispute. Besides, her loyalty to Tish made
her want to take Tish's side in the quarrel, and she could not.
She was too much in sympathy with Robert.

Chloe's immediate instinct was to turn to Gil. She had no
clear idea what he could do, but she felt sure he would think
of something. At any rate, it would make her feel better to
pour the story into his sympathetic ear. Just being in his
comforting presence, even if it did nothing for Tish, would
make *her* feel better! So she sent one of the footmen round
with a note for him and settled in to wait.

Gil did not appear. Chloe finally confronted the footman
and was informed that the note had been dutifully left, but
that Mr. Gilliland had been away from home when it was delivered. Her heart sank. All she could do was possess her
soul in patience and hope that he would return to his flat be-
times. If he did not receive her note in time to intervene, she
would have to face the task of dissuading Tish herself. It was
a daunting thought.

The hours crawled by. Dinner arrived, with still no word
from Gil. It was a silent, strained meal. Mr. and Mrs. Dalrymple exchanged only as many words as were necessary to
direct the servants and complete the rituals of a multicourse
meal, and Chloe felt unequal to the task of maintaining a
conversation without the assistance of her hosts. No one ate
much. The food must have seemed as tasteless to Tish and
Robert as it did to Chloe.

She reluctantly decided that she must make a last-ditch

effort to persuade Tish not to go. She peeped into Tish's dressing room just as her friend, beautifully gowned, was completing her toilette by leaning into her looking glass to fasten her earrings. Chloe was a little surprised to see that instead of Tish's maid, Bobby and his nurse were present. Tish's eyes met Chloe's in the mirror as she entered, and Tish smiled. She looked more relaxed than Chloe had seen her all day.

"Come in, Chloe! Quite the family party, as you see." She waved a hand to indicate the child and his nurse, a diffident young woman scarcely older than Tish herself. The nurse ducked a shy curtsey as Chloe closed the door behind her. Freed momentarily from Nursie's grasp, Bobby ran toward his mother on sturdy little legs, crowing with delight. Tish scooped the child up and kissed him with a resounding smack. He instantly struggled to get down, and she set him on the floor again, laughing.

"Men are fickle creatures," she remarked, turning back to her mirror. As if contradicting her statement, Bobby threw his plump arms around his mother's knees and clutched as much of her as he could reach.

"Up," he demanded. But his nurse quickly seized him, gulping an apology to Tish, and bore him to the opposite end of the room. Bobby roared his disapproval of this treatment.

"Mercy on us!" exclaimed Tish, rummaging swiftly through the drawers of her dressing table. She unearthed a paper of sweetmeats and handed one to the nurse, whereupon Bobby's howls swiftly subsided. Tish smiled apologetically at Chloe. "I see so little of him during the day, you know, that I miss him terribly. I'm afraid I rather spoil him when I do see him."

"I would, too," admitted Chloe. "I do envy you little Bobby. He's such a poppet! Does he always help you dress?"

"Oh, yes! Just at the end. He chooses which jewels I should wear." Her nose wrinkled comically as she fastened a garnet necklace round her slender throat. "And then I put them back and choose for myself!"

It was past Bobby's bedtime, so Tish soon bade him good

night, watching rather wistfully as he was carried from the room. "There goes *one* man who truly loves me," she said, half to herself. She caught Chloe's sympathetic look and smiled wryly. "I am feeling sorry for myself tonight. Pray do not regard it! I will recover my temper by morning." With a little sigh, she picked up a hairbrush and began carefully repairing the damage that Bobby's parting caress had inflicted.

Chloe sank onto a spindle-legged chair beside the dressing table and watched her gravely. "Must you go to this party tonight? I don't believe you really expect to enjoy it."

Tish shrugged. Her expression became guarded. "I suppose I will like it well enough, once I am there."

"If you stayed here with me, you could teach me piquet. Or help me improve my wretched whist game," offered Chloe coaxingly. "And then we could attend the next card party together."

The hairbrush faltered for a moment, but then Tish shook her head and continued working. "I am already dressed. And I daresay Mr. Choate will arrive at any moment. It's far too late for me to change my mind."

"You could plead a headache."

Again Tish hesitated, but then her face hardened. "No. I have said I am going, and I am going."

Chloe knew better than to coax or argue once Tish's mulish streak had asserted itself. She said no more, but her mind was far from easy. Tish's cheerfulness had vanished with little Bobby, and it was plain that she shrank from the duty her own stubbornness had imposed upon her. She no more wanted to go to Mrs. Budleigh's party than Chloe did. But go she would, and nothing could prevent her.

The house seemed very silent once Tish had gone. Chloe settled herself in the Dalrymples' small library with a novel chosen at random from the shelves. She had a cozy fire and a loudly ticking clock to keep her company, and the library was directly off the entrance hall. She was determined to sit up until Tish returned, and she wanted to remain within earshot of the front door.

At first it appeared that staying awake would be easy to accomplish. Her nerves were on the stretch. Her mind tugged and worried at the tangle her affairs were in, going endlessly round and round the various difficulties she faced. The novel was powerless to divert her from her problems, and for a long time she stared, unseeing, at the fire. A dreadful feeling of foreboding stole over her, worsening as the evening wore on. She hoped it was only the effect of silence, and darkness, and isolation in this rather depressing little room. Disaster seemed to be hanging over her head like the sword of Damocles, and she knew not when the sword would fall or what form the fatal blow would take.

The room grew colder. Chloe curled her small body in the chair before the fire, throwing a shawl across her lap. This must have made her a little too comfortable, for the clock chiming twelve caused her to jump, startled. She realized it had awakened her. She sat up, stretching, and became aware that footsteps were crossing the hall outside the library door. Was it the sound of Tish entering the house that had actually awakened her? Chloe tossed the shawl aside and darted to the door, almost sick with relief. But when she threw it open, it was Robert Dalrymple whose startled face greeted hers.

"Oh!" stammered Chloe, taking a step backward. "I—I thought you were Tish."

His smile was strained. "I thought the same. I saw the light under the door, and hoped— She is not here, then? No. Of course not." The candle he held lit Chloe's face, which apparently was telling him everything he needed to know. He suddenly looked very tired. "I take it she went to Mrs. Budleigh's party," he said dully.

"Yes," said Chloe, feeling foolishly guilty. "She has not yet returned."

"No, I suppose not." He heaved a small sigh. "I would not be home at this hour myself, had I not left my party early. It was—dull." He smiled bleakly. "Or perhaps it was I who was dull. At any rate, I left it. Good night, Miss Littlefield."

He bowed and would have gone, but Chloe put out a swift hand to stop him. "Will you not wait up for her? The library is quite comfortable."

He hesitated, but only for a moment. Then he gave her

that slight, bitter smile again. "I think not, thank you. She would not be pleased to see me."

He turned to head toward the stairs, but then stopped and looked back at Chloe. "By the by, have you and Gil set a date yet?"

"A date?" Chloe was genuinely puzzled. Then, as his brows flew up, she understood, and blushed for her slowness. "Oh! That! No, I—no, we have not. In fact, I rather think—that is, I am not perfectly sure—well, I don't know *when* we will actually marry. Or—or *if!*" she blurted, in a burst of candor.

His brows climbed higher. "Oh. That's the way the land lies, is it?"

"Well, yes, I'm afraid so. I mean well, I don't know what I mean. It's just that . . ." her voice trailed off.

"I hope the glimpse of wedded bliss you have seen in this house has not given you cold feet," he said dryly.

"Certainly not!" she assured him. "I had cold feet long before I saw—that is, I—I have never really wished to marry. I still do not wish to marry. Anyone."

"Ah. Well, if you should ever change your mind, take my advice and don't marry for love. Whatever other mistakes you make in your life, do not make that one. Don't marry for love. I have learned that lesson the hard way."

Chloe thought she had never seen a man look more despondent than Robert Dalrymple did at that moment. The stark despair on his face was very hard to witness. She had seen that expression often, on the face of one dear to her, and it was terrible to see it again. Her heart went out to him.

"I understand you," she whispered, her eyes blurring with tears. "My mother married for love. And my father for money. Of the two, my father received the better bargain. He got what he wanted. My mother, naturally, did not." Chloe swallowed painfully. "My mother was the unhappiest woman I have ever known."

He nodded quietly. And then he turned and walked, silent as a ghost, up the stairs to bed. Chloe returned to her sanctuary before the fire, deeply shaken. Robert's misery had touched her to the quick, bringing back all her saddest memories of her mother. Poor Mama, grieving endlessly for the love denied her. It was ghastly to have been reminded so vividly of her, and of all the reasons why Chloe had vowed she would never, ever, step into the trap that had ensnared her mother.

The episode had touched her so personally, it took some time before she realized that Robert's pain had a meaning far removed from her mother's sufferings. When the notion struck her, she sat suddenly upright in the chair, actually gasping aloud. Robert Dalrymple loved his wife! That was what he meant. And she had irrationally attached her own emotional response to the news—based on the past situation she had known, not the present. What a shatterbrained thing to do! Why, this wasn't sad news at all. It was *good* news.

Unless—was it possible that Tish no longer cared for Robert? Chloe nibbled a fingertip, frowning. She swiftly reviewed everything she could recall of Tish's behavior since she had come to London, but could draw no real conclusion from her observations. She had assumed that Tish's recklessness was rooted in her reaction to Robert's aloofness. But was the shoe, perhaps, on the other foot? Was Robert's aloofness a response to Tish's wildness? She had to admit she did not know.

A prodigious yawn seized her. My, she was tired. She had spent almost an entire evening *thinking*. Who would have believed it was such arduous work? She curled up in the chair once more, drowsily blinking at the clock. Ten past one. Perhaps she should try the novel again.

That was her last conscious thought until a cold draft stole under the library door, awakening her. She struggled to sit up, disoriented. A soft murmur of voices sounded in the hall, and a stifled giggle. Tish!

Chloe, still throwing off the effects of sleep, was halfway to the door before she realized that Tish's escort had come into the hall with her. She halted, unsure whether throwing open the library door would make her look foolish, like an anxious parent awaiting the return of a wayward daughter. The cold draft still swept under the library door, telling her that the front door in the hall stood open yet. She heard Tish say something, and a low rumble of male laughter reply. Tish must be bidding good night to Mr. Choate; he would soon be on his way.

But the baritone voice continued, and although Chloe could not make out the words, she recognized the voice with a shock. She would know that teasing note anywhere. It was Lord Rival, not the harmless Mr. Choate, who was bidding good night to Tish.

Now nothing would prevail upon Chloe to open that door. She stood, in an agony of disturbed emotions, and unwillingly listened to another minute or two of murmured conversation and stifled laughter—all of it containing a provocative and, to Chloe, extremely distasteful undercurrent of stealth. But at last she heard the closing of the front door and the scrape of a tinderbox. Only then did she dare to peep out into the hall.

Tish was lighting a candle. The task was presenting some difficulty because her hand was none too steady. When the light from the library spilled across the hall, she whirled round, burning her finger.

"Ouch!"

"Oh, Tish, I'm sorry! I didn't mean to startle you."

Tish blinked at Chloe in momentary surprise, then smiled. "Did you wait up for me? S-silly!"

Chloe tried to speak lightly. "Well, after all the things Robert said about this party, and how gloomy you looked while you were getting ready for it, I thought you were embarking on some dangerous exploit. I was half afraid we'd be fishing your lifeless body out of the Thames tomorrow." She held the door to the library invitingly open as she spoke.

Tish giggled, wandering obligingly in to cast herself on the sofa. "It wasn't as bad as that. Bad, but not as bad as that."

Chloe closed the door carefully behind her and sat across from Tish. Tish had brought the pungent smell of alcohol in with her. This would definitely not be the time to talk to her of Robert's love.

"You stayed quite late. Was the party agreeable after all?"

"Oh, it was great fun! At first." Tish squinted sleepily at

the fire. "I thought I might not know anyone in the Budleigh set, but I was acquainted with most of the gentlemen there. 'Course, the only lady I knew was Letty Lade." She lifted an unsteady finger to her lips. "Don't tell Robert! He would say she's no lady at all."

"Oh, dear," said Chloe faintly. "But surely you were acquainted with the hostess?"

Tish struggled upright on the sofa, frowning in concentration. "I must have been. But I don't recall it. If it weren't for the invitation, I'd say I'd never met her before tonight. But I must have, mustn't I? Wouldn't invite a stranger to her party. Doesn't make sense." Tish was seized by a sudden yawn. "But, then, for all I know, she might have invited all of London," she admitted, still yawning. "There were a great many people there."

"I wouldn't have liked that."

"No. They were a very friendly lot, though." Tish sank back into the depths of the sofa. "Too friendly, some of them."

Chloe shuddered. "I wouldn't have liked that, either."

Tish stifled another giggle with one gloved hand and became a little more animated. "Oh, Chloe, there was the most dreadful creature! Just the sort of female my mama-in-law warned me I would meet—one of these encroaching souls, you know, trying to wheedle her way into my company. She followed me about, boring on forever about her dear friends Lord So-and-so and Lady Such-and-such, trying to hoax me into thinking she was hand-in-glove with these persons who, I daresay, would not recognize her if they saw her on the street! I suppose I will now figure in her conversation as her *dear friend* Mrs. Dalrymple! And I gave her such a setdown, too—I wish you could have heard me! But mushrooms are impervious to snubs."

"How ghastly!"

"Yes. But that wasn't the worst. That frightful Wilford Yarborough was present. *He* was the worst." Tish shivered, and crossed her arms as if unconsciously protecting herself. "He hung about, and hung about, grinning at me with that horrible wet mouth of his, and he kept *touching* me."

"Good heavens! I thought you told me you had fun? It sounds appalling!"

"Well, the *party* was fun. The champagne was very good. And George was there, you know, so he finally put Wilford Yarborough to rout. Thank goodness."

Chloe reflected for a moment on the evils of jealousy. It was certainly an unpleasant emotion to experience. "Did you play piquet?" she asked cautiously.

Tish shook her head. "Something new." She leaned toward Chloe, her eyes dancing with slightly tipsy mischief. "I had never seen a roulette wheel before. Have you?"

Chloe now perceived that Tish had spent the evening in some very fast company indeed. Her eyes grew round. "You played *roulette?*" she exclaimed, awestruck.

Tish nodded, beaming. "Yes, I did. And I won, too!" Her eyes clouded again. "At first."

To Chloe's surprise, Tish's eyes suddenly filled with tears and she dropped her head in her hands. "Oh, Chloe, what am I to do?" she moaned. "I can't t-tell Robert. Oh, I am in such a coil!"

Chloe flew to her friend's side and put a sustaining arm around her shoulders. "What is wrong? Tish, what is it?"

Tish raised her eyes, bleared with alcohol and tears, and uttered tragically, "I wagered my garnets. And I lost them."

Chloe's eyes darted, horrified, to her friend's bare neck and earlobes. "Merciful heavens. Oh, Tish, don't cry! We'll get them back."

"We can't get them back. I lost them in fair play! How can I get them back?"

"Well—can't you buy them back? Redeem them?"

Tish's face crumpled in shame. "I haven't any money!" she wailed. "I lost it all. I won't have a p-penny until next quarter-day!" She thumped the arm of the sofa in a rage of frustration. "Stupid, stupid, *stupid!* I don't deserve to live!"

"Oh, hush! You mustn't say such things. It's not as bad as all that, is it? You can't be the only woman who has wagered her jewelry and lost."

"No, but I must be the only *Dalrymple* who has done so!"

Chloe found herself with nothing to say in reply to that.

She patted Tish silently and handed her the handkerchief she had tucked in her sleeve.

Tish sniffed, mopping her eyes. "Robert's mother was right," she said dolefully. "He ought never to have married me. I am a disgrace to the family. And I did so want to be a good wife!" Her eyes filled with fresh tears.

If this was Tish's ambition, she did not seem to be going about it properly. But Chloe did not suppose this was the best moment to point that out.

"Poor Tish! We must think how to tell him. I will help you if I can."

Tish bounced upright, her wet eyes wide with horror. "Tell Robert? I would rather die!"

"But, Tish, Robert will know just what to do! I cannot help you; I haven't a clue how to get your garnets back! And only think, if you say nothing to him, and one day he sees jewelry he gave you on some other woman—why, that would be worse than anything!"

Tish shuddered, gulped, and buried her face in her hands with an inarticulate moan.

Chloe put her arm round Tish's shoulders again. "If you go to him tomorrow and explain exactly how it was, and tell him you are very, very sorry, and promise never to do such a thing again—"

"He will be so angry," Tish whispered miserably. "He told me not to go to that wretched party."

Chloe sought for something encouraging to say. "He told you not to go because he must have *known* the sort of party it would be. He may have expected that something like this would occur. Why, perhaps he will not be surprised at all, but will be so touched by your contrition that he will forgive you at once."

But Chloe's flight of optimism did not inspire Tish with hope. The stubborn look was creeping back into her face. She pulled away from Chloe abruptly. "I will not apologize to Robert. The garnets were mine, weren't they? It's no business of Robert's what I do with them."

"But, Tish—"

"No! Not another word!" Tish's eyes blazed with sudden

anger, and she fairly leaped off the sofa. "*Don't* tell me what to do! Why is everyone always telling me what to do? First Robert, and now you. Ordering me about—advising me— correcting me—lecturing me! Well, I won't have it! I won't! I can't bear it another instant!"

Chloe, utterly confounded, watched helplessly as Tish stormed out of the room.

Chapter 13

Chloe did not sleep well. Her dreams were uneasy, filled with a sense of impending disaster and haunted by the echo of Lord Rival's mocking laughter. After tossing restlessly in her bed for several hours, pummeling the pillows and tugging her coverlet this way and that, she eventually gave it up and faced the day, dragging herself downstairs to a late and solitary breakfast. Robert Dalrymple had left the house and Tish was still abed. Chloe was moodily sipping her second dish of tea when she heard Gil's voice in the hall.

In a flash, she set down her teacup and flew joyously out of her chair, ignoring propriety to rush to him. Since she was the only member of the household who was up and dressed, she was half afraid the servants would turn him away. Fortunately, she arrived upon the scene before this disaster could occur. There stood Gil, hat in hand, not a hair out of place, and wearing a very beautiful morning coat. He looked splendid, and she had never been so glad to see anyone in her life. Were it not for the quelling presence of the Dalrymples' butler, she believed she would have hugged him.

Gil forestalled her by crossing the hall to her side and casually dropping a light kiss on her cheek. "Hallo, Chloe," he greeted her. "Starting a new fashion?"

He indicated the egg-stained napkin in her hand. A sputter of laughter escaped her. "Will it catch on, do you think?"

"Bound to," he assured her. "I say, are you really breakfasting? I could toddle round again in a half hour or so."

But Chloe impulsively clutched his hand. "Don't go!" she

begged. "I am quite alone and feeling so dismal! Besides, I need to talk to you."

"Yes, I received your note—at long last." Gil glanced at the butler, who still hovered nearby, stiff with disapproval. "No need for you to hang about, Snead. Miss Littlefield can show me to the breakfast room," he said outrageously.

The butler visibly swelled with emotion. "H'if you will be so good as to follow me, sir," he uttered, "H'i will show you to the morning room!"

"That won't be necessary," said Chloe hastily. "Mr. Gilliland may join me in the breakfast room if he wishes."

"I do wish," said Gil firmly. "And I hope there is a ham."

Snead bowed, his expression of sour incredulity expressing to a nicety his opinion of Young Persons who insisted on behaving with an informality bordering on licentiousness. He stalked silently before them to the breakfast room and held the door open while they entered, then pointedly left the door open behind him as he retired. Chloe sank back into her chair, quite cowed by this treatment, but Gil grinned and cheekily closed the door on his way to the sideboard.

"Oh, Gil, do you think we ought? Snead already does not approve of me," said Chloe nervously.

Gil, helping himself to buttered eggs, cocked a knowing eyebrow at her. "It's not you, Clo. It's Tish he dislikes. You and I are equally in his black books—we are connections of hers."

Chloe was amazed. "How is that possible?"

"Oh, it's always that way with these family retainers. Snead has been a member of the Dalrymple household since he was in short coats, I daresay. Sides with the countess on everything."

"The countess," repeated Chloe thoughtfully. "Tish said something last night about her mama-in-law disapproving of Robert's marriage. It's true, then? I thought she was merely overwrought when she said it."

"No, it's true enough." Gil seated himself across from Chloe and shook out his napkin. "Had her eye on some other female for Robert. Took a pet when Robert chose Tish instead. Our family's fairly well connected, but nowhere near well enough for her la'ship. Very high in the instep, Robert's mama."

This was disturbing news. Chloe rested her chin on her hands, her forehead puckering, and absently watched Gil dig into the buttered eggs and ham. Tish's recklessness, even if her motive was merely to gain Robert's attention, had obviously raised doubts in his mind about the wisdom of marrying her. If, in addition to the unfortunate example his wife's behavior set daily before him, Robert heard her constantly disparaged by his family, it was a miracle that he still spoke of loving her.

"What was it you wanted to say to me?" asked Gil, momentarily between mouthfuls. He continued to eat steadily, washing everything down with black coffee, while Chloe poured out the tale of Robert and Tish's row the previous morning, Tish's attendance at a very *fast* card party against her husband's wishes, Robert's admission that he had married Tish for love, and Tish's returning from her party inebriated and without her garnets. She discovered within herself an odd reluctance to tell Gil that Lord Rival had escorted Tish home, so she omitted that detail and finished her story. She then searched Gil's face anxiously for some clue to his opinion, but he seemed oddly expressionless.

"Gil, what do you think we ought to do? Can you get Tish's garnets back for her? I will gladly lend her the money if you know how it can be accomplished."

Gil methodically wiped his mouth, pushed back his chair, rose, and walked to the window. He stood for a moment staring into the street. Chloe pressed her palms together and waited, holding her breath. When he did not immediately reply, her heart sank. "Are the garnets gone forever, then? Oh, dear! I thought surely you could find a way to redeem them."

"I probably could," he said slowly. Then he looked at Chloe, his gaze troubled. "But I don't believe I will."

Chloe's mouth formed an astonished O. "You won't? Why not?"

"Been giving it a deal of thought lately. Know what I

think? I think we're behaving like a pair of dashed busybodies."

"What!"

"I don't mind our helping Tish out of the basket—well, that's why I asked you to come! But I draw the line at meddling in her marriage. Have a notion we might do more harm than good. And as for helping her to deceive Robert— no, I won't do it. Tish lost those garnets through her own folly, and she can dashed well face the consequences. I believe a crisis will do her more good than any rescue we can devise."

This way of looking at the matter had not occurred to Chloe. "You mean—if we retrieve Tish's garnets, we are not really helping her."

Gil nodded. "I don't mean to be disobliging, but that's the way I see it."

Chloe smiled blindingly at him. "Oh, Gil, how clever you are!" she exclaimed. "And how wise! Here I've been fretting myself to flinders, trying to think of a way to get those silly garnets back, and now I see it would be the worst thing we could do! You are quite right. Tish must suffer just a little at present, or there will be worse heartbreak for her down the road. If only she would confide in Robert! I feel sure he would forgive her."

"Aye. But we can't make her do so if she don't choose to."

"I suppose not. And of course we cannot tell him ourselves." Chloe rested her chin in her hands again, thinking. "Would it be meddling if we dropped Robert a hint?"

Gil choked. "Yes, it would!"

"I was afraid you would think so. Very well!" She pushed back from the table and rose briskly. "In that case, come with me to the morning room. I think we can best help Tish if you teach me piquet."

"Piquet!" Gil burst out laughing. "Clo, you can barely tell clubs from spades! Why the dickens do you want to learn piquet?"

But Chloe was in earnest. She struck her small fist into a determined palm. "I know you don't approve of it, Gil, but I *must* find a way to spend more time with Lord Rival.

An unmarried girl has very little opportunity to encounter single gentlemen, and already, on at least two occasions, I have been excluded from his notice merely through my inability to play piquet." An idea occurred to her, and she brightened a little. "Of course, if you don't wish to teach me, I suppose I could ask him to do so. That might be better yet."

Gil had not moved from his place by the window. The laughter died from his face. He said brusquely, "Rival won't teach you how to play. He'll teach you how to lose."

That unfamiliar, set expression had descended again onto Gil's beloved features. Alarmed, Chloe went to him and placed her hand coaxingly on his sleeve. "Oh, Gil, pray—! You mustn't worry so. Lord Rival is not so very bad, once one comes to know him. He really can be quite—quite pleasant." Her voice faltered as Gil's expression hardened.

Was he *angry* with her? Impossible! Gil was never angry with her. But he held himself so stiffly, and stared down at her so queerly! The morning light streaming in at the window beside them threw the planes of his face into relief, making him look older, and somehow stern. She had never seen him look so. "What is the matter?" she asked, bewildered.

"You do not listen to me," he told her. His voice was very quiet. Pain moved in his eyes. "I have told you repeatedly that I do not like this scheme of yours, and yet you persist in it. You are too naive to understand the dangers you face."

She moved impatiently, and he covered her hand with his own. "Chloe, you're too innocent to comprehend your own innocence!" he said urgently. "You always think the best of everyone, and you refuse to believe that there are some people who do not deserve your trust. But there are, and Lord Rival is one of them. You are throwing yourself at a man who cares nothing for you. A man who will not hesitate to ruin you."

Chloe shook her head in instinctive denial. Gil did not know everything. George *must* feel something for her, to kiss her the way he had. "You are too severe. He is not as bad as people say he is. And he does care for me a little. He and I are—friends."

She heard the sharp intake of Gil's breath. He seized her by the shoulders and stared at her as if he had never seen her before. "Chloe, do you *like* the fellow?" he asked incredulously.

His vehemence was confusing. Puzzled, she looked into his eyes. She saw emotions there that made no sense to her. "Well, yes! Sometimes. Is that so very dreadful?"

He thrust her aside with a bitter exclamation and began pacing the tiny breakfast room, apparently deeply agitated. She watched him, doubt and perturbation creasing her brow. "There is nothing wrong with liking the man a little, is there?"

George's voice echoed in her thoughts: *Oh, Chloe. I think you do like me a little.* She tucked the memory hastily away, before it could make her blush. "Well? Is there?" she persisted. "I still think that my cultivating his friendship is the best way to solve two problems at one stroke. I haven't heard you offer any better idea for ending our engagement. And we *must* lure him away from Tish while Robert still loves her."

Gil halted for a moment in his pacing. "The rogue has already alienated Tish's affections from her husband—this fine fellow, this friend whom you *like* so well! Why, she spoke of putting a period to her existence the other day, just at the thought of being separated from him! How do you like that?"

Chloe's eyes widened in startled denial. "No! You must have misunderstood her."

It was terrible to think that Tish's infatuation might have taken such strong possession of her. A nightmarish image of George kissing *Tish* suddenly flashed into her mind. Chloe shrank from the idea in horror.

Gil saw her recoil, and a bitter smile twisted his features. "Vile, isn't it?" he agreed. "I only hope poor Robert can win her back."

"Oh, yes! I'm *sure* he can," averred Chloe feverishly. "He must! Otherwise—oh, what a calamity!"

It was now Chloe's turn to pace the room. Gil leaned against the mantelpiece and watched her. As he did, his wry smile faded, leaving him grim and white-lipped. "What is distressing you so?"

She waved her hands incoherently. "Everything! Tish! I— I do hate to think of injuring poor Tish. I mean, I knew it would upset her if George were seen to be flirting with me— well, that was part of the *plan!* But if what you say is true, I am afraid she will be more overset than—than I had thought." Chloe brought her disjointed speech to a stumbling conclusion and bit her lip shamefacedly.

Gil stood motionless, his eyes blazing like blue coals. He gazed levelly at her. "*George,* is it? Just how far has your flirtation with Rival gone?"

Chloe blushed, but lifted her chin defiantly. "It is coming along quite well, thank you," she said, trying to sound as airy as possible. Something frightening flashed across Gil's face. She added quickly, "But there is nothing to cause you the least anxiety, after all!"

Gil had gone white and tense. When he spoke, it was clear he was controlling his voice with an effort. "Chloe, I am asking you to call a halt," he said carefully. "I want you to stop flirting with Lord Rival. Now."

Chloe's eyes widened in surprise. "But there's no *harm* in it!" she exclaimed. "And it might do so much good!" She had no desire whatsoever to stop flirting with George. Flirting with George, she realized, had become her favorite pastime. In fact, it was the thing she most looked forward to every day. She would not willingly give it up—and for no good reason!

"For my sake." His voice sounded strained. "Will you do that? Will you leave him alone for my sake?"

Baffled, Chloe placed her hands on her hips and glared at him. "Now, Gil, you know perfectly well that I would do anything for you. But this is nonsense! I am *pursuing* him for your sake! Partly."

Suddenly Gil's control slipped, and fury jumped in his voice. "That's a loud one! Did you consult me first? Did you ask my advice? Did you even bother to discover my *opinion* before you plunged ahead with this crazy scheme? Stop trying to do me favors I don't want!"

"Well, if you're trying to save me from making some silly mistake, that's a favor *I* don't want! I do wish you would trust me a little! You are leaping to absurd conclusions."

"So now I'm *absurd,* am I?" He was on her in two strides, grabbing her by the arms and forcing her to face him. "You have seen the damage Rival has done to Tish! You've seen it with your own eyes, and *still* you persist! Have you no common sense at all? How can I get it through that stubborn, willful little skull of yours? I beg you to stop and you laugh at me."

Astonished and frightened, Chloe felt Gil's hands shaking with the force of his emotions. She stared up into his contorted face. It was like looking into the face of a stranger. "I am not laughing!" she protested, her own voice quavering. "Gil, I have never seen you like this. Why—"

"I see what it is," he interrupted roughly. "You already care more for Rival than you do for me."

Chloe was stung. "Oh, Gil, no! No, you are wrong!"

"Well? What is it, then? Don't blather any more about Tish, or about ending our wretched engagement! Tell me the truth! Why is it so hard for you to stop flirting with that man?"

At a loss, she hesitated. She was angry, but Gil's anger was so disproportionately intense that concern for him blotted out part of her wrath. Her troubled eyes searched his face. "It's—it's fun," she said lamely. "And I just don't see why I *should* stop. I think—I think you're behaving very oddly, Gil. It's not like you to be unreasonable. Are you quite well?"

Gil seemed to struggle with himself for a moment. He took a deep breath and removed his hands from her, clenching them at his sides. "Sorry," he said tersely. "I'm sorry, Clo. You must think I've run mad."

He turned and walked away from her, returning to the window. "I've made a few inquiries about Rival," he said. He was no longer looking at her, and his voice was so low she had to strain to hear him. "It's difficult to find out anything precise. He makes a great joke out of living hand-to-mouth. I daresay there's nothing in that; a man can't be on the town without running into dun territory. But there's something smoky about him, Clo. Can't quite put my finger on it."

He glanced back at her, and she was again struck by the change in him. He looked deadly serious. "It was easy to learn the identities of a few of his recent flirts. They were all married, all very silly. And each and every one of them was rich. Might be a coincidence, of course; plenty of wealthy women in the *ton*. No one says outright that he fleeced them. But there are some deuced ugly rumors floating about."

Chloe's eyes flashed. "Why, that is slander! What next will you say? You cannot expect me to heed such ill-founded and malicious gossip!"

"You told me yourself he was winning money from Tish."

"Yes, but I also told you his skill was greater than hers! It would have been remarkable had he *not* won! And I believe he rescued Tish last night from a very dangerous set of people. It was he who brought her home from that dreadful card party."

"Did he? What a hero!" scoffed Gil, animation returning to his features. "A pity he did not think to do so before she had lost every penny, and her jewelry as well!"

"You are determined to think ill of him!"

"You are determined to defend him. Chloe, for God's sake, take care!"

She was amazed by the real anguish he seemed to feel. "Why are you in such a taking? Anyone would think I was in mortal danger!"

"Chloe, don't you remember your mother? Don't you remember what happened to her? What her life was like? Horace Littlefield is a prince among men, compared to Rival!"

"Well, for heaven's sake!" she cried, exasperated. "I would never consider *marrying* him!"

The instant the words left her mouth, she realized they were false. And the look on Gil's face told her that he knew it too. They had both heard the unmistakable hollow ring of a lie at the heart of her statement.

Gil had always had an uncanny ability to perceive the very things she most wished to keep secret. But this was something she had managed to keep secret even from herself. Feeling as shocked as Gil, she sank onto a chair, one hand fluttering instinctively up to press her cheek.

She *would* consider marrying George. Had been toying with the idea, in fact, since that night in the garden. Well, he was so very handsome! And clever. And charming. And—kissable. Who could resist fantasizing, just a little, about what marriage to such a man might be like? Even a girl who was completely uninterested in marriage—as she was—enjoyed daydreaming about an attractive man.

Chloe drew herself up and faced Gil with dignity. "Even if I were considering such a thing, which I am not—not *really*—there is a vast difference between considering it and *seriously* considering it."

"I will not split hairs with you," said Gil unsteadily. He rubbed his face wearily, sighed, and crossed the room to pick up his hat. He stood for a moment, turning it absently in his hands and staring down at it. "All my life I've heard you rail against the evils of fortune hunters," he said quietly. "You vowed you would never trust a man enough to marry him. Now I see you slipping under the spell of a thorough-going villain who, if he wed you at all, would wed you for your fortune. You are rushing to embrace the very fate you have feared all these years. And I am powerless to prevent it." He looked up at Chloe again and gave her a bitter smile. "You could do worse than to trust me, Clo."

"I do trust you," she said quickly. "You know that. There is no one whose advice I more willingly follow! But this is a situation in which you must trust *me*. You cannot advise me in a matter about which you know nothing! You are barely acquainted with Lord Rival. You have based your opinion of his character on rumor and hearsay."

"I am fairly well acquainted with you, however," said Gil. "You always fire up in defense of those you love."

Chloe felt her cheeks grow hot with embarrassment. "I do not *love* Lord Rival!"

Gil looked at her with a sort of critical detachment. "No, I don't believe you do," he said at last. "But I think, if he plays his cards well, he could easily make you love him. And he's a man who plays his cards very well indeed."

"Oh, pooh!" said Chloe bracingly, although she knew she was still blushing. "I see no reason why Lord Rival should *want* me to love him."

"No mystery about that. Even a rake must marry one day. And apparently this rake must marry money."

And with that stunningly hurtful pronouncement, he crossed to the door, opened it, and left her. Without another word. With no farewell. Chloe, stricken, stared at the place where Gil had just been standing.

Anger surged through her. It was clear that Gil could not conceive that a man might marry her for some *other* reason than her wretched fortune! He found her so unattractive, he could not even imagine that another man might find her lovable. Tears stung her eyes.

She loved Gil more than she loved anyone else on earth. She had always believed he loved her the same way she loved him. Well, he obviously did not. She thought he was the handsomest young man of her acquaintance. He must think she was plain.

Chloe rose and went to the mirror hanging over the sideboard and scrutinized her face. Even with her eyes full of tears, and her complexion blotchy with incipient weeping, and her expression woebegone, there was nothing fundamentally wrong with her features. Why couldn't Gil see that?

But that was not really the point, she realized, as fresh tears spilled down her cheeks. If Gil were plain, it would not change how she felt about him one whit. If his face were ugly as an old boot, it would still be the face most dear to her, and looking at him would give her more pleasure than gazing at an Adonis. It would never have occurred to her, she was sure, no matter *how* unattractive Gil might be, that no one could fall in love with him—which seemed to be what he thought of her.

Chloe, pronounced unlovable by the person she loved most, was forced to run upstairs to her bedchamber to hide her sobs. Once there, she flung herself facedown on the bed and cried into her pillow as though her heart would break.

Chapter 14

"What I find astonishing," confided Mr. Crawley earnestly, "is the number of persons who willingly subject themselves to it. Why, there must be a hundred people here."

"Mr. Crawley, pray take care!" whispered Chloe, agonized. He had a rather penetrating voice, and standing not ten feet from them was the soprano whose voice Jack was astonished that people wished to hear.

He looked round mildly, recognized the soprano, and leaned a little closer to Chloe. "Sorry!" he whispered hoarsely. "But you needn't blush, Miss Littlefield; I daresay she is quite deaf. Can't spend one's life howling loud enough to overpower an orchestra blasting away at one's feet and not suffer the consequences. Stands to reason."

Chloe, who was fairly certain that a deaf singer would find it difficult to attain the level of fame enjoyed by this woman, could only hope that the chatter of genteel conversation surrounding them had drowned out Mr. Crawley's remarks. He was correct, however, in his comments regarding the size of the crowd. Chloe wondered if they would be able to find seats among the press of people squeezing into the salon.

The instant she and Tish had arrived, Jack Crawley had attached himself to their party. It was almost as if he had been lying in wait for them. Since Mr. Crawley was obviously not musical, Chloe was at a loss to explain his presence at a *soirée musicale*. She was even more at a loss to explain his increasingly assiduous attentions. Once he had glued himself to her, he maneuvered to separate her from

Tish and be alone with her in the crowd. She liked Mr. Crawley very well and supposed his friendship with Gil caused him to seek her out—but if she were an unattached female, she would suspect him of *courting* her. Most puzzling.

She did wish Gil were here. He would easily prevent Jack from monopolizing her. He would probably monopolize her himself, but that was a much pleasanter prospect. Chloe banished the agreeable picture with an inward sigh. She had not seen Gil since that terrible scene this morning, and she still felt very low. She had almost begged off attending tonight's musical evening, but decided that staying at home with nothing to distract her would only deepen her depression.

Meanwhile, Mr. Crawley had taken possession of her hand and tucked it into his elbow. "High time we claimed our places," he announced cheerfully and began to steer her toward the rows of closely packed chairs.

Their progress was impeded by the throng of chattering guests. Chloe was too short to see her way through the crowd and had, perforce, to follow Jack's lead. As he propelled her determinedly forward, a pair of elegantly clad legs materialized before her, stepping into her path and causing her to halt. She looked up and met Lord Rival's smiling eyes. It seemed her heart skipped a beat. A wavering smile came unbidden to her face.

"Miss Littlefield, your servant," said Rival easily, somehow managing to bow as though there were no surrounding crowd to hamper his movements. Chloe dipped a small, demure curtsey. She felt Jack's arm stiffen beneath her fingertips, but he exchanged nods with Lord Rival quite civilly.

"How d'ye do? Pleasant evening, what?" said Jack hastily. "Daresay the program will begin at any moment. You'll excuse us, my lord? Must find a seat for Miss Littlefield, you know!"

"I have done so," said Lord Rival. He smiled kindly at Jack. "Very good of you to offer your assistance, but quite unnecessary. You may relinquish her to me now." He nodded a friendly dismissal.

Jack was clearly nonplussed by these masterful tactics. Chloe had to stifle a laugh. Really, George was the most complete hand!

Jack sputtered for a moment, then succeeded in saying sarcastically, "I did not know Miss Littlefield was in your charge, sir!"

"I am not," said Chloe calmly. She peeped naughtily up at Lord Rival, waiting to see how he would handle that. She felt quite certain that he would win the battle, with or without her assistance.

She was not disappointed. Appreciative laughter lit his eyes, and his mouth quirked at her. Then he turned back to Mr. Crawley, the picture of polite boredom. "She *was* not," he said. "She is now." And with the blandest of smiles, Lord Rival reached out and detached Chloe's hand from Jack's outraged arm. Nodding carelessly over his shoulder at poor Mr. Crawley, Lord Rival tucked Chloe's hand into his own elbow and walked off with her.

She looked back guiltily at Jack, offering him a little moue of apology. After all, it would have been most undignified for her to *resist* Lord Rival's audacious action. She saw Mr. Crawley for a moment, looking both indignant and chagrined, and then the crowd cut off her view. Chloe turned to her new partner and rapped him smartly on the forearm with her fan.

"That was very bad of you," she told him primly.

His eyes gleamed wickedly. "I am yours to command. Shall I restore you to your spindleshanked admirer? Say the word and I will do so."

The bubble of laughter she had been repressing escaped, and she giggled. "No, pray do not! I had no notion how to escape his clutches, and really, I do hate to encourage him. It is the oddest thing, for of course he knows I am engaged to Gil, but he *will* hang about! I cannot understand it."

"Can you not? I can."

"Really?" She looked up at him in surprise, meaning to inquire, but her questions died on her lips. What she saw in

George's face almost seemed to stop her breath. She stared, thrilled and astonished, at the tender smile playing round Lord Rival's mouth and the hunger in his eyes.

"You may have noticed that I, too, am hanging about," he said softly. "Perhaps Mr. Crawley can no more help himself than I can."

Confusion rushed through her. She tore her gaze away, disturbed by what she feared his meaning was. And yet, it was irresistibly exciting to think she might have—was it *possible?*—captured the heart of the elusive Lord Rival. Her first, ignoble, thought was a triumphant: Take *that,* Sylvester Gilliland! But then her thoughts jumbled chaotically as she tried frantically to think what her response ought to be. It was difficult to keep in mind what the purpose of all this flirtation originally had been. What on earth should she do?

Fortunately, it was not necessary to respond immediately. They had now reached the seats that he had reserved for them, and she had to bow to the persons in the neighboring chairs, see to the disposition of the diaphanous folds of her evening shawl, and otherwise busy herself in preparation for the upcoming entertainment.

She sat through the first portion of the musicale with an interested, attentive smile pasted on her face and her ears hearing none of it. She was acutely aware of Lord Rival's sleeve beside her bare arm, and his muscular thigh less than an inch from her silk-covered knee. In an agony of attraction and apprehension, she struggled unsuccessfully to sort through her own feelings. It was almost a relief when, at the first interval, he whispered to her that he had promised to speak to a friend and, with every appearance of reluctance, excused himself. His gaze lingered on her before he walked away, and he gave her a hot, secret smile that brought the color to her cheeks. But then he was gone, and Chloe was at leisure to compose herself.

She fell into conversation with the elderly lady seated directly in front of her, and had nearly recovered her equilibrium when Jack Crawley intruded. He gave her a look filled with reproach, and seemed quite aggrieved. As soon as the dowager's attention was claimed by another, Chloe made haste to soothe Mr. Crawley's ruffled feelings.

"Mr. Crawley, I believe you may have misinterpreted my actions," she began, contrition in her voice.

"No," he said unexpectedly. "Gil told me what you were about. Throwing yourself at Lord Rival—a deuced silly thing to do! Tell you what, Miss Littlefield—if you and Gil don't wish to marry, you needn't go to such lengths. There are other ways to escape the obligation."

She almost gasped aloud in surprise. "You—you knew? I did not realize you were so deep in Gil's confidence!"

"Oh, aye. He told me of it before he ever introduced me to you." Jack was still quivering with injured feelings. "I offered to court you instead, but anyone can see you've a preference for that rapscallion Rival." He shook his head in disgust. "Don't know what all the ladies see in him, upon my soul! I may not be a handsome chap, but at least I don't try to tumble every wench I meet!" A look of horror suddenly engulfed Jack's features. He turned beet red and floundered in a morass of stammered apologies. "Speaking to a lady!" he gasped. "Forgot!"

But Chloe's stunned expression was not due to maidenly embarrassment. Her fingers clenched numbly on her fan. How many other people knew that her engagement was a sham? Was that Gil's way of scotching it—simply telling everyone in town that he did not wish to marry her? A blush of mortification stained her face, and a lump of tears rose up to choke her. Why did Gil not *tell* her that he had set Jack on to court her? Was he determined to make her look a complete fool? She wished there were somewhere she could go to have a good cry.

There was not, of course. She stared fiercely at the back of the chair in front of her, gulping deep draughts of air and fighting to control herself. Beside her, Jack sank miserably onto the next chair and clumsily patted her hand, apologizing disjointedly until she wanted to scream.

Then someone was bending over her, his voice warm with concern. "Miss Littlefield, are you all right?"

She looked dazedly up into the face of Robert Dalrymple.

Surprise drove her tears away. "Mr. Dalrymple! I did not know you were here."

"I have only just arrived. But really, Miss Littlefield, you do not look well. Have you the headache? Ought I to take you home?"

Mr. Crawley had risen and was standing unhappily by. Now he said eagerly, "Aye, that may be just the thing. A good idea, what?"

"Oh, no—no," said Chloe faintly. Her eyes pleaded with Robert. "I think, perhaps, I should like a little air."

He immediately offered his arm and she rose to take it. "Mr. Crawley, I wish you a very good evening," she said, by way of dismissal. He seemed so relieved that she was not giving him the cut direct, he bowed with considerable poise. Then Robert was escorting her toward the French windows at the side of the room.

"Thank you," she told him, with real gratitude. "I feel better already." She would not think of Gil, she promised herself. She took a deep breath, and smiled.

A slight smile answered hers. "You look better," he admitted.

He seemed so approachable that Chloe plucked up her courage and asked, if not the question clamoring most loudly for her attention, at least a question she would be glad to have answered. "Did Tish know you were coming? She did not mention it to me."

She watched his face curiously. It seemed to her that his color heightened a trifle. "I was not intending to come, or I would have escorted you. But I thought—I thought I might show a little interest in—in the sorts of entertainment my wife enjoys. For a change."

She thought she understood him, and gave him a warm smile. "I am sure she will be very, *very* pleased to see you."

"I hope so," he said, his voice a little strained. Then he held the door open for her, and together they passed out into the coolness of the night.

Lord Rival strolled idly about the room, inwardly calculating how much longer it might take him to steal Chloe's heart. He was fairly pleased with the results of tonight's labors. He'd bet a pony that Chloe had no idea whether she had just listened to a set of operatic arias or a concert upon the pianoforte. She had sat beside him, all aquiver, with the color in that exquisite little face of hers fluctuating delightfully throughout the entire first half of the program. He had obviously cast her into a complete flutter.

She would have to love him, of course, or she would never do anything so outrageous as to break her engagement to a respectable young man. A young man she apparently held in considerable affection, too. And thank God for it, he thought, stifling a yawn. Otherwise there'd be so little challenge involved in winning her that the courtship would be a complete bore.

Well, almost a complete bore, he amended, recalling the times when she had made him laugh with her quaint mixture of innocence and sauciness. She even showed flashes of wit from time to time. And she would doubtless improve with age. A pity she wouldn't grow any taller, but that could not be helped.

Ah, there was Tish. He placed himself by a branch of candles at the edge of the room and waited for her to see him. Finally her eyes flicked toward him, and he saw them light up. He grinned and winked at her. Predictably, she blushed. He strolled over to her group and engaged in a little desultory conversation with the cluster of idiots voicing their puerile opinions of the musicians, the composer, and the state of modern music. Then he neatly detached Tish from their midst and piloted her out the nearest door.

She laughed up at him. "What is your hurry, George?"

"The interval won't last forever, my sweet."

They had stepped through some French windows onto a stone-paved terrace. His practiced gaze swept the darkness, ensuring that they were quite alone. Then he drew Tish close to him and bent to kiss her. She immediately stiffened and pulled away as she always did, murmuring something inaudible. He quelled his irritation with an effort.

"Tish," he whispered, lightly stroking her bare arm. "Why do you deny me? Don't you trust me, my darling?" He bent to her lips again, but she turned her face so his mouth glanced along her cheek.

"It's not that I don't trust you," she said breathlessly, with a completely unconvincing giggle. "Although I suppose I *shouldn't* trust you, should I? Everyone tells me you are a— a rake."

His hand made soothing little circular motions against the small of her back. "It's the garnets, isn't it?" he said ruefully. "I ought never to have accepted that stake."

She gave an unhappy little shrug. "It was I who wagered them," she said listlessly.

He thought swiftly. Yes, it was worth the gamble. He cradled her chin in the warm palm of his hand and said, with all the seriousness he could muster, "It was wrong of me to take them. Shall I give them back to you? Let me, Tish. They are not worth one moment of distrust between us."

He had no power to restore her garnets, since he had already sold them, but his luck held. As he had hoped, relief rushed into her face and she relaxed against him. "Oh, thank you, George," she said gratefully. "I couldn't possibly accept them, but thank you. Thank you for offering. I own, it did make me feel a little—oh, I don't know what! Suspicious of you, I am afraid." She was blushing again. "How silly of me! I lost them fairly, after all. But it means a great deal to me, to know that you did not wish to take advantage of me."

"Take advantage of you!" he exclaimed, folding her tenderly in his arms. "Certainly not."

God help him. What a scoundrel he had become. What a worthless, disgusting, lying blackguard. He turned his face toward the darkness so she could not see his expression of self-loathing.

A bar of light streamed across the terrace, but with his face toward the garden George did not immediately perceive its source. It was Tish throwing herself violently out of his arms that caused him to turn, startled. There, framed in the lit French window behind them and frozen in shock, stood Robert Dalrymple and Chloe Littlefield.

Chapter 15

For a moment the four of them stood like so many wax-works. Then Tish soundlessly crumpled onto the pavement. In a flash, her husband was at her side, kneeling on the cold stone and lifting her head to cradle it in his lap. His face was pale with anguish, but not as pale as hers. Tish looked like death.

George stood, bemusedly watching. He could feel the danger in the moment, but for once it failed to stimulate him. There was nothing thrilling about this adventure. It was sordid, shameful, and entirely of his own making. If Robert Dalrymple wished to put a bullet through him some gray dawn, George could hardly blame him. Would not, in fact, blame him.

"Tish," said Robert hoarsely. "Tish." He chafed his wife's limp hands.

Tish gave a low moan and turned her face into her husband's waistcoat. George watched, feeling oddly detached, as Tish's eyes fluttered open. She weakly turned her head to stare dazedly into her husband's strained, white face. "Robert," she whispered. Her eyes filled with tears. "Oh, God!"

Her sobbing cry was both prayerful and despairing. It seemed wrenched from the depths of her soul. She covered her face with hands that were visibly shaking. The scene was too intimate, and far too painful, to continue watching. It would take more than a fainting spell to heal this marriage. Robert still held his wife, but his body was rigid with rejection and affront. This would be no sentimental, all-is-forgiven reunion. George averted his eyes.

They fell on Chloe. She was standing, just as he was, exactly where she had been when Tish swooned. The light from the room behind her outlined her petite form and made a halo of her pale ringlets. Her blue eyes were huge with shock as she gazed at the Dalrymples. She looked like a cherub horrified by its first glimpse of evil.

Well. Here was another problem he must address. Was there any dignified way to approach it? He thought for a moment, and decided there was not. He had always been lucky, but there was not enough luck in the world to salvage his embryonic courtship of Miss Littlefield from the wreckage that lay at his feet. It would take a miracle. Under the circumstances, he did not expect divine intervention on his behalf.

As if feeling his eyes upon her, Chloe turned her head slightly and looked at him. There was something chilling in her gaze, although her expression did not alter. It took him a moment to recognize what it was, and then it hit him—for the first time, she was looking at him without desire. There was no spark of attraction, nor even friendship. She simply looked at him, and waited.

He approached her, feeling almost diffident. It was strange to have a woman look at him so gravely. He cleared his throat. "Miss Littlefield, I believe I owe you an explanation."

"No. I don't think you can explain this."

Her tone was polite. He had rather she showed a little emotion. Even anger would give him something to work with. But she remained perfectly composed, gazing levelly at him with that bone-freezing lack of interest.

There it went. *Poof!* There should have been a whiff of smoke or a clap of thunder to mark its passage. He saw, in her complete withdrawal, the utter ruination of his hopes. He would have to strike her name from his list of heiresses. There would be no wooing of Chloe Littlefield, at least not by this sorry excuse for a suitor.

An ironic smile twisted his lips, and he bowed deeply. There was nothing whatsoever to say. He glanced once more at Robert and Tish, who still formed a tableau of misery on the terrace pavement behind him, and mentally drew a line through Tish's name as well.

Should he stay, and allow Robert Dalrymple to call him out? No. He probably could not do so, in the presence of ladies. Besides, it was rather late in the day for George to start acting the part of an honorable man.

"Nevertheless," he said quietly, "I offer my apologies. Inadequate as they doubtless are. I shall not inflict my presence on you further." He bowed again, hesitating, but no one moved or spoke to him. He left.

Some of the color had returned to Tish's face, although she still huddled on the pavement, a portrait of grief. Robert held her stiffly, looking as if he would like very much to drop her. It was all so frightful. Chloe felt she had stumbled into a nightmare. She heard footsteps behind her and turned, trying to shield Robert and Tish from whoever was coming through the door. But it was only a footman, coming to close the window before the entertainment resumed. He looked very much astonished by the scene that met his gaze.

"Mrs. Dalrymple was overcome by the heat," said Chloe swiftly. "Could you fetch us some help, please?"

It was a silly thing to say, since there was no heat to speak of. The footman, however, was well trained. He immediately bowed, his features expressing appropriate concern, and vanished to bring assistance. Chloe crossed to her friends.

"They will be on us at any moment," she said in a low voice. "Tish, you must try to get up now."

Robert said nothing. He appeared to be containing his emotions by keeping his lips firmly shut. He rose, however, and helped Tish to her feet. She staggered a little, but Chloe quickly slipped an arm around her waist. Tish collapsed against her, her head on Chloe's shoulder. Robert made no move to take his wife from Chloe, but stood like a statue while Chloe made soothing noises and encouraged Tish to stand. Fortunately the footman reappeared, bringing reinforcements in the form of two stout underlings.

"I shall call for my carriage," said Robert tonelessly. He

departed to perform this task before the footman had a chance to do it for him.

The footmen carried Tish on a complicated route through the garden and out to the street rather than drag her through the company and disrupt the party. Chloe was grateful for their quick thinking. The last thing any of them wanted was to excite interest among the *ton* and start tongues wagging more than they already were.

The ride home was harrowing. Chloe sat beside Tish, facing forward, and Robert sat facing them. No one spoke. No one touched. Robert stared out the window with eyes that obviously saw nothing. He looked extremely grim. Tish stared straight ahead, an expression of utter hopelessness on her face. She looked wretched. Chloe felt herself beginning to tremble with reaction, and was very glad indeed when they reached the Dalrymples' town house. She stammered a hasty good night, whisked herself upstairs to her room, and firmly closed the door. A sleepy housemaid helped her to undress and put on her night rail, then curtseyed and departed. Chloe heaved a huge sigh of relief to find herself, at last, alone.

What a monstrous tangle they were in. What a frightful, ghastly, appalling tangle! Her nerves on the stretch, Chloe paced back and forth across the hearth rug in her bare feet, trying to make sense of her chaotic thoughts. She blushed with mortification to think how completely the tables had been turned on her. It was Tish, not Chloe, who was supposed to discover Lord Rival's duplicity! It was Tish, not Chloe, who was supposed to have her eyes opened! What an idiot she had been, blithely planning how to extricate Tish from the clutches of a rake, foolishly confident that she was less susceptible than Tish to his allure. Why had she believed that? With what evidence? In hindsight, her cocksure naivete, her willful, stubborn *blindness* seemed almost incredible.

And what a close call she had had. She crossed her arms over her chest, shivering with the horror of it. Thank God she had only felt attraction. Gil was right; the man could have made her love him. And what a terrible fate that would have been. Her mother's unending sorrow was nothing to what Chloe's would have been, married to a man like George Carstairs. Horace Littlefield was frequently unfaithful, but at least he did not inspire women with an overwhelming desire to fall at his feet. Lord Rival's unhappy bride would never know a moment's peace.

A dull rumble of shouting penetrated the walls of her chamber. Chloe halted, holding her breath in dread. The deep shouting subsided, then rose again. An answering voice, higher-pitched, also sounded. This voice had a rather hysterical edge. Chloe was deeply thankful that she could not decipher the words either voice was shouting. Next came an unmistakable faint crash, as of glass or china breaking. Chloe rushed to her bed and scrambled between the clothes, covering her ears with a pillow and screwing her eyes tight shut.

This had to be the most horrible of horrible nights. How she wished she had stayed at Brookhollow rather than subject herself to this! She had posted down to London, stupidly thinking she could help Tish—what vanity! What breathtaking arrogance! All she had done was thrust her own hand into the hornet's nest. She had done nothing whatsoever to pull Tish out.

Cowering in her bed, hiding from the sounds of Tish and Robert's row, she wished desperately that Gil were here. Even in her bedchamber, even at midnight, even in her night rail, if Gil were to walk through the door she would run to him! Just as well, however, that that was *not* going to occur. Her face burned as she pictured trying to explain to Gil the events that had just transpired. What a muttonhead she would appear!

She would have to tell Gil sometime. Probably as soon as tomorrow. She deserved that humiliation, she supposed. Still, she kicked the coverlet in frustration at the idea of having to confess to him just how wrong she had been, and how right he had been. Maddening!

But he had been wrong, too. Chloe suddenly remembered that Gil had set Jack on to woo her, without saying a word to her about it. Why on earth would he do such a thing? This seemed, to her, a question of far more importance than the state of the Dalrymples' tumultuous marriage. She instantly forgot the skirmish down the hall and sat up in bed, scowling ferociously at the dying fire.

So flirting with Lord Rival was a silly thing to do, was it? At least it had seemed *plausible!* What girl in her right mind, and possessed of two good eyes, would jilt Gil for *Jack Crawley?* What was he thinking, encouraging Jack to wedge his bony self between them?

An answer suggested itself. A monstrous, terrible answer. Chloe grew very still as she considered the possibility that Gil found her so unattractive, he believed that his gawky, kindly, rattlepated friend was a good match for her. He probably lumped them together in his mind—thought of them both as plain and puddingheaded. The perfect couple.

She hugged her pillow forlornly, blinking back tears. No, she would *not* cry. She would not. If that was Gil's opinion of her—even now, when she knew she looked better than she ever had in her life—why, there was nothing she could do about it. If he did not find her pretty now, he never would.

This avenue of thought proved ineffective in stemming the tide of tears. If anything, it made them flow faster. But *why?* she argued with herself. What did it matter, after all? Gil's friendship with Jack was unaffected by Jack's homeliness. His friendship with Chloe would be likewise unaffected. Why did she want Gil to feel something different for her than he felt for his other friends?

Oh, no.

A thought, even more monstrous than the one before, began to rear its ugly head. Impossible! It was impossible. Chloe struggled to fight the idea, to force the notion back into the deep, unthinking recesses of her soul where it belonged. She almost cried aloud, *Get back!* She was not even aware that her tears had stopped as she panted, terrified, wrestling with the absurd, ridiculous idea that she might feel something for Gil that—

But this was nonsense. Gil was her best friend. It had never mattered at all that he was male and she was female.

Neither of them had, even once, given the snap of their fingers for . . .

It had never crossed their minds that . . .

Why, she was tired, that was all. All sorts of mad ideas occurred to one when one was tired. She would lie down and go to sleep, and banish this terrible idea. By morning, she would blush to think she had ever, for one moment, considered . . .

She lay hastily down. The house was completely silent. When had Tish and Robert's quarrel ended, she wondered. She stared tensely into the darkness and forced her body to relax. She would think of something else. She would think of *anything* else.

Chloe closed her eyes and began determinedly counting sheep. She had slept so little the night before, and was so completely worn out, that despite her unruly emotions she somehow drifted off. When next she opened her eyes, sunlight was streaming through the chinks in the draperies.

She found Tish in the breakfast room, sipping black coffee. She looked so pale and unhappy that Chloe's heart went out to her. It was impossible to speak of anything while the servants crept about, discreetly filling their cups and replenishing the platters on the table in a silence that would have done credit to a house of mourning. Naturally, the entire staff was aware that their master and mistress were at odds. If Chloe had heard the row last night, it was a safe bet that at least some of the servants had heard it as well.

Chloe was wondering how best to broach the subject of ending her London visit and returning to Brookhollow when a tiny sound caught her attention. She glanced at Tish, who had been listlessly going through her morning's correspondence. Tish was staring disbelievingly at a sheet of hot-pressed paper clutched in one hand, while her other hand traveled, as if unconsciously, up to her throat. Fortunately, the door closed at that moment behind Snead. The two friends were momentarily alone.

"What is it?" asked Chloe anxiously.

Tish looked up, appearing rather dazed. She gave an uncertain laugh. "Well, I—I am not sure, but I think—" She set the paper carefully down and hunted swiftly through her stack of invitations. A very odd expression settled upon her features. "Chloe," she whispered, "I think I am being cut."

"Cut?"

"Yes. It is the most extraordinary thing, but I—I have not been invited to Lady Selcroft's rout party. I have a note from an acquaintance expressing the expectation that she will see me there, and, indeed, I have heard others mention it, but—but I am quite certain that I haven't received an invitation. Lady Selcroft is a very old friend of my mother's, so I hardly think—" She stopped, swallowing hard. "Perhaps there has been some mistake."

"Oh, yes, of course there has been! It must be merely an oversight."

"Except that—oh, Chloe, there are so few invitations here! Much fewer than there should be, this time of year. And two of them—" Tish hung her head, her cheeks flushing scarlet. "Two of them are from Mrs. Budleigh."

Chloe sat in shocked silence. She did not know what to say. Tish dropped her head in her hands, tears beginning to slip through her fingers. "It's all of a piece. I am ruined. Oh, what am I to do?"

Chloe rose from her place at the breakfast table and came round to sit by Tish, putting an arm around her friend's shoulders. "I cannot advise you," she said, with difficulty. "I know so little of these things. Indeed, I—I have lately discovered that I know even less than I thought I did."

Tish sniffed and mopped her eyes with her serviette. "Even *that* is my fault," she said drearily. "I ought to have done things properly, and taken you to be presented, and given parties in your honor, and—oh, Chloe, I have made a mull of *everything*. I wanted you to have a good time, and I wanted to m-make Robert love me again, and I wanted everyone to admire me, and I have behaved like a complete ninny all S-Season!"

Tish's wail of despair wrung Chloe's heart. "Oh, Tish, no! I *have* had a good time. I've had a wonderful time. And everyone does admire you. Why, I've seen the way they all crowd round you! And Robert loves you—"

But at that, Tish broke into heartrending sobs and completely buried her face in her breakfast napkin. Between sobs, she gasped, "We have—agreed—to live apart!"

This was dreadful enough, but then Tish lifted her face, swollen and tearstained, and said, "Robert is t-taking Bobby away."

"No! Oh, Tish, he *mustn't!*"

She shook her head despairingly. "There is nothing I can do. A man's children belong to him, and him alone. That is the law."

"But—but *why?* Robert cannot wish to rear a small child!"

"He says he will take Bobby to my mama-in-law. He d-doesn't wish for Bobby to grow up under m-my influence." Tish gulped, and her fingers twisted the napkin convulsively. "I have been a bad wife. He fears I will be a bad m-mother as well."

Chloe took a deep breath and expelled it on a sigh. "Tish, you know I will always stand your friend. Give me a round tale, if you please! *Have* you been a bad wife? I could have sworn you loved Robert when you married him."

"Of course I loved Robert! I love him still." Tish's face crumpled again. "I could never love anyone but Robert."

Chloe was bewildered. "But Gil told me you were cast into despair at the notion that Robert might separate you from George."

Tish stared uncomprehendingly at Chloe's puzzled face. "Wh-what made him think such a thing?"

"Why, you told him you cared for George so much that you threatened to put a period to your existence if Robert sent you away from him—"

Tish interrupted impatiently. "From *Robert.* Gil would have it that Robert might pack me off to Bath, and I told Gil that if he sent me away, it would be the end of everything, and—" Tish's red-rimmed eyes filled again. "And so it is! How could Gil think I cared for *George?* I told him in so many words there was nothing in that!"

"Oh, dear."

"But none of that matters now. I *behaved* as if I cared for

George, and that has ruined everything." Tish's shoulders slumped in defeat. "I only wanted to—to make Robert jealous. Just a *little*. He—he stopped spending time with me while I was increasing. I was so ill, and I suppose I was often cross with him, and he was afraid of hurting me, or hurting the baby, I suppose—and—well, he fell into a habit of keeping his distance. And then, after Bobby was born, he—he simply drifted away. I thought—" Tish blushed vividly. "I thought if other men seemed to admire me, Robert might—might *look* at me again. I never wanted anything serious to happen with George. George understood that, but it seems he is the only person who d-did."

Chloe felt even more foolish now. Even Lord Rival had understood matters more clearly than she had! He had told her Tish was not deeply infatuated with him, and Chloe had not believed it. But he had been right. She had misunderstood even Tish, whom she thought she knew so well. What a terrible lesson in humility Chloe was learning! It seemed she had been wrong about everything and everyone.

"But—last night?" inquired Chloe hesitantly.

Tish covered her face with her hands again and shuddered. "There is no excuse for last night. If you must know, it was George who won the garnets from me."

"Good gracious!"

Tish looked up and sighed. "Yes. But I had always thought of him as a friend, you know. And he offered to give them back to me, so I—I suppose I hugged him. And there you have it."

"Oh, what a chapter of accidents!"

"Yes," said Tish dully. She looked drained and worn. Chloe could not wonder at it, with the emotional storms poor Tish had had to weather lately.

"You must be wishing me at Jericho," said Chloe sadly. "I came to London intending to help you, Tish, but I think I have done more harm than good. I shall make arrangements to return to Brookhollow on the morrow."

A bitter half smile twisted Tish's mouth. "This can't be comfortable for you," she admitted. "I am so sorry, Chloe."

The smile faded, and her voice sank to a whisper. "I am sorry. For everything."

Chloe, with a heavy heart, spent the rest of her morning making the necessary arrangements for going home. She dashed off a note to Gil apprising him of her plans, sent a footman out to purchase two bandboxes and an additional trunk to hold her London purchases, set a maid to repacking the trunks she originally brought, arranged for a post chaise, and busied herself sufficiently to keep her thoughts at bay. She was standing in her bedchamber, knee-deep in stacks of neatly folded garments and drifts of tissue paper, and directing the disposition of her hats, when Snead appeared in the open doorway. He delicately averted his eyes from the spectacle of feminine trappings spread all round the room, fixed his gaze on the middle distance, and coughed.

"Beg pardon, Miss Littlefield, but Mr. Gilliland is h'asking to see you."

Chloe, much harassed, looked up and blew a curl out of her eye. "Botheration!" she muttered.

Snead's upper lip lengthened in disapproval. "Shall I send him away?" he inquired frostily.

"No, no! I will come down, of course. Where is he?"

"H'i took the liberty of showing him to the library."

"Pray tell him I will be with him directly."

Snead bowed, his professional equilibrium restored by her return to propriety. "Very good, miss."

Chloe hopped over a pile of petticoats and chemises to reach the looking glass and peered distractedly at her reflection. She ran her fingers quickly through the worst of her tangles, retied the riband that threaded through the curls, and trotted downstairs to the library. She felt unaccountably nervous. *It is only Gil!* she reminded herself firmly, banishing, as best she could, the odd thoughts she had had about him lately.

But then she came round the corner and stepped into the library, and there he was.

He was just the same as he always was, just as he always had been. He was handsome and funny and clever and kind, but Gil had always been handsome and funny and clever and kind. Why did her heart leap and swoop and flutter like a hummingbird at the sight of him?

And how long has this been happening? she thought, confused and frightened. For now she realized that this was not the first time that the sight of Gil had affected her this way. She had been ascribing her increasing pleasure in his company to their long-standing friendship, and the newness of her friendship with everyone else in London. But there was a tender edge to this happiness she felt, this elation at the mere *sight* of him. Her delight was out of proportion, she now perceived. In fact, it was dangerous. Foolish!

She clutched the doorjamb, feeling suddenly almost faint. Too many conflicting feelings swamped her: joy, and longing, and panic. And pure embarrassment. What an *idiot* he would think her, if he discovered how she felt! And Gil always discovered how one felt.

Oh, dear. High time she went home.

Chapter 16

Gil, standing by the fireplace, heard the rustle of a skirt in the doorway behind him and turned. Chloe stood on the threshold of the library, one white hand gracefully touching the doorjamb. She looked so lovely that he had to clear his throat before he could speak.

"Hallo, Clo," he finally managed. "You look just like a sunbeam."

She was wearing a butter-yellow half-dress over a white satin slip, and with her golden hair threaded with a yellow ribbon she did, indeed, give the impression that a ray of sunshine had entered the somber confines of the room. She hovered in the doorway, though, as if poised for flight.

"Hallo, Gil," she said faintly. "Did you get my message?"

"Yes. I couldn't make it out, as usual, so I popped round to inquire." He paused, then tried to remove the emotion from his voice. "Tish tells me you're leaving tomorrow."

"Oh. You've seen Tish, then." Chloe took a step into the room, then stopped. He noted, with a pang, that she looked almost nervous of him.

"Yes. I say, Clo, I'm awfully sorry about yesterday morning," he said in a rush. "Don't know what came over me. I shouldn't have carried on like I did. Daresay it gave you a fright."

"Oh! That," said Chloe, her cheeks turning faintly pink. "No, I—I understand perfectly . . . now. Did—did Tish tell you what happened last night?"

"Aye," he said gruffly. "Looks like we've made a proper mull of things, between the three of us."

"You mean Tish and I have made a proper mull of things,"

said Chloe miserably. "You were right all along, Gil. About everything."

At that, she finally entered the room and sank onto a chair. She perched tensely on the edge of the seat and twisted her fingers in her lap. "I haven't been any use whatsoever. I would have done better to have stayed at Brookhollow! I haven't helped Tish, and I haven't helped Robert, and, worst of all, I've placed *you* at fiddlestick's end. Because now all of London knows me as your fiancée." Tears gathered in her eyes. "Had I stayed where I belonged, you might have found a way to end *that* business, at least. But what will we do now? I've been staying as a guest of your *sister*—and she has been the one introducing me—and I've met simply *everyone*—and now no one will believe that our engagement was none of our doing, because we ought to have said so at the start. And, oh, Gil, I am so sorry!"

Gil was only sorry that she was sorry. But as long as she *was* sorry, he could not say so. He ached to comfort her, but feared that if he touched her he would no longer be able to contain his pent-up emotions. He could not even hand her his handkerchief, since he had given it to Tish a quarter of an hour since. He jammed his hands in his pockets and inwardly cursed his helplessness while Chloe sniffed and wiped her tears away with the back of her hand. The childlike gesture was oddly endearing.

"Is that why you are going home?" he asked, his voice sounding strained and harsh in his own ears.

She nodded, gulping. "That, and the fact that it is excessively awkward for me to remain. I can do nothing to help matters, and I am very much in the way. I'm sure it's painful for Robert and Tish to have me here, watching their marriage disintegrate."

"I wish I could think of somewhere else for you to go. Somewhere here in Town." He clasped his hands tightly behind his back, afraid that they would reach for her in a moment if he did not. "I don't suppose you would consider going to the Westwoods?"

"Oh, I couldn't bear it! Besides, Grandmama washed her hands of me after that dreadful summer when—*you* know."

Aye. He remembered very clearly. At the age of seventeen, a rebellious Chloe had been sent, at her father's insistence, to spend a summer with his mother. It had not gone well. According to Chloe, Lady Maria had spent the entire summer criticizing Chloe's beloved mother, correcting Chloe's manners, forbidding Chloe to engage in all her favorite pursuits, and attempting to force her into a mold she refused to fit, in order to groom her for a life she did not want. The summer had culminated in an offer of marriage from a man handpicked by Lady Maria for his title and his supposed ability to control Chloe. Chloe's scornful rejection of this eligible *parti,* and the bitter clash of wills that had ensued, had completed the estrangement between Chloe and her autocratic grandmother.

No, he had had no real expectation that Chloe would consent to stay with the Westwoods. Nor had he any expectation that they would invite her. He sighed. "I thought as much. I wouldn't have suggested it, but—I do wish you would stay, at least through the Season. Selfish of me, I suppose."

"Selfish?" A faint smile flickered across her tearstained features. "You are never selfish."

A lump rose in Gil's throat as he gazed at Chloe's sweet little face. This was the sort of thing, he mused, that made a chap fall for Chloe. Her habit of blurting out whatever came into her head, and the fact that the things that came into her head were simply adorable. Her sweetness was as unthinking and innate as her loyalty, and her optimism, and her sunny temperament, and the thousand other lovable qualities he had taken for granted all his life. It was hard to think he might not see her again for months. He supposed he would make a point of going home this summer, where he might see her regularly, but—dash it all—he didn't like the idea of her going out of reach tomorrow, even so far as Brookhollow. He didn't wish to be separated from her for a week, let alone for the rest of the Season.

"I shall miss you, Chloe," he said unsteadily.

Her wet blue eyes lifted to his. "I shall miss you, too," she whispered.

The clock ticked loudly in the silence that followed. Gil

stared at Chloe's woebegone face, holding his breath. There was something in her eyes—

He almost dared to hope—

It was not the time to speak. Every instinct clamored against it, and yet he could not help himself. He took a deep breath and plunged recklessly over the precipice.

"I have thought of a way we could end our engagement," he said.

Chloe immediately dropped her eyes, but not before he saw something painful flicker in their blue depths. "Oh?" she said.

The polite note of inquiry sounded less than enthusiastic. Gil told himself that that, in itself, was encouraging. He had believed she was *eager* to end their engagement. If she was not—

He ploughed ahead.

"Yes." He found it necessary to clear his throat again. "But I have only been able to think of one way we might end it respectably."

"Oh." She gave an uncertain little laugh. "That is one more than I have come up with. What is it?"

Confound it, his palms were sweating. He wiped them nervously on his trousers. "Chloe—"

By Jove, he had to clear his throat again! "Chloe—"

A sudden shriek sounded in the hall. Startled, both Chloe and Gil swiveled to look. The library door still stood open, and a blur of lilac dimity flew past their field of vision.

"Mama!" cried Tish, sounding almost hysterical with joy.

As one, Chloe and Gil ran to the library door and peered into the hall. Snead stood sourly beside the open front door. Lady Gilliland, majestic in a voluminous traveling cloak, enormous hat, and gloves of English kid, was standing in the center of the hall, enveloping the weeping Tish in a fond embrace. An ancient traveling coach, mud-spattered and piled with trunks, was visible in the street outside. And a chorus of frenzied barking, its shrillness only slightly muffled by the confines of the coach, informed the interested that Lady Gilliland had seen fit to bring her Yorkshire terriers with her to London.

"Leticia, my own!" uttered Lady Gilliland. "I know you will forgive my foisting myself upon you with no warning. Gil, how do you do? I am not surprised to see you here; I daresay you haunt the house, now that Chloe is in residence." Reaching calmly over Tish's head, Lady Gilliland extended her hand. Gil walked forth and bowed over it, feeling somewhat dazed.

"Mother! What brings you to Town?"

Lady Gilliland's expression became Sphinxlike in its inscrutability. "Dear boy," she said cryptically, patting him. The hand was extended to Chloe. "Chloe, my love! How pretty you look."

"Thank you, Lady Gilliland," murmured Chloe, obediently stepping forward to make her curtsey.

Lady Gilliland's gaze traveled to the stairs. Her son-in-law had materialized at the foot of them. "Ah. Robert," she observed placidly.

It seemed to Gil that his mother's eyes narrowed a trifle, as if something in Robert's appearance made her thoughtful. She said nothing, however, but moved forward to greet him. Robert stood rather stiffly, and Gil thought he looked pale and tired. No wonder! But Mother was always up to every rig; she would be far too needlewitted to remark on it.

"How do you do, ma'am?" said Robert, apparently with an effort.

"Very well, thank you, my dear." She offered him her cheek and, hesitating only slightly, he dutifully kissed it. She shot him another keen glance, but her smile did not waver. "So unconscionable of me to descend upon you like this! But I left home all in a quack; there simply wasn't time to send word. I trust a brief visit will not discommode you overmuch?"

"Certainly not," said Robert, although his tightlipped expression contradicted his words. "You are always welcome here."

Tish still clung to her mother's side. "Chloe is in the best bedchamber, Mama, but—"

"But I will be leaving tomorrow," interposed Chloe

quickly. "Pray do not inconvenience your mother on my behalf, Tish! I can easily quit the room today."

Lady Gilliland's brows climbed. "Leaving, my dear? Oh,
you mustn't do that. Only think what an off appearance it
would present! If you leave Town the instant I arrive, everyone will assume that you dislike me."

This view of the situation had obviously not occurred to
Chloe. Flustered, she began to stammer a disjointed series of
disclaimers and apologies, but Lady Gilliland had already
turned her attention elsewhere. "Where is Logan? Ah,
Logan, there you are. Have you shown my dear doggies the
garden? Yes? Then you may hand them to me, if you please.
Pray see to the disposal of my trunks—no, I am not in the
least tired, thank you, and it is immaterial to me which bedchamber I am given. Tish will accompany me to the drawing
room meanwhile, won't you, my love? Or shall we go to the
nursery? I am excessively anxious to see Bobby, but really,
I almost think—yes, yes, my precious widdy doggies! Yes,
we've arrived! Journey's end, my sweetings! Journey's end,
my poppets!"

And, thus cooing to the two tiny creatures now nestled in
each arm and still hysterically barking, she sailed up the
stairs with Tish trailing in her wake. Robert, Gil, and Chloe,
standing in the hall below, stared bemusedly after her.

"She scarcely ever comes to Town, you know," remarked
Gil, stepping aside to allow a parade of servants carrying
trunks, boxes, presents for Bobby, and various canine accoutrements to pass. "I wonder what has brought her here?"

"Your father's traveling coach, apparently," said Robert
acidly. "Really, I hate to seem uncivil, but I am, myself,
preparing to leave Town for an extended visit with my own
mother. Lady Gilliland could not have chosen a worse time
to land, unannounced, on my doorstep! I do wish—" he
broke off, seeming to recall where he was and to whom he
was speaking. "I beg your pardon, Gil," he said stiffly.

"Oh, no need!" said Gil cheerfully. "All in the family,
dear chap. Besides, can't tell me anything about Mother I
don't already know. She's always been like that, you
know—carries everything off with a high hand, and there's

never any gainsaying her. She'll have her way in the end, so we generally let her have it to begin with. Saves trouble."

Chloe's pretty forehead had puckered in a perplexed frown. "Yes, that's all very well, but what am I to do? I had already begun packing—all the arrangements have been made—"

"Unmake 'em," recommended Gil. "You know Mother. She'll hammer at you all evening otherwise. You'll fall in with her ideas eventually, because she'll somehow make it impossible for you to do anything else. Agree with her now! Then you won't have to change everything at the last minute."

"Oh, dear!"

Gil grinned affectionately at her. He felt so confident of his mother's ability to keep Chloe in London, since she had expressed such a decided opinion on the matter, that an overwhelming sense of relief was buoying his spirits. He shook Robert's unresponsive hand energetically. "Expect me for dinner, old man," he advised him happily and departed in a much more cheerful frame of mind than he had enjoyed for some time.

Lady Gilliland, meanwhile, had succeeded in settling her excited pets and was seated on a sofa in the drawing room, listening with careful concentration to her daughter. Tish was pouring into her mother's ears a stream of impassioned and rather incoherent confidences, accompanied by much uncontrolled weeping. It was all very difficult to follow, but Aurelia thought it best to let the child unburden herself without interruption. She sat in sympathetic silence, therefore, merely patting Tish from time to time and making soothing sounds.

Although the tales Tish told were disturbing, Aurelia was not surprised by them. She had received not one, but three letters in the past two days warning her that her daughter's behavior, coupled with her preferred mode of dress, was causing a great deal of gossip and rapidly deteriorating her social standing. If her behavior continued unchecked, Tish would soon find herself beyond the pale. Matters had not been helped by her mother-in-law's indifference. Had the countess championed her, it might have made all the difference in the world; but as it was, more than one influential hostess was whispering that Robert Dalrymple had made a shocking *mesalliance*.

Far from resenting the interference of her well-meaning friends, Aurelia was extremely grateful for their warnings. She swallowed her anger at Robert's mother, whom she was much inclined to blame for not quashing Tish's excesses before they had reached this point, and immediately set out for London. She deliberately neglected to send word of her imminent arrival. Aurelia wanted to see for herself how matters stood, without giving Tish and Robert an opportunity to don smiling faces for her benefit.

Well. It was every bit as bad as she had feared, and very likely worse. Robert had aged ten years, and Tish looked on the brink of a decline. Another woman might have bowed to the inevitable and taken Tish home in disgrace. Aurelia Gilliland, however, was made of sterner stuff. A baronet's wife was hardly as powerful as a countess, but after all, she was not a *complete* nobody. Any steps that could be taken would be taken.

Amid Tish's catalogue of woes, she discerned that Robert had threatened to take Bobby away, and that Tish had morbidly convinced herself that he was serious. Aurelia supposed that he was, in fact, serious, but deemed it best, for the time being, to pooh-pooh the idea.

"Nonsense, my dear. I shall soon put a stop to that, I promise you! Now sit up, Tish, and compose yourself. You have wept long enough."

Tish was so much in the habit of obeying her mother that she actually sat upright and heeded this crisp admonition. Aurelia ran her eyes over her critically. "You are grown quite thin, and you are much paler than I like to see you. I daresay it is the fashion to be slender, but I fancy you have gone a trifle overboard. You do have a fatal tendency to go to extremes, my love."

"I know it, Mama," said Tish listlessly. Her dejected and apprehensive aspect indicated that she clearly expected to receive a severe scold from her mother, or worse. And so she would, but not immediately. The exigency of this hour called for deeds, not words.

Aurelia rose and adjusted her tippet briskly. "Well! I see little sense in sitting about, weeping and wringing our hands. Matters have clearly reached a crisis, and swift action must be taken. We shall tackle your difficulties one at a time. Go and splash some water on your face, my dear, and change your clothes. We are going to pay some morning calls together—not, I am afraid, very amusing ones, but I trust we may be able to repair at least some of the damage you have done."

Tish blinked. "I—I never pay morning calls."

Just as she feared. Aurelia drew herself up to her full imposing height and fixed Tish with a baleful glare. "Leticia Dalrymple, you were *not* reared in the Antipodes! You have just been telling me that you believe hostesses are dropping you from their invitation lists. How can you wonder at it, if you do not adhere to the most *basic* conventions? Why, even if your conduct were otherwise quite unexceptionable, which it clearly has not been, you would find yourself courting disaster by pursuing such a course." Her foot tapped impatiently as she watched a painful blush creep up her daughter's neck. "How many rules have you broken? Have you taken Chloe to be presented?"

"No, Mama. But Chloe does not wish to be presented. She—"

"Chloe's wishes are entirely beside the point. You ought to have insisted! Why did you not? I am much inclined to believe that all your troubles are rooted in want of firmness. Had you shown just a little resolve, a little tenacity of purpose—"

"Oh, Mama, I cannot order Chloe about! She—"

"Well, I can. I shall speak to her the instant we return. No presentation, and yet you have been taking her with you to party after party! *Really,* Tish! I am extremely vexed with you."

"Yes, Mama." Tish hung her head like a child.

"When is the last time you issued invitations?"

"Invitations? For—for what?"

"For anything, child! Do people dine with you? Do you hold rout parties, or card parties? You haven't the space for dancing, of course, but—" She stopped, her nostrils flaring with displeasure. "Well. I can see by your face that you do not entertain."

"No, Mama." The words came out in a whisper.

A dreadful pause ensued, wherein Aurelia struggled to quell her emotions. When she spoke, she spoke carefully. "Leticia, I do not wish to minimize the seriousness of what I fear has been grossly improper behavior on your part, by leading you to believe that I ascribe your social ostracism solely to your neglect of etiquette. From what you have told me, I believe you to have been at fault—grievously at fault—in your public behavior, your private neglect of your marriage, and your encouragement of Lord Rival's attentions. But I *will* say that to crown your indiscretions with *carelessness* is doubtless adding significantly to your dilemma! If you have alienated and offended the arbiters of society, through nothing more than simple laziness and inattention, you have indulged in folly that borders on the suicidal! If you do not court these women, if you do not dispose them to think kindly of you, who will stand your friend? Who will intervene to shield you from malicious gossip?"

Tish, not unnaturally, was drooping wretchedly beneath this blistering onslaught. She was well aware that her mother addressed her as "Leticia," and spoke in flowing periods, only when she was deeply moved.

Aurelia watched her squirm, listened to her halting apologies, and was satisfied that Tish made no attempt to defend her conduct and offered no excuses for it. She supposed the consequences of Tish's behavior were providing sufficient punishment, and so she sent her daughter off to don something chaste and tasteful, suitable for accompanying her mother on a round of calls upon those persons who were most likely to prove useful—houses where Tish alone might have met with polite denials that the hostess was at home, but where, accompanied by Lady Gilliland, she might gain entrance. Aurelia trusted that her own influence, small as it might be, coupled with Tish's meek and newly humble demeanor, might do much to soften the hearts of those women whom Gil irreverently apostrophized as "the beau monde biddies." Aurelia meant to waste no time in reassuring these women that Tish's conduct had fallen once more under the influence and protection of someone able to direct it into proper channels.

Chapter 17

Chloe, who was well acquainted with the redoubtable Lady Gilliland, took Gil's advice. With this caveat, however: she was determined not to delay her return to Brookhollow for longer than a se'nnight. She therefore moved her travel arrangements out only one week, then spent the afternoon undoing everything she had done that morning, soothing the disgruntled servants who had assisted her, and trying not to think too much.

She could not stay in London. She simply could not. Even with Lady Gilliland to support her, the atmosphere in the Dalrymples' home was oppressive—and then there was Gil. Try as she might to banish them from her thoughts, his words kept coming back to her. *I have thought of a way we could end our engagement.* Every time she recalled it, a fresh wave of depression afflicted her. He had sounded so hopeful! So eager!

Well, why should he not? From the day it was announced, both of them had done their utmost to wriggle out of their betrothal. She had worked harder at it than Gil had, in truth. The more fool she.

Nonsense, she scolded herself, shaking out her folded muslins and returning them to the clothespress. She had never wished to marry. Her life was full without it. And no matter *what* her feelings for Gil, she certainly could not marry a man who did not feel the same for her.

Now, *that* admonition had some teeth. She recalled her mother's unrequited love for her father in all its slow, unfolding misery. She would not go down that path. She would not. Better a solitary life at Brookhollow, tending the land she loved and interesting herself in the comings and goings of her tenants, charity work for the parish, and a life of comfortable friendship with her neighbors.

Why, she looked *forward* to going home, she reminded herself. Apart from her father, who was often a thorn in her side, everyone and everything she loved was there. She would go home and resume her old life, and prepare for the day when she would be old enough to truly be regarded as the lady of the manor. Respected. Perhaps beloved. A part of the community.

It had always seemed a pleasant, peaceful prospect. Now it seemed incomplete to her, as if such a life would have something hollow and aching at the core.

A terrible loneliness suddenly gripped her, so intense that it halted her movements. She stood for a moment, blinded by emotion, her hands stilled in their task. *Gil.* She would never get him out of her heart. How could she forget him? He would always be in her life—but not where he belonged, at the center. He would be on the fringes. A friend. Dear, but infrequently seen. It would be torture, struggling forever to hide her feelings from him.

And one day he would marry. He would marry, and she would have to welcome his wife into her circle of friends or risk losing Gil's precious presence, even at the fringes of her life. What if his wife recognized the longing in Chloe's eyes? Oh, dreadful. Surely she would ban Gil from Chloe's presence, or find a dozen small, spiteful ways to separate them.

Chloe leaned forward and pressed her forehead against the cool wood of the cupboard door, her throat aching with unshed tears. She couldn't think about it now. She would go mad if she thought about it now. Besides, her time would be better spent learning to bear this terrible cross. She took a deep breath. "What can't be cured must be endured," she whispered aloud to herself. Then she resolutely opened her eyes, straightened, and resumed her tasks. There was nothing else to do.

She happened to be crossing the hall when Tish and Lady Gilliland returned from their round of morning calls. Tish seemed exhausted, but her mother looked, if anything, refreshed and energized. Battle evidently agreed with her.

"Did you have a pleasant time?" asked Chloe.

Lady Gilliland smiled. "Pleasure, my dear, was not what we were seeking. I believe we have enjoyed some *success,* and that is all that matters. Lady Selcroft was excessively kind, and Sally Jersey was at least cordial, for which I am most grateful. Tish, my love, I think it would be best if you go directly upstairs. You look worn to a thread, and you must, you really must, make some effort to recruit your strength. Recollect, pray, that your brother will be here for dinner; I have every expectation that Robert will refrain from insulting Gil, not to mention me, by disappearing to his club. Do you wish to show your husband that pale face and those great circles beneath your eyes? I thought not! Run along, sweeting. Chloe and I have much to discuss."

This was news to Chloe. Her eyes widened apprehensively. "I am persuaded, ma'am, that you would rather lie down for an hour than talk to me. You must have risen at first light, to arrive in London by midday. Pray do not exhaust yourself on my account! I have much to do—"

"Nonsense, child, I am not such a poor creature. I assure you, I do not regard a trifling journey of sixteen or eighteen miles as an excuse to cosset myself for the remainder of the day. Come along!"

Lady Gilliland beckoned imperiously and swept into the library. Thus commanded, Chloe trailed helplessly behind her. Lady Gilliland stood before the fire, vigorously tugging at her gloves. Chloe closed the door behind her, but hovered nervously by it, ready to open it again and escape if need be.

Lady Gilliland glanced up from her gloves. "You look extremely well, Chloe. London appears to agree with you."

"Thank you, ma'am. I—I have enjoyed myself very much."

The gloves off and folded, Lady Gilliland tossed them neatly onto a cherrywood table and, peering into the looking glass above the mantel, began working the hatpin out of her hat. "I am glad to hear it. Tish tells me, however, that you have not yet been presented."

Chloe swallowed. "No, ma'am. It—it did not seem necessary."

Lady Gilliland's eyes met Chloe's in the mirror. "It is extremely necessary, as Tish knew well," she said crisply. "I have already spoken with her, my dear, and I promise you that this household will not, in future, be run in such a ramshackle fashion. Come! What is that face you are pulling? It will not be much of an ordeal. We will procure suitable clothing for you, teach you a few simple rules of protocol, and the thing is done."

"Ma'am, I am returning to Brookhollow this Thursday week," said Chloe, trying to speak with a firmness to match Lady Gilliland's. "I cannot think it necessary to go through the ritual of a court presentation if—"

"Returning to Brookhollow! Why, the Season is only half over."

"Nevertheless, ma'am, I—"

"And do you think never to return to London? My dear Chloe, you cannot have *half* a Season, short of illness or death! It simply isn't done. A green girl, a girl whom no one knows, cannot appear and disappear at will, attend only the parties that take her fancy, snub the royal family—yes, I see that you are shocked by the very idea, but I assure you that is how your behavior would appear! And appearances are everything in this part of the world, as I believe you may have learned by now."

She swept the hat from her head and placed it beside the gloves, then seated herself gracefully on a sofa. "I was a little surprised, you know, that we heard nothing from you after the engagement notice was published." Her eyes met Chloe's with unnerving keenness.

Chloe, already knocked off balance by Lady Gilliland's frontal attack regarding her social obligations, was completely nonplussed by this abrupt change of subject. Speechless, she could only stare at her would-be mother-in-law, terrified that her every fleeting thought must be plainly legible in her face. Lady Gilliland studied her for a moment before she went on.

"It must have given you quite a turn, to see those notices.

I fully expected you to come back, posthaste, to rake us all over the coals. At the very least, I was in daily expectation of receiving a stinging letter from either you or Gil. Especially you, my love! You were so adamantly against the idea of marrying Gil before you left. Or so you said."

Chloe flushed scarlet. "Why—so I was! I was very much against it!" she stammered.

"Are you still?"

Chloe realized that her jaw had dropped. She carefully closed it, then said, as simply and as carefully as she could: "Yes."

Lady Gilliland patted the sofa beside her invitingly. "Come and tell me about it, my poor child. Has it been miserable, then, finding yourself engaged to my son out-of-hand?"

Chloe approached cautiously and sat, but on the extreme edge of the sofa. "Well, I wouldn't describe it as *miserable*. It was certainly embarrassing, and we were both very angry at first."

"I daresay." Lady Gilliland looked sympathetic. "But that is what struck me as so extraordinary, you know. We haven't heard a peep out of either one of you. Why is that?"

Chloe blinked. "Well—well—I don't suppose it occurred to us—it certainly did not occur to *me*—that there was anything to be said. After all, the damage had been done." She lifted her chin as some of her anger returned. "And I think it's as well that we refrained from expressing ourselves to you, ma'am, and especially to my father! You would not have enjoyed hearing what we had to say."

"I see." Lady Gilliland seemed completely unperturbed. She continued to regard Chloe fixedly. "Do you and Gil plan to marry?"

"No!" cried Chloe, in a strangled voice.

"No? Then what, precisely, do you mean to do? From aught I can tell, neither of you has repudiated the engagement. I have been receiving felicitations all afternoon."

"And I suppose you accepted them without a blink," said Chloe bitterly.

"Of course, my dear." An amused smile curved Lady

Gilliland's lips. "I would indeed count myself fortunate, and Gil as well, if you married him."

Pain tugged at Chloe's heart. She found she had to look away. "Well, I am not going to marry him," she said. Her voice sounded a trifle too loud. "I am not going to marry anyone."

To her surprise, Lady Gilliland's cool, strong hand reached out and covered her own. "You have not known many examples of a happy marriage, have you, my dear?" she said quietly. The hand patted hers, then removed itself. Lady Gilliland looked pensively off into space. "Not every couple is as fortunate as Sir Walter and I have been. We had not met above a dozen times, I fancy, before we found ourselves at the altar. That is the way things were done in those days, you know—not so long ago. But our parents had chosen well. We suited admirably, and soon became fast friends."

Chloe was both startled and touched that Lady Gilliland would confide in her. She must have looked a little dubious, however, for Lady Gilliland, catching her expression out of the corner of her eye, laughed a little and turned back to her. "You are thinking that we are seldom to be seen in each other's company? Very true, my love, but we are happy nonetheless. Sir Walter has his books and his garden, and I my dogs and my house to run, and we share a healthy respect and affection for one another. I am utterly persuaded that a strong marriage is, of all possible experiences in life, the one most likely to result in sustained happiness. And my own experience has shown that true friendship is the best foundation for such a marriage. And true friendship, my dear, is what you have with Gil."

Chloe nodded, but could not speak. It was hard to meet Lady Gilliland's eyes, gazing at her so kindly. She stared, instead, at her hands twisting tensely in her lap. It was all very well for Lady Gilliland to speak of *friendship* with Sir Walter. But Chloe knew she would be desperately unhappy, married to a man she adored—as she adored Gil—if what he felt for her was only "respect and affection." Besides, Gil did not wish to marry her, so it was foolish even to entertain the idea, let alone to have this conversation with his mother.

She took a deep breath. "Lady Gilliland, I feel honored by your confidence," she said haltingly. "And of course I—I am glad that you would welcome me as an addition to your family. Thank you. But—I cannot marry Gil. You must put the notion out of your head. It is—it is unthinkable."

"Unthinkable. Why? Forgive me, but you must make some allowance for the partiality of a mother. Gil seems to me a most unexceptionable young man."

Chloe looked up swiftly. "Oh, yes! That is not what I meant. That has nothing to do with it. It's just—"

"I would even call him handsome."

"Oh, yes, exceedingly handsome! But—"

"And I have always had the impression he was well liked around Town. That must count for something, does it not?"

"Of course! Everyone likes Gil. He is so very—"

"I know for a fact that he has a kind heart and a sweet temper. Why, even as a boy, he was never one to tease the smaller children, or torment insects, or anything of that sort."

"Oh, no, never! Why, he allowed Tish and me to follow him about, and was so patient with us, even when the other boys would taunt him for it. He has always been—"

"He is not foulmouthed, is he? That is the kind of thing a mother might not know."

"Gracious, no! At least—"

"And he has always been quite fastidious in his personal habits, so I cannot imagine you finding him repellent in that way."

"Oh, of course not! There is never anything offensive about Gil. In fact—"

"He is not addicted to gaming, or drink."

"Far from it. He—"

"I have not perceived any annoying habits, such as cracking his knuckles, or smoking tobacco, or anything of that nature."

"Oh, no! He does not even take snuff. Gil is—"

"Frankly, Chloe, I believe you could do much worse than to marry my son."

"Frankly, Lady Gilliland, I believe I could not do better!"

The words were scarcely out before Chloe clapped her hands over her mouth, as if she could call them back and stop them.

Lady Gilliland regarded her thoughtfully. "Ah," was all she said.

Chloe found that she was trembling. "Lady Gilliland, pray do not misunderstand me," she said desperately. "I have the highest opinion of Gil—I have always had the highest opinion of Gil—but I tell you truly, I cannot marry him. Indeed, we have both been doing our utmost to discover a way we can respectably end our betrothal, and Gil has told me—only this morning, just as you arrived—that he has found a way. There was not time for him to tell me what it was, but I assure you, whatever it may be, I mean to abide by his decision." Her voice trailed off at the end of her speech. She blinked to clear the tears that had stupidly welled up, and turned her face away, fervently hoping that Lady Gilliland would not notice her emotion.

But it was not from Sir Walter that Gil had inherited his perspicacity. Lady Gilliland continued to regard her fixedly, and Chloe felt herself growing more transparent by the moment. She folded her arms tightly, as if unconsciously protecting herself, and drew herself carefully upright on the sofa. "You know I have never thought of marriage," she said with simple dignity.

"Yes, I know that. I have already given you my views on the felicity of married life, and will therefore say no more on that head. I do not wish to browbeat you, my dear." Lady Gilliland still watched her intently, her head cocked like a bird. "If you and Gil are in agreement—and, I must say, you generally are, which is one of the reasons why I believed— well! Talking pays no toll. If you and Gil are in agreement on this, and do not wish to marry, I suppose a way must be found to break the engagement. I only hope you will find a way to do so with a minimum of scandal. I should not like to have Gil's future chances of forming an eligible alliance harmed. I understand that you mean to never marry, but I believe Gil feels far otherwise."

"Yes," said Chloe faintly. If only she could stop trembling! If only Lady Gilliland would not treat her so kindly! Somehow it made everything worse. "We might have ended the matter at once, you know, but Gil—Gil wanted to find a way that—that would not—" She raised a shaking hand to cover her eyes before the tears started falling. "Forgive me, ma'am, but—I think—I think I am not quite well!"

And, not knowing what else to do, Chloe rose blindly from the sofa and fled, nearly tripping over the tiny dog that trotted in the instant the library door opened. She hastened up the stairs to her bedchamber, as embarrassed as she was unhappy. She had made a complete fool of herself! Useless to hope Lady Gilliland would believe she had been taken ill! Oh, but what did it matter? What did *anything* matter? She would think of some excuse to offer Lady Gilliland at dinner. Right now, she was going to have a good cry.

Lady Gilliland watched Chloe's precipitate departure with sympathy—and great interest. She picked up the squirming terrier and stroked it absently, gazing thoughtfully at the doorway Chloe had just vacated.

"So much weeping and misery in this household!" she remarked to the dog. A slow smile crept across her face. "Really, it makes me feel quite optimistic."

Chapter 18

The group that gathered in the Dalrymples' small drawing room before dinner suffered from a surfeit of nerves. The only calm member of the party was Lady Gilliland, and the only cheerful one was Gil.

Seldom had a mere family dinner occurred in such a highly charged atmosphere. Everyone had dressed with elaborate care, each for his own reasons; the assembled company could not have appeared more correct, or more gorgeous, if the Regent himself was to join them. Lady Gilliland, however, was the only member of the party who was at leisure to appreciate this. The others were too busy struggling to maintain their composure, achieve an air of normalcy, and keep their eyes off the one person present who was irresistibly drawing their attention like a magnet.

Lady Gilliland was enjoying herself hugely. Her only regret was that Sir Walter was not present to share the exquisite entertainment provided by the children's unintentional theatrics. She did hope that one day in the not-too-distant future she could describe it all to the present company and enjoy a good laugh with the very persons now unconsciously providing this diverting spectacle. At the moment, of course, it would not strike a single one of them as amusing in the least.

Poor Robert, standing so stiff and grim-faced by the fire, looked absolutely haunted. He was clutching a glass of untasted Madeira and trying to keep his eyes from following Tish everywhere she went. Tish fluttered aimlessly about the room, lovely in a spangled gown of clinging spider-gauze that glittered when she moved. She was pale, but two spots of feverish color on her cheeks gave her the burning, intense beauty of a consumptive. Lady Gilliland devoutly hoped that matters would resolve before Tish made herself ill with excessive emotion. Whenever Robert succeeded in tearing his eyes away from Tish, hers would compulsively flit to him, and her brittle, brilliant smile would become ragged with anguish.

Gil and Chloe, seated across from one another on twin settees, were providing comic counterpoint to Robert and Tish's melodrama. Chloe, like Tish, had arrayed herself in what surely must be her most becoming dinner dress; Lady Gilliland had never seen her look so beautiful. She perched on the settee, doing her best to appear at ease, while Gil sat and stared at her in frank admiration. Lady Gilliland had to bite back a laugh as she watched them. Since Gil's gaze was riveted on Chloe, whenever she glanced at him her eyes caught his. They would both immediately look away, blushing hotly, and then, since Chloe seemed better able to command herself than Gil, she would resolutely fix her gaze on someone else and attempt to join in the conversation. At which point Gil's eyes would irresistibly return to Chloe, and stay there until the dance repeated itself. *Friendship,* pish-tosh! The entire room smelled of April and May!

She supposed that she would be the only member of the party who would be aware of what was served or taste the dinner at all. In fact, she was fairly certain that the others would eat little and spend their time stirring their food this way and that, going through the motions rather than actually chewing and swallowing. This supposition proved true, for the most part, but one member of the party defied her expectations. Gil may have been unaware of what he was eating, since his attention was fixed unwaveringly on Chloe throughout the meal, but he ate steadily, with a young man's appetite, and managed to put quite a bit of it away.

The Dalrymples' servants had outdone themselves. Lady Gilliland wondered cynically if they were feeling some concern over which household, if any, would employ them if and when the master left the mistress. There was never any hope of hiding marital discord from the servants, of course.

Doubtless rumors had been flying all day. The dinner certainly appeared designed to remind its consumers of the excellence of the present staff. Fresh flowers adorned the table, which was perfectly set with gleaming china, highly polished silver, wax candles, and sparkling cut crystal. The linens were spotless. The meal itself was excellent, and the service attentive and unobtrusive. What a pity, thought Lady Gilliland, that she was probably the only person at the table who noticed any of it.

Conversation was sporadic and desultory. Lady Gilliland peacefully consumed her dinner and bided her time. Eventually Robert turned to her, with an obvious effort, and politely inquired how she had left Sir Walter and whether things were going well in the neighborhood. Lady Gilliland smiled.

"Sir Walter is quite well, as always, thank you. Everything has been most quiet; scarcely any news or gossip to report. Except, of course, for the Ewings."

A pause ensued. Lady Gilliland tranquilly sipped her wine and waited. It was Tish who asked, "Who are the Ewings, Mama?"

Lady Gilliland opened her eyes in what she hoped would seem an expression of mild surprise. "Surely you remember Mr. and Mrs. Ewing, Tish? Such a lovely couple, and so fond of one another! I believe you missed their wedding—well, of course, you would have been in London. What a picture they made! I believe I never saw a couple more besotted, and their feelings perfectly mutual. Why, everyone expected them to live in blissful harmony! But, alas, it was not to be. As Shakespeare said, 'The course of true love never did run smooth.'"

Four pairs of eyes fastened on her. Tish, especially, seemed painfully interested. "What happened to them?" she asked, sounding as if she dreaded the answer.

"Oh, nothing, my dear. Nothing in the world. It was what they *thought* had happened to them that was nearly their undoing."

Aurelia's eyes traveled round the table. Certain that she held everyone's undivided attention, she blandly continued.

"No one seems quite sure how it began, or which of them was more at fault, but a certain *distance* crept into the Ewings' marriage. Little misunderstandings arose. Feelings were injured. Doubtless each of them contributed to this, of course; that is always the way of it. I never yet knew a marriage that soured through the fault of one spouse alone."

She paused again, ostensibly to sip her wine, and covertly noted the arrested expression on Robert's face. Robert was no fool! She continued, still in the same gentle, offhand way.

"Be that as it may, eventually people began to notice that the Ewings scarcely ever appeared in public together. We all commented on it, of course. It seemed a shame, after such a promising beginning. And any fool could see that both of them were unhappy, but what can one do?" She shrugged. "Fatal to interfere in someone's marriage, even with the best intentions! I daresay there were any number of us who were simply longing to give them both a good talking-to, but naturally one does not dare. We hoped that Mr. Ewing's mother might intervene, but unfortunately she was a jealous, spiteful woman and had taken poor Mrs. Ewing in dislike. So the last thing she was inclined to do was help her daughter-in-law. If anything, she made matters worse by continually finding fault with her. And, I am afraid, she had no hesitation in complaining to her son about his bride. Most unfortunate. You can easily imagine the damage that was done."

Robert's color was a trifle heightened. "I suppose Mrs. Ewing was completely blameless in every way," he said dryly.

"Oh, by no means!" said Lady Gilliland promptly. "Quite the contrary. In fact, it was Mrs. Ewing's behavior that brought matters to a head."

"What did she do?" asked Tish. Her voice quavered a little.

Aurelia shook her head gravely. "Indeed, I hesitate to tell you, for it's enough to make you all think ill of her. And I believe she meant nothing by it. In fact, I thought it rather pathetic, for everything she did was merely an attempt to regain her husband's attention. But the foolish creature deliberately began dressing in the most outlandish mode—really, some of the things she wore were nothing short of scandalous! And I'm afraid she adopted a flirtatious manner to match her wardrobe. And several of the young men in the neighborhood received quite the wrong impression."

"Oh, dear," said Tish. She was blushing. "Mama, would you care for a little more of the duck? Allow me to—"

"But the worst of it was," resumed Aurelia, smoothly quashing Tish's misguided effort to change the subject, "that there was one man in particular whose attentions she encouraged. And he had a most unsavory reputation."

"Did he?" said Robert grimly. "Pray continue, ma'am. You interest me extremely."

"Well, it is an interesting tale," said Aurelia modestly. "At any rate, I believe this dreadful man would not have hesitated to ruin Mrs. Ewing. And the silly creature was so innocent, at heart, that she ran headlong into danger."

"She sounds a perfect idiot," said Gil. Seeing that her son's eyes were alight with unholy laughter, Lady Gilliland shot him a quelling glance.

"She was not, I am afraid, very wise," said Aurelia repressively. "And I always thought her stubborn, and unwilling to take the advice of those older and wiser than herself. But I am convinced that her heart was ever in the right place. And I am perfectly sure that, despite all appearances to the contrary, she never allowed this man to take liberties with her, even when alone with him." Aurelia touched her napkin delicately to the corners of her mouth. "Mrs. Ewing," she said softly, "never, for one moment, stopped loving her husband."

Tish, motionless, stared at her dinner plate. Chloe's blue eyes were fixed thoughtfully on Lady Gilliland's face. "How did things come to such a pass, between two people who loved one another?" she asked quietly. "I always thought that mutual love brought understanding."

"Oh, my dear, nothing could be farther from the truth! Love brings misunderstanding, more often than not."

"Why is that?" asked Tish, almost inaudibly.

Aurelia smiled fondly at her daughter. "Because to love someone, Tish, means giving that person the power to hurt you. It is really rather frightening to love anyone as much as the Ewings loved one another. The more one loves, the more power the beloved has, for good or ill—to make one happy, or to make one desperately unhappy. Tiny flaws become magnified. Slights are imagined. And then pride rears its ugly head, and soon the entire relationship is poisoned."

Robert's brows rose. "Pride?"

"Oh, yes. Simple human pride. One feels wounded, and often the other person has no notion of it, and that hurts even more. And one tells oneself, Well, I sha'n't let on. So instead of having it out, one is silent, and nurses the injury, and broods, and allows it to fester. Eventually one tries to get a bit of one's own back. And everything goes from bad to worse. A little of that happens in every marriage, you know."

Robert set his fork carefully beside his plate, and took a deep breath. "What happened to the Ewings?" he asked quietly.

"Oh, they came very near the brink. Very near indeed. Each of them believed that the other had stopped loving, you see. I believe they actually had plans to separate, although they were both heartsick about it. Such a pity! So much needless suffering! All that was really required was a simple, honest confession of their feelings. But pride kept them silent."

"You say they came *near* the brink. They did not separate, then?"

Aurelia smiled serenely. "No. They swallowed their pride and spoke their love before it was too late," she said. "And all's well that ends well."

A brief, but pregnant, silence fell. It was broken by the scrape of Robert's chair as he pushed it back from the table. He was pale and moved awkwardly, but he rose and held out his hand to Tish.

"May I speak with you alone for a moment?" he asked, none too steadily.

Tish raised her eyes to her husband's face. She did not speak, but placed her hand in his and rose. Robert faced the room, said, "Pray excuse us," bowed, and led his wife out the door. It closed behind them, but not before Lady

Gilliland, Chloe, and Gil saw Robert's arms go round Tish in a crushing embrace.

Another silence fell in the dining room. Lady Gilliland looked extremely pleased with herself. Gil shook his head admiringly. "Mother, you are the most complete hand," he exclaimed softly.

"Nonsense," said his mother, keeping her mouth very prim. "And I haven't the foggiest notion what you mean by that remark," she added belatedly.

Gil chuckled and threw his napkin down beside his plate. "Well, if the host and hostess see nothing untoward in abandoning their guests in this shocking manner, I daresay you will not take it amiss if Chloe and I compound the error by leaving you quite alone?"

"Not at all," said Lady Gilliland graciously.

Chloe looked up at Gil, her eyes suddenly wide with apprehension. "I will stay here with Lady Gilliland," she said.

"No, you won't. Come along, Clo! Step lively, or she'll start spinning another tale to pull *us* out of the briars. And I mean to pull myself out, thank you."

"Run along, my love," said Lady Gilliland placidly. "I daresay Gil has something very particular he wishes to say to you. I shall meet you later in the drawing room."

Chloe's knees felt unaccountably wobbly as she rose. Gil took her hand and led her from the room. A bar of light beneath the library door informed them that Robert and Tish were closeted there, so Gil took the lamp from the hall table and began pulling Chloe peremptorily up the stairs.

"We'll try the morning room," he whispered.

"There won't be a fire there."

"We'll light one. Come on, Chloe—What's the matter?"

"Nothing!" Chloe lied. She still hung back. "I don't know what you can possibly have to say to me that you couldn't say in front of Lady Gilliland."

"Come with me and you'll find out," Gil promised.

She followed him up the stairs, guiltily aware that the clasp of Gil's strong, warm hand secretly gave her much pleasure. How often would she feel his hand closing over hers from now on? she wondered wistfully. Not often enough. She could not bring herself, therefore, to waste this precious opportunity by deliberately pulling her hand out of his. Instead, she swallowed her misgivings, clung to his hand, and accompanied him to the morning room.

By now she had realized what Gil had to say to her, and why he did not wish to say it in his mother's presence. He was going to tell her his idea of how they might end their engagement. And no matter what his idea was, Lady Gilliland would oppose it. He was right, of course; it would be best to tell Chloe alone. Perhaps they could present it to their families as a fait accompli, thus avoiding a series of tiresome scenes. She hoped so. It would be difficult enough to maintain her resolve without being buffeted by argument.

The morning room was, as she had predicted, dark and cold. Gil closed the door behind them and knelt to light the fire the servants had laid ready for tomorrow. She watched, her heart aching with love for him, as the light bloomed beneath his fingers and illuminated the strong, clean planes of his face. It was almost as if she had never really *looked* at Gil before. Why had she never noticed these little things about him? How could she have seen him day after day, for most of her life, and remained oblivious to his manifold perfections? Soon she would return to Brookhollow, and he would be out of reach. While she could, she would look at him, and commit every detail to memory.

When the fire was burning to his satisfaction, Gil rose and glanced back at her. She looked hastily away, afraid that he would read her thoughts.

"You'll be cold," he told her. "Come closer to the fire."

She moved to a spindle-legged chair near the fire and sat, clasping her hands in her lap. *Here it comes,* she told herself.

To her surprise, Gil did not sit in a neighboring chair, but on the footstool at her feet. He took her hand again and gazed into the fire, frowning a little. "Do you remember, the morning the engagement notices were posted, Tish said that we might enjoy being engaged?"

Chloe nodded, not trusting her voice.

"Well, I *have* enjoyed it. I didn't expect I would, but there it is."

"Yes. I didn't expect to, either, but . . ." Her voice trailed off.

"But you did?"

"Well, yes. I've liked not having to worry about—about keeping fortune hunters at bay. Or unfairly raising anyone's expectations. Or things of that nature."

Gil's frown was now fixed on their linked hands. "It hasn't been so awfully bad, has it, Clo? Spending time with me? You haven't grown tired of it, have you?"

He sounded almost shy. Instinctively, she pressed his hand. "Of course not," she said warmly. "Why, I'd rather spend time with you than anyone."

His frown cleared. "I feel the same."

Chloe felt herself to be on dangerous ground. She forced herself to pull her hand out of his. "But we can't stay engaged forever," she said bracingly. "What was it you were going to say to me, Gil?"

He faced her then, his expression troubled. "You won't like it."

He rose and began pacing the room. After several moments had passed and he still had not spoken, Chloe prodded tentatively. "Is it the idea you had? The one for ending our engagement?"

"Yes," he said curtly.

She could not bring herself to encourage him further, or beg him to explain it. Her thoughts churned chaotically, trying to think what on earth it could be. Something she would not like! Oh, dear. It must be really dreadful, to throw Gil into such a taking that he dared not even tell her! She watched in increasing alarm as he prowled back and forth, restlessly picking up small objects and setting them back down. He finally jammed his hands in his pockets and faced her. His expression was grim.

"We can't stay engaged," he said.

"No."

"And if we cry off, it will cause the very devil of a scandal."

She nodded, mystified, and waited for his solution.

"So I think we should marry."

Chloe's jaw dropped. She felt the color draining from her face. But Gil raised a hand, as if to ward off argument, and rushed into speech. "Now, hear me out! I know you don't wish to marry, but I always thought it was because you were afraid some fortune hunter would cast out lures to you and you'd find yourself in your mother's situation. Well, you can't think *I* care about your stupid fortune! It's you I care for, Chloe. Always have. Always will." Gil's voice was choked with emotion.

And suddenly he was back at her feet, both her hands in his. "Please, Chloe. I was never more in earnest in my life. Please. Will you think on it?"

She stared dazedly down at Gil's face. There was a strange roaring in her ears; she wondered if she were about to faint. "Marry you?" she repeated. She could barely get the words out. Her lips felt numb.

"Yes, that's right. Marry me. I—I know it's not what you wanted, and I daresay the notion comes as a bit of a shock, but—"

"*M-marry* you?"

"Yes, dash it! Why not?"

"Because—because—oh, Gil, you don't want to marry me! Friendship isn't enough. Yes, I know you love me, and I love you, but there's more to marriage than—"

She barely had time to register the fact that Gil had pulled her to her feet before he was kissing her, kissing her with a ferocity and a tenderness that robbed her of all reason. Objections vanished, reservations melted away, and all hope of hiding her feelings from him utterly disappeared, forgotten. After the swift, initial shock of astonishment—and perhaps because of it—she was powerless to control her response. Far from hiding her feelings, she found herself expressing them, responding to his touch with an abandonment she would have thought shameful, had she been able to think.

Gil did not appear to be thinking clearly, either, for he did not seem to find her eagerness the least bit repellent or shocking. On the contrary, it was evident, amazingly and wondrously evident, that their passion was entirely mutual. It was surprise, more than anything else, that caused them both eventually to tear themselves apart and open their eyes, blinking at one another like creatures who had lived their lives underground, never knowing what sunlight was until this moment.

Now Chloe blushed. She ducked her head into Gil's waistcoat to hide her embarrassment, but he took her face in his hands and held it, his eyes studying her features in bemused wonder. "Chloe, I love you. How did that happen?"

A tremulous smile wavered across her face. "I don't know. But I love you, too."

He took a deep breath and hugged her to him, expelling it in a blissful sigh. Chloe listened happily to his heartbeat. His voice rumbled in her ear when he spoke. "You *will* marry me, won't you?"

She nodded shyly against his chest. "I rather think I will."

Gil spent the next several minutes expressing his delight in no uncertain terms, and by the time Chloe was able to speak again, she was curled on his lap on the sofa. But there was something in the back of her mind, something bothering her that needed explanation. She sat up and pointed an accusing finger at him. "*Why* did you ask Jack Crawley to court me?"

Gil looked mildly surprised. "I didn't."

"He said you did! At least—" she stopped, blinking in momentary doubt. "That's what I understood him to say."

"Well, what a whisker! It was entirely his own idea. I told him you'd have none of it, but he *would* do it. Seemed vastly taken with you. Can't say I blame him." He chuckled. "You and Crawley! What an idea!"

"It was a *dreadful* idea. And I thought it was yours! Which made me think—well, never mind."

Gil cocked a knowing eyebrow. "Made you think I had a low opinion of your—er—personal attributes?"

When Chloe nodded, blushing, Gil shouted with laughter. She pounded his chest in mock fury. "It was not funny to *me!*"

Gil speedily convinced her that his appreciation of her was all that it should be, but the methods he employed, although delightful, soon made her think it might be prudent for them to join the others in the drawing room. He agreed, albeit reluctantly.

"Marry me *soon,* Clo," he whispered, and she, giddily throwing caution to the winds, rather breathlessly promised that she would.

The drawing room was deliciously warm, well-lit, and crowded with inhabitants. Bobby and his grandmother's terriers were romping on the hearth rug, their combined squeals and yelps rendering conversation impossible. Lady Gilliland looked on fondly, occasionally offering deft interference when either her grandson or her dogs ran the risk of serious injury or mutual misunderstanding. Robert and Tish were seated side by side on a settee, tenderly holding hands. When the door opened to admit Gil and Chloe, both looking a trifle rumpled and sheepish, Lady Gilliland beamed triumphantly. "Ah!" was all she said, but she said it in a tone of great satisfaction.

Tish rose from the settee and flew to hug Chloe, her own joy so great it blinded her to the new glow of happiness surrounding her friend and her brother. "Oh, Chloe, I am the happiest creature on earth!" she exclaimed.

"I am so glad," said Chloe warmly, smiling first at Tish and then at Robert. "You are—both—staying in London, then?"

"For the present," said Robert. He held out his hand and Tish fluttered back to him like a tamed bird. He smiled at her. "When we do go to visit my mother, I believe Tish and Bobby and I will go together."

"Excellent!" exclaimed Gil, crossing to shake Robert's hand.

Chloe reflected that the entire time she had been in London, she had never before seen Robert grin. But now he turned his grin toward her, saying, "I take it you will stay with us for a while yet?"

Chloe blushed and nodded.

"Not too long," said Gil, in a voice that intensified Chloe's blush. "I fancy she'll be leaving you before the end of the Season."

Lady Gilliland had watched these exchanges with a tolerant eye. She rose gracefully from her seat by the hearth, and began gathering her evening wrap, her spectacles, and her dogs. "It has been an interesting day," she commented. "Interesting, and most satisfactory."

Gil grinned. "And busy! Mother, you are a marvel."

Her eyes twinkled. "Pooh! I do not begrudge a little exertion on my children's behalf. I am glad to have been of assistance, of course, but I always depended upon Tish's affectionate heart, and Robert's good sense. And, of course, on the strength of the bond between you and Chloe." On her way to the door, she reached out and patted Chloe's cheek. "Dear girl," she murmured. "You have made us all very happy."

Chloe smiled mistily. "You were right all along, ma'am. Gil and I were meant for each other."

"Yes," said Lady Gilliland simply. "But do not allow him to rush you to the altar, my dear. There is really no reason why you shouldn't finish out the Season here, and marry at home."

Gil opened his mouth, then shut it again. He looked as if he had a reason, and a very good one, for marrying Chloe as soon as possible. He seemed to feel disinclined, however, to tell his mother what it was.

Chloe's eyes searched Lady Gilliland's anxiously. "But— the entire Season! I don't know if I ought to stay away from Brookhollow for such a period."

"Nonsense, child. You will find when you arrive home that Fanshaw has matters well in hand. You will be able to take up the reins again at whatever moment you choose." Lady Gilliland smiled faintly. "Your father, my dear, has not been allowed to meddle. In fact, he is no longer on the premises."

A ripple of surprise ran through the room. Chloe stared. "Not on the premises! Why, how is this?"

"He has purchased a home of his own," said Lady Gilliland calmly. "Near Welwyn, I believe. I rather thought Gil would not care to live with his father-in-law. And—forgive me, Chloe, if I speak a trifle too frankly—but you never seemed quite comfortable with him yourself."

"But—but—*how*—?" Chloe's voice failed her. Gil crossed swiftly to her side and put a sustaining arm round her. She clung to him gratefully.

"Mother, you are frightening Chloe," said Gil severely. "Has that blighter been embezzling from her estate?"

Lady Gilliland opened her eyes at this. "Heavens, no! Gil, I am grieved to hear you express yourself so unbecomingly. I hope you will refrain, in future, from apostrophizing your papa-in-law as a *blighter.* But do not put yourself in a taking, Chloe! Your father has come into some funds. He has naturally taken the opportunity to set himself up on his own."

"F-father? Came into *funds?* Forgive me, but I—I don't quite see."

Lady Gilliland looked a little vague. She waved a languid hand. "Well, it does not matter, does it? The important thing is, he has removed himself from the neighborhood. Good night, my dears."

She would have gone, but Gil put out a hand to stop her. He had turned a little pale. "Mother, I hope you did not—" he swallowed, then smiled weakly. "But of course you did not. The idea's absurd! You and Father did not—" he stopped, as if unable to go on.

Lady Gilliland attempted a frosty stare. "If we did, it is none of your concern."

"Good God!"

Chloe, bewildered, glanced first at Gil and then at Lady Gilliland. "What? What are you speaking of?"

"Marriage settlements!" uttered Gil in a strangled voice.

Chloe and Tish both cried out at this. Even Robert looked a little startled.

"But—dear ma'am—what would you and Sir Walter have done, had Gil and I broken our engagement?" uttered Chloe, horrified.

Lady Gilliland appeared in no way discomposed. Her expression was perfectly serene. "Oh, there was never any fear of that. I would not have placed the notices, my dears, had I not been quite certain."

An audible gasp arose from Chloe, Gil, and Tish. "*You*

placed the notices?" three voices exclaimed in unison. Robert gave a crack of laughter.

Lady Gilliland had moved to the door and opened it. But she turned and gazed mildly back at the astonishment and chagrin on the faces staring at her. A gentle smile lifted the corners of her mouth. "Officious of me, wasn't it? I daresay you all assumed Horace Littlefield did it."

She waited briefly for a response, but the children had apparently been struck dumb. Her smile widened. "I suppose I should have told you," she mused. "Had you known it was *I* who placed the notices, then Gil, at least, might have realized that his union with Chloe was inevitable. You might all have relied upon my judgment, thus sparing yourselves several weeks of anxiety. But, on the whole, I must say I am pleased with the way events transpired. They do say suffering is good for the soul. Well! You have all managed to suffer a little, and yet have sustained no actual damage. A very happy outcome! Good night."

PENGUIN PUTNAM INC.
Online

Your Internet gateway to a virtual environment with
hundreds of entertaining and enlightening books
from Penguin Putnam Inc.

While you're there, get the latest buzz on the best authors and books around—

Tom Clancy, Patricia Cornwell, W.E.B. Griffin,
Nora Roberts, William Gibson, Robin Cook,
Brian Jacques, Catherine Coulter, Stephen King,
Jacquelyn Mitchard, and many more!

**Penguin Putnam Online is located at
http://www.penguinputnam.com**

PENGUIN PUTNAM NEWS

Every month you'll get an inside look at our upcoming books and new features on our site. This is an
ongoing effort to provide you with the most
up-to-date information about
our books and authors.

**Subscribe to Penguin Putnam News at
http://www.penguinputnam.com/ClubPPI**